Welcome To Norse America

COLIN TABER

Other books by
COLIN TABER

The Ossard Trilogy
The Fall of Ossard
Ossard's Hope
Lae Ossard (2013)

The United States of Vinland Series

The Markland Trilogy:
The Landing
Loki's Rage (2013)
Markland Aflame (TBC)

Future episodes will progress this
unique alternate history.

For new release information visit
www.UnitedStatesOfVinland.com
and register for new release email alerts

The United States Of Vinland

The Landing

Book one
The Markland Trilogy

By Colin Taber

COLIN TABER

Thought Stream Creative Services
P O Box 562 Mount Lawley
Western Australia 6929

www.UnitedStatesOfVinland.com

First Published 2013

Editors:
Content editing by Harry Dewulf, www.densewords.com
Copy Editing by Laurie Skemp, www.authors-editing-assistant.com

Cover Art: Athanasios, www.mad-gods.com

Paperback Distributed in Australia by
Dennis Jones & Associates
www.dennisjones.com.au

US edition: ISBN: 978-1451569667
Australian: ISBN: 978-0980658637

Set in Goudy Old Style 11/18/36

The Landing

-

Contents

COLIN TABER

THE LANDING

For Mum & Dad

Thanks for believing.

COLIN TABER

Part I

The Landing

COLIN TABER

Chapter 1

-

The Landing Squall

All Eskil knew was the smothering chill of the embracing sea. As the waves passed, they rhythmically lifted and lowered him and the broken mast to which he clung. But he was not able to focus on any of that; his body was numb, his thoughts slow and thick.

Death beckoned.

A storm had come from nowhere, to darken the sky and push their two ships off course. Fierce winds and mountainous waves had driven them well away from their Greenland heading, and then, after what seemed an eternity of battling the tempest, both had stolen the other ship out of sight. At that point, with a prayer to Odin, Eskil could only focus on his own ship and people.

They struggled with exhaustion, until their limbs ached, hoping to handle the protesting ship through the heaving seas. But it was finally swamped by a monstrous wave. His last memories of the chaos were of his crew's desperate attempts to hold the craft together, until a final wall of brine had come to tear it all apart. Eskil found himself alone in the water, not remembering where he had last seen his expecting wife,

Gudrid.

The worst of the weather then dissipated, as if its job was complete.

To lose out at the end of such an elemental fight was maddening, but rage was an emotion Eskil could no longer conjure. Not now, for he was drained and battered, overcome by the chill of the sea.

He knew it would not be long before the cold would claim him, stealing his last breath as it kissed his shivering lips.

He dimly noted the clouds beginning to break up, although the rain continued. Such a thing at least declared that the storm was well and truly past.

Maybe it was a victory of sorts that he had survived such a vile tempest.

He clung to the ruin of the ship's mast and sail, still bound to the rigging, the best manoeuvre he had been able to manage after finding himself in the sea. Once secured, he had begun calling out, seeking his beloved Gudrid. But because of the continuing rain, he had neither seen nor heard her or any of the others.

Bound to the floating timbers, he was relatively safe from the threat of the sea finding his lungs, although it left him with only one other task – trying to stay awake. If he did not, he would die. He knew the icy water was far more likely to kill him than anything else.

He seemed otherwise alone, if not for the ship's ruin, the soft call of the wind, and the grey curtain of rain.

Eskil faded, his fatigue rising to overwhelm him, as the rhythmic motion of the waves continued to gently lift and drop him. Around him the wind droned on and the rain eased.

Jerking awake, thus setting his sodden blonde hair to flick about his face, Eskil realised he had blacked out for a moment, or perhaps longer; he was not certain. He tried to curse, but his voice failed him, coming out as a shivering rasp. He should have been frightened, but instead lay his forehead back down against the timber of the mast.

A feeling stirred in him; perhaps his spirit was trying to rally

12

whatever remained. Finally roused, he hissed out across the waves, "Odin, help me! Take me to this new land you have led me to seek!"

There was no answer.

Eskil's grip began to slacken and his mind began to fall to grim and dark thoughts.

Then he heard a sound, a sound not of the wind or the waves, or even of the gods. The noise grabbed his attention.

What could it be?

It sounded again: the call of a bird, the caw of a raven.

A raven meant land!

He fought to awaken himself, to focus, as he tightened his grip.

The raven sounded again, this time joined by another's call.

Land!

And then, after that sweet chorus, came the crash of rolling surf.

Land was near!

He lifted his head to look about, seeing nothing but the tight, blue-grey valleys of water between the passing waves. Once it moved on, he roused in time to make a new discovery: beneath the waterline, his numb feet briefly stirred gravel as they dragged along the seabed.

Shallows!

He looked past the mast and tangled lines, and the cloth of the ship's sail in front of him, to the overcast western sky, where the grey shroud of rain was brighter because it hid the sun.

To the west, where yet more land was reputed to be.

His feet then found the shallows again.

While still hugging the mast and up to his neck in the chilled sea, Eskil took a step forward, only to find yet more rising seabed.

The curtain of rain continued to fade, revealing huge but distant silhouettes. The dark, steep-sided forms loomed as if they mouthed a great fjord. With each moment, more land became visible, in shades of grey, as a rugged coastline opened up in front of him.

"By Odin!" he whispered through chattering teeth.

Eskil took another step on the stones of the seabed, only to find the water so shallow that he stumbled to his knees. His spirit soared as he worked with numb and awkward fingers to untangle himself from the rigging that had bound him to the mast. Finally breaking free, he rose and stepped forward as he sought to escape the water.

He would live!

He looked at the land emerging from the receding drizzle as he stumbled forward. His mind, still half lost, began to stir, but for now he noted the green of grass and grey of rock ahead; he realized he remained alone. Gazing up and down the shoreline, he searched for a sign that the others had also made it to land.

Anyone, but most especially his Gudrid!

The thought overcame him, setting him to shake and shiver as he staggered out of the foaming surf. He had promised his thirty followers a new life of land and freedom, a life away from the rising kings and the creeping influence of the White Christ.

They would only honour the old gods!

Just ahead of him, the rocky shore ascended to a narrow pasture, a few shrubs and a tumble of larger stones before the side of a low green hill began. The steeper entry into the fjord rose farther along the shore as it ran away to meet with other valleys. Yet, much remained lost in the colourless haze of drizzle.

After a few more exhausted steps, he was out of the water, across the stony shore, and onto the pasture.

He dropped to his knees.

Here he was alone in the wilds, lost on the rugged shores of Markland, or another place beyond Greenland.

THE LANDING

But he had survived!

Behind him, debris from the ship washed up, stranded next to a large, already-beached section of the hull. He could also see one of his people bobbing face down in the water.

He got up and stumbled back to the surf, reaching Drifa's body. He pulled her up to the gravel – but to no avail – she was still and dead.

"Damn you, Odin," he growled, "I was doing this for you! To bring your faith to a new land, away from those who have turned from your might!" Exhausted, verging on delirium, he collapsed onto the rocks leading up to the pasture, his spirit all but broken. "You led me here, you whispered to me in my dreams of a westerly land that I should seek. Well, I did as you directed; now I am here!"

And then the wind died, as the last of the squall's clouds and rain parted, allowing the mid-afternoon sun to shine down from over the distant heart of the fjord. The light washed over him, golden, generous and warm.

Eskil slowly rose back to his feet as he called out, "Odin, give me this land and I shall give it back to you a thousand-fold!"

A raven called, drawing his attention.

Amidst the golden glare, briefly highlighted by the departing showers, Eskil saw a raven perched on a tall stone rising straight and true by the tumbled boulders at the base of the hill.

He stepped forward, drawn to it.

The raven watched his approach.

He slowed, with each step, not believing what he saw: a stone, taller than a man, marked by the runes of his people.

The runes read: "The Landing".

"By the gods!"

He then heard another voice, the sound of which made his heart jump.

"Eskil?" It was his wife, Gudrid.

He looked down at the base of the standing stone and noticed wet cloth on the grass, trailing away behind it. Putting a hand to the runestone, he leaned on it for support as he stepped around it, holding his breath.

There she sat, with her back to the stone, her woollens still damp from the sea, but lit by the warm sunlight. Already her long blonde hair was mostly dry.

"Gudda!" he whispered in disbelief, using his pet name for her.

She looked up to him, her hands over the small bulge of her expectant belly, her blue eyes sparkling with relief. "Oh, Eskil!"

He dropped to his knees beside her and took her into his arms.

"I thought I had lost you!"

"And I you. But Odin has spared us." Pulling away from her, he surveyed the green slopes of the hill in front of them and then turned to the steep sides and rocky crests at the entry to the fjord rising farther down the coast. "He has brought us here."

"But where are we?"

"I'm not sure, perhaps Markland."

"Markland?"

"I think we passed Greenland." He pointed to the distant fjord. "And I can see thickets of trees farther down the sound. They might simply be willow and birch, but others will be deeper inland, where they are better sheltered from the fury of the sea. Markland is named after the trees."

"Markland?" she whispered again.

"Yes. The sailors in Iceland described it as a rugged and harsh land said to be beyond Greenland, but a place with more timber."

They both turned to take in the view - low green hills behind the beach, running west onto a deep and wide sound along the coast. The steep sides of the fjord rose in the far distance, occasionally edged by narrow, sun-warmed pastures. Glimpses of waterfalls spilled down like white ribbons between exposed rocks and thin woodlands. By the golden light of a summer afternoon, Markland seemed a land of rugged beauty and promise.

Eskil stood and offered his hand to Gudrid; she took it and rose. "Are you hurt?"

She smiled. "Merely tired and cold, although I feel sickly." One of her hands went to her belly again as she spoke, "I think I swallowed a lot of seawater."

He nodded as he put an arm about her. "And how long have you been here, sitting against this runestone?"

They both turned to examine the etchings, the raven watching them from above.

"Not long, although to be truthful, I find it hard to think of how it all came about. I grabbed at some wood from the ship and was brought here by the waves. I do not think I was in the water for long, and I did not realise this stone was special until now. I simply came ashore and sought to escape the last of the rain and wind."

Eskil ran his hand over the stone's weathered face, his fingers tracing over the rough runes. The stone faced out towards the open sea as a marker.

The raven watched them for a moment, and then jumped into the air, spreading its black wings. The bird flew above their heads and dove down towards the shore. It did not land, instead gliding to pass over the breaking waves. The raven then rose again and turned to land on the broken timbers of the beached hull lying in the shallows. It looked back at them and cried out.

The wet sounds of splashing came to Eskil and Gudrid as something stirred the water nearby. Another part of the ruined ship drifted into view. A small, partially hidden section of timbers emerged from behind the bulk of the beached hull the raven was using as a perch.

Eskil and Gudrid could see three of their people clinging to the timbers as they tried to get to shore, their kicks and strokes heavy with exhaustion.

"Quickly!" Eskil called out as he led Gudrid racing down to the water, wading into the chilly surf to reach them.

They grabbed the three men, one by one, and dragged them to the gravel beach.

The men collapsed. Torrador coughed up water while the blonde brothers, Steinarr and Samr, both gasped for breath.

The raven called out again before leaving the hull, flying up and over them. It turned and dove again, down towards the breakers, as it headed along the shallows and towards the distant fjord. With another call, it flew towards the glare of the sun, but not before drawing Gudrid's attention up the beach.

Two figures, silhouettes against the golden glare, waved as they staggered towards them.

"More of our people!" Gudrid exclaimed as she left Eskil with the recovering men.

Torrador began a fresh round of choking and retching, ending with a hoarse gasp. "By Odin, thank you, Eskil!"

Eskil knelt beside the big man, relieved to hear his voice. "Only concentrate on getting the sea out and some air in." He patted the big man firmly on the back, setting his brown hair to jiggle.

Beside them, Steinarr was now on all fours, as was Samr, who was trying to rise.

Gudrid called from down the beach. "Erik is over here!"

Eskil watched the silhouette of the Dane as he crawled from the water, amongst the bobbing timbers and other debris from their ship.

She went to the wretching man who was slumped onto the gravel. As he gathered himself, she called back to Eskil and the others, "There is much here we can use, including the rigging and sail."

THE LANDING

Eskil patted Torrador on the back again as he looked at his wife and whispered, "Thank you, Odin."

Gudrid remained with Erik as he recovered.

Beyond her, a man and woman approached from down the beach, both moving heavily with fatigue.

Before turning to face the newcomers, she called back to Eskil, "Get the wood and rope, and the sail as well. We will need it for shelter."

Torrador paused in his recovery and let out a chuckle, despite trying to stifle his mirth in case he embarrassed his leader.

Eskil grinned. That was his Gudda; she was never shy in voicing her opinion. He stood and said, "Come, she talks to you, too!" He glanced at the other men and added, "Steinarr and Samr, we have work to do!"

His friends, coughing to clear their lungs, did as bidden and got to their feet. The four of them began grabbing at any useful debris they found in the surf, pulling it up onto the beach.

Gudrid moved on and met the other survivors, bringing them back to Erik.

Eskil could see it was the Icelandic couple, Ballr and Halla. He liked them; Ballr was a resourceful and trustworthy man.

When Erik the Dane recovered and was on his feet, Gudrid sent him and the Icelanders back to Eskil, as she continued to walk along the beach, looking for more survivors and salvage. Occasionally, she would turn and call back, telling of particular items washed up on shore. After a good while, she turned and made her way back to them, holding a box in her arms.

The survivors reunited; Gudrid returned to Eskil, Torrador and Erik, the brothers Steinarr and young Samr, and Ballr and his wife, Halla. As the afternoon waned, they also collected much of the salvage and began sorting it into piles on the pasture. At one end of their work lay Drifa, her body waiting for their tending.

Eskil looked at his wife, her face now pale, as she cradled the small and familiar wooden box in her arms. "Come, my Gudda, you have done well, but you are exhausting yourself."

"I shall be alright."

"No, come and let me sit you back in the sun, against the runestone."

"There is so much to be done."

"You can direct us from the runestone, and you can even grumble at me if you like when I do it all wrong, but I will not have you risking your health and that of our unborn." He led her back up the gravel beach and onto the green pasture before reaching the runestone.

"What of Drifa? She must be put to rest."

"We will tend to her, but first we must get the salvage before the tide takes it away."

She nodded, accepting his wisdom.

He added, "We also need to get a shelter up while we have light."

"Yes; the needs of the living first."

Helping her down, he knelt beside her. "We will set Drifa to rest when our work is done, after sunset if we must."

She nodded. "Where will we build?"

"Here."

"It is too exposed."

"Yes, but it will do for now. Tomorrow we will look for a better site."

She gave a weak nod and leaned back against the runestone. "If you build it here, use the stone: It called us here."

He nodded. "I was going to. Now rest."

"Eskil?" Her eyes were growing heavy, the lids drooping as she tried to make one last command.

"Yes, my wife?"

She weakly offered the wooden box up to him. "I found these; put them in pride of place, as they are what kept us safe."

He took the offered box, handling it with care, as it had been handed-down to her by her mother. He unlatched the lid and looked inside, checking that the wood-carved statuettes of the gods remained intact. "I will, my wife, for the gods brought us here after testing us."

"Yes, to here; to a gods' land."

"Yes, to Godsland."

She nodded and then let her eyes close as she sought sleep.

Gudrid slept, weary first from her own near drowning, and then from her efforts to revive friends and crew. In a slumber bathed in the glow of the afternoon's summer sun, she dreamt of her babe due to be born in autumn, feeling the innocent's eagerness to come into this new world. She found comfort in those dreams, watching her child grow in both wisdom and strength. In them, she witnessed a son's coming of age, of his own fatherhood, and of him finally leading the people of Markland into a grand, god-gifted age.

Here, by the runestone, they would birth a mighty future!

Chapter 2

-

Markland

While Gudrid slept, the men fashioned a simple tent from salvaged rigging, timber and sailcloth. The shelter, pitched at the runestone, was basic, but it would do.

When Gudrid awoke, it was to find her new world falling into twilight, the distant view one of silhouettes and gloom. A good fire burned half-a-dozen paces away, at the edge of the tumbled rocks, much of its light and warmth reaching her while also illuminating the rising hillside behind. The flames' flickering light also reached the pasture that separated them from the gravel beach. Scattered across the space were piles of salvage – mostly bits of timber, some cloth, rope and other items – all of it helpful, if but basic. A few baskets and three small chests were stacked aside of this. Gudrid felt great relief to see them, for in them should be a mix of blades, tools and seed stock.

Eskil stepped out of the shadows, his stride purposeful as he came to kneel beside her. "How are you?"

She smiled. "Well."

He took her hands and cupped them in his own. "We have finished the shelter and Halla is preparing some fish."

"Are we safe?"

"Not from the weather, no; not as safe as I would like us to be. A wind is blowing up and more clouds are appearing, but at sunset, it did not look too bad. We should be alright for one night."

She asked, "And what of the skraelings?" All of them knew of the tales to come out of Greenland; they had heard of them in Iceland before sailing, of new lands and new peoples.

"We have seen no one. I have sent Steinarr and Samr to walk the beaches and climb the nearest hills. They will be back soon to tell us what they have seen." He looked out into the dusk. "Or they should be; I need to check on them."

"And what of the others we dragged from the sea?"

"They are alright, but busy with tasks."

As he spoke, Halla appeared out of the darkness and walked with a basket in hand. She turned to Gudrid, smiling to see her awake. "I am here if you need anything."

Gudrid gave a grateful nod and then turned back to Eskil as he continued, "We have also found a few tools and gear amongst the timber salvage, as well as some clothes, cloth and rope. The real problem is that we are mostly unarmed, without any means of going back to sea. I think we will be staying here."

"That might not be so bad."

He nodded, but his jaw firmed; he was holding something back.

"What is wrong?"

He grimaced before answering, "We found one of the men, dead."

"Who?"

"Manni."

She nodded.

"He was missing a leg, gone just over the knee. A bite was taken out of him."

"A serpent?"

"I suppose; the lesson is we should be wary of the water."

She nodded again. "And what of the others?"

"No sign, not yet. Nor any of Leif's ship."

She pursed her lips. "Perhaps they have also survived?"

"It is possible, but more likely the sea has taken them."

"We need him and his people."

Eskil nodded. "He is a good man, the kind you want by your side." He shivered, thinking back to how close he had also come to death. "Yes." He considered his next words before continuing, "We were all lucky. We should be dead."

"Yet here we are, at the foot of a runestone?"

"It seems the gods wanted us spared."

She nodded.

"Come, let us get you into the tent. The air is getting cold." He helped her up and then led her around the runestone and into the shelter, the structure aglow by a small fire within.

Halla was inside tending the fire, a basket by her side.

Eskil said, "I need to check on the others. I will be back soon." He turned and walked out into the deepening night.

Gudrid overheard Torrador ask Eskil after her health.

Her husband answered him, before asking, "What of Steinarr and Samr?"

"The brothers have gone onto the stream to get some water. The others should also be back soon."

As Gudrid listened, she realised she had missed out on yet more discoveries. The thought faded though, quickly lost to the smell of cooking fish.

Halla said, "Gudrid, just get comfortable, the fish will be ready soon enough."

"Who caught the fish?"

"Me, would you believe? I caught them myself!"

"Really?" Gudrid laughed as she stepped towards the Icelander, ready to help, and to also share the fire's heat.

"I saw some of our baskets floating in the surf, swamped by the waves. When I went to fetch them, I discovered two fish trapped inside one of them."

Gudrid laughed as she looked down at the fire, the low flames held within a skirting circle of rocks. Two gutted fish lay to the side, spread across a flat stone, surrounded by glowing coals. "You are a fine fisherwoman!"

"A good piece of luck."

"Or a gift?"

Halla gave a nod before turning back to check on the fish. "We have received more than one gift. Every one of us is alive because the gods want us to be."

Gudrid nodded.

"How are you feeling?"

"Tired, but better, and hungry, after smelling your fish."

Halla sighed. "If only there was more to eat!"

"Do not fret."

"And what of this place; Markland, your Eskil calls it? It is not far removed from Vinland, and it is also bound to harbour skraelings."

"We will simply have to see. We are camping by a runestone, a marker carved by our own kind. This place is already given; not to the skraelings, but to our own people."

Halla smiled. "Do you think they are here?"

"Our own kind?"

"Yes."

"They have at least passed through, and most likely would not have carved a runestone if they were just exploring. Maybe farms are farther up the fjord, or maybe they come here in the summer, perhaps for furs or iron, or maybe even timber. Greenland is supposedly not rich in any of those things."

"Yes, that is why they were supposedly excited about Vinland."

Gudrid went on, "Let us hope the others are back soon so we can eat. It will be good to bed down for what at least will be a dry night, better than what the storm gave us."

Halla looked out into the night, through a gap in the sail. A weak breeze stirred, its song backed by the regular crash of surf. "Yes, a dry night and, thanks be to Freya, one during which we will be warm and sheltered. But we will need to head farther up the fjord tomorrow and seek a better place."

"Have Drifa and Manni been tended to?"

"No, we ran out of light. We laid them out just beyond the salvage. I think the men mean to deal with them soon."

Gudrid turned her back to the fire to feel its warmth. "And where are the others?"

"They are checking over what has washed up. With the light nearly gone, they all shall be back soon enough."

Gudrid hoped so.

The weak wind died at last, bringing an almost complete silence to the night. The fire crackled occasionally, but the crash of the surf, as the low waves came to skirmish with the rocks and gravel of the shoreline, was the only other sound.

The world seemed to slip into a sleepier calm, but the silent women were suddenly roused by a slapping thud from somewhere in the gloom.

THE LANDING

They tensed and turned to the dark beyond the tent's opening.

"What was that?" Halla asked.

Gudrid stepped across to look outside, trying to make out what might cause such a sound. She wondered; perhaps a boulder coming to rest after it rolled down the hill that climbed up over the beach? Or perhaps the landing of a beast after bounding down from the same hillside?

With a soft voice, Halla asked, "Can you see anything down along the beach?"

"No."

Halla stepped across to join her.

Both women stared out into the night.

The light was weak as dusk faded away. They could discern little, with any certainty, particularly on an unfamiliar shoreline littered with rocks, piles of salvage, and other shadowed shapes, either real or imagined.

From the rhythm of crashing waves came a sudden splash at the water's edge, about sixty paces away, a sound so stark that Halla gave out a gasp. "Something is there!"

Gudrid silenced her with a hand. "Hush, Halla. Do we have any weapons?"

"Only the fire and a small knife...I have the blade here." She was clutching it tightly in her white-knuckled fist, the blade still slick from gutting the fish.

"Give it to me."

Halla passed it across, releasing the blade from her shaking grip.

Staring into the night, Gudrid asked, "Can you lift any brands from the fire?"

"There is one long enough."

"Get it."

Another series of splashes sounded, these quieter, but coming steadily closer, as whatever lurked came towards the camp from along the beach.

"There," Gudrid hissed, pointing down to where an indistinct but large silhouette moved from the edge of the surf to the pasture, and slunk closer.

"What is it?"

"I do not know, but it must be a hunter, as it is not shy about closing in."

"What is it doing?"

"Watching, I think."

"Why?"

"Perhaps the smell of the fish attracted it?"

Next came the sounds of timber and rock being pushed aside.

Gudrid stepped out into the night, leaving the tent behind.

Halla followed, raising the flaming torch.

"It has found what it seeks. What is down there besides the salvage we dragged from the sea?"

Halla cursed, "Gods, it will have found Manni and Drifa!"

"No!" Gudrid hissed.

A low and guttural rumble sounded as the beast began tearing at the bodies.

Gudrid continued forward, with the knife held out in front of her. "Is it a wolf or could it be a bear?"

Halla also took another step, but grabbed at Gudrid, "No, you cannot go any farther!"

"We have to stop it."

Then came more sounds of wet and hungry feeding.

THE LANDING

Halla's eyes dropped down for a moment, to the swell of Gudrid's belly, before she said, "You stay here; I will go and send it on its way," but a tremor in her voice betrayed her.

"We will both go, together."

Halla hesitated, but finally gave a nod.

After a deep breath, they stepped forward.

Slowly, one step after another, they closed on where the beast loomed. While they advanced, the dark silhouette continued to feed, choosing to ignore them.

They closed to within ten paces of it.

The creature finally stopped its meal to lift its head and stare. A rumbling growl rose from deep within its chest. It was a wolf, a powerfully large and ragged beast.

It was hard to see anything in the gloom, apart from its size and the glint of its eyes as they reflected the flame of Halla's brand.

She moved the torch, lowering it to hold it in front of them. Beside her, Gudrid gripped the knife, both feeling braver for having weapons in their hands.

One thing was certain; the beast had come for meat. The creature tensed, lowering its head as it continued to rumble in anger at the two women for disturbing its bloody feast.

Gudrid cursed, realising that having come so close, they now could not back up. At the very least, they should have brought another burning brand - not merely for light, but also to bolster their meagre armoury.

The wolf blinked, the reflected light of its eyes winking out, then reappearing half a pace away. It happened so quickly, showing Gudrid and Halla that this thing, despite its size, could move with speed.

Side by side, they stood both tense and still.

Halla whispered, "We need the others; we never should have left the tent."

Gudrid nodded, but neither could take her gaze from the gleaming eyes in front of them.

The reek of one of the bodies reached them, its belly torn open to release the rankness of its guts. Manni, his corpse already missing a limb, had been astink with the richness of blood, drawing the wild beast.

Gudrid looked for any advantage, but only noticed that far out to the east, the horizon sported a rising glow that hinted at the rising moon.

The giant wolf brought its head down and tensed its haunches.

Both Halla and Gudrid sensed the dark beast was about to strike.

A patter then came to them, one with rhythm, as if something rushed along the hilltop to their side. But a rising wind quickly drowned out the new sound.

The breeze whistled as it flew over rocks, danced through pasture, and even worked to take off the tops of waves. A moment later, flaring lightning lit the land, finally revealing their adversary.

Large, but rangy, with a dishevelled, dark coat, the wolf looked half-starved. Most of all, the beast looked desperate.

The dazzling cloud display faded, replaced by the deep crack and rumble of thunder.

Halla started.

Gudrid said, "Be steady; that is Thor's hammer. The gods are with us."

"What should we do?"

"We must back away. We have to move slowly and not turn our backs. If we can get to the fire, we can get some more torches that might keep it from coming at us."

Halla nodded. "Let us try."

The wolf suddenly turned its head to the side and sniffed the air. A voice came to them at the same time, rising above the wind from the hillside to their right.

"Gudda, Halla, stay still and do not move. Keep your weapons in front of you!" It was Eskil.

Gudrid's heart fluttered at the sound.

Halla sighed with relief.

From behind them, to their left, perhaps only twenty paces away, another voice called out, "You are not alone; we are here." It was Ballr.

His voice was followed by others from the hillside – the brothers Steinarr and Samr.

"What should we do?" Gudrid called out.

Eskil answered, "Nothing sudden, let us force it to turn."

Steinarr said, "I have no axe or blade, as the sea has taken them, but I have plenty of stones." And, with that, a rock the size of a fist landed between the women and the beast, causing all three to start.

The animal took a step back, its voice rumbling again.

Another stone landed in front of it, followed by one that hit it in the side, and finally one that smacked it squarely on its head.

The great wolf whined as it fell back, skipping to the side. The beast moved away from the bodies to go behind some brush, trying to shelter its too-large form. With a throaty growl, it raised its head and looked for a moment as if it would stand its ground, but another hail of stones came at it, one again hitting it on the head.

The beast yelped, and then turned and ran.

Ballr arrived beside the women, followed by Eskil, as well as Steinarr and Samr. The men let fly with another round of stones as the beast disappeared into the gloom down the beach.

Steinarr growled after it, "Markland is ours, not yours, ragged beast!"

Lightning flashed, and a heartbeat later, a loud clap of thunder hammered the air, as if punctuating the end of the encounter.

Eskil laughed. "A land that is indeed ours, given to us by the gods themselves; first Odin this afternoon, and now Thor, to protect us by calling us together in a moment of need."

Gudrid smiled. "Godsland it is, and that is what you called it earlier."

Eskil nodded. "Godsland, indeed."

Halla turned back to their camp, the tent aglow because of the fire, reminding her of their meal. "Oh, the fish!" She hurried to check on their food.

Gudrid chuckled and followed.

Eskil turned to the other men. "Drifa and Manni will draw back the beast. We need to tend to them now."

Steinarr offered, "We can bury them with stone. They need a cairn."

Ballr gave a nod. "You are right that it cannot wait, although it is a shame we lack enough timber to build a pyre. I think that is what they would have preferred."

Eskil said, "Anything, over flame or under rock, would be better than being feasted upon by that ragged beast."

The men agreed.

Eskil announced, "We have plenty of rocks, so a cairn is what we will build to mark their passing."

Torrador and Erik soon returned to join in the toil.

As they worked, gathering loose stones to pile atop the two bodies, Ballr said, "This is no burning ship, nor blazing pyre, but still fitting in its own way, as they shall live on in this new land by joining the soil."

Eskil nodded. "Those are fine words. Let us hope their burial brings their spirits peace."

The others agreed.

THE LANDING

Before long, it was done.

The men returned to the tent and a meal of fish, which they hungrily devoured. Divided eight ways the food did not stretch far, but it was enough.

After they ate, Steinarr shook out a cloth he had rolled up, its importance clear only when it was unfurled and free. He stood there proudly, letting the firelight show its truth – a black raven, on a blue field – the banner salvaged from their wreck. He announced, "The raven flies over Godsland, having beaten off the wolf!"

A cheer rang around them.

Erik the Dane laughed and offered, "We need something to drink!"

The others murmured in agreement.

Steinarr nodded and offered the banner to Eskil.

Sharing a smile, with Gudrid beside him, Eskil stood and took the banner. "A drink would be good, but that will have to wait for another day. For now, let us celebrate that we sailed under the raven, the symbol of Odin, who delivered us here. We came looking for a new home, one free from the influence of the White Christ and rising kings, and we have found it. Together, we will build a great land to honour him!"

They called out their agreement.

Chapter 3

-

Godsland

Exploration and discovery, under cool and mostly dry skies, filled the next few days. In that time, it seemed the wolf was unwilling to face them again, although they often found fresh signs of its passing. Those days also brought sorrowful moments often paired with hope: The bodies of three more of their crew were found, along with the half-eaten remains of some of their livestock; three drowned and savaged sheep. They also happened upon more salvage, including a chest holding a small iron axe – and that, at least, was welcome.

Much of the debris from their ship was close to the site of their beaching, but the farther west they ranged from the runestone, the better the land. With every step they took from the open sea, the more the low, rock-studded hills, along the windswept and stony coast gained shelter from the nearby islands edging a broad channel that seemed to funnel them towards the fjord's mouth.

Away from the beach, areas of the hills often revealed sheltered gullies with pastures, streams and even struggling copses of trees. They were unlike the steeper, western shores, where the fjord cut into Markland's rugged interior. But they were close, and more welcoming than the harsh land about the runestone.

They also noticed how the shore curved around, beginning to head north. Eventually, when another channel ran into the one beside them, they realised they were on a large, sea battered island at the fjord's mouth. The slopes and vales across the water were tighter and deeper, with occasional woodland-cover. It looked to be not only birch and willow, but also taller timbers such as pine and larch. To see this range of terrain and timber was a comfort, even if it was unreachable – at least for now.

The island promised to be a harsh place. Thin soils hid under the turf, but improved in the gullies, similar to those inland along the fjord. The summer weather was cool, as was the water, but they had expected Greenland and the adjacent new lands to be as such. The long, white winter would be their real challenge. Nonetheless, the vales, woods and pastures they saw about them had potential.

They spent their second night at a more sheltered campsite featuring deep stone overhangs, along one side of a gully, as well as several small caves. Here they feasted on the meat from the sheep carcasses they had recovered, and smoked what they could of the rest.

Eskil spoke as they sat around a noisy fire fed by driftwood and timber gathered from a nearby copse. "It looks as if we have found all we are going to, in the way of survivors and salvage, though we must keep watch for whatever else may come. Yet, a question remains. Should we stay on this island or take to the mainland that from a distance looks promising, with better pastures and thicker woods? If any of you have concerns on this matter, now is the time to voice them."

No one immediately answered since they were busy with their mutton. In truth, Eskil had planned it that way; he wanted his people to consider their words carefully.

Halla spoke first, not surprising anyone, as she had again worked to cook and serve, and was still cutting her own portion of meat with one of their few blades. "What of the wolf? If we are on the island, then so is the beast."

Eskil nodded as others murmured their own concerns. After swallowing a mouthful of meat, he said, "The wolf is a danger, I agree. The huge beast looked crazed and half starved. Perhaps it crossed ice to the island during the winter and became stranded at the thaw.

Regardless, we will need better weapons, as one wood axe, a few knives and a generous supply of stones may work against the wolf when we are together, but not if any of us are caught out alone. We will have to watch for signs of it, to see if we can find its lair. As for our meagre arms, we need to improve them, since they will not do against the skraelings."

"Skraelings?" Torrador asked with a frown.

"They may not be on the island, but we know they are in Greenland and also most certainly in Vinland. Some must be nearby, even if they are in the depths of the fjords. Eventually we will run into them."

Halla finally sat, with her own serving of meat, but instead of eating, she asked, "How would we stand against them?"

"We are too few to wage any meaningful war with them, regardless of how many of them Markland hides. For now, we must be armed and ready as best we can, and that means creating a home we can defend."

Gudrid spoke up. "Staying on the island may keep them at bay."

Eskil smiled at her with pride, for she was right. "For a while, at least."

"Should we work to build a boat and sail for Greenland," Erik asked, "thus seeking the company of our own kind?"

"They are giving themselves to the White Christ. They are no longer our kind!" Torrador snapped, drawing sharp nods of agreement.

Eskil agreed. "That is reason enough to stay here, on the land Odin chose for us."

Steinarr sat beside his younger brother, Samr, both men nodding as they ate. The older man swallowed some mutton before saying, "We will need to build a boat in any case – and eventually a ship."

Gudrid answered him, "Yes, we have the skills, but the tools are gone, stolen away by the sea. We could still build a ship, but such a thing would take more time than we can give it before winter settles in."

Many of them considered her words before turning to Eskil, who gave a nod. "While we lack the tools to easily make a ship capable of crossing to Greenland or back to Iceland, we will be able to create them in time. We first need a boat for the local waterways. And we need to consider the winter, for it will be long and harsh."

Steinarr shrugged. "Winter will be hard, but it is almost two full seasons away."

Gudrid grimaced. "If we had Manni or Leif here with their tools and skills, we might finish a ship over summer, but not by ourselves. It will take longer. At the same time, we will need to be hunting and gathering food, as there is no farm yard here to harvest."

Eskil nodded, pleased with how sound a thought it was. "Yes, we must consider our other needs as well."

"We need iron," Steinarr grumbled. "A few knives and a poor wood axe will win us no skraeling war."

Erik the Dane agreed. "We will not find iron on this island. In order to make the tools and weapons needed to defend ourselves, we will need to go to the mainland and find a bog that will provide the necessary metal for smelting." Murmurs of agreement rose from the group.

Eskil announced, "So, Godsland is our home for now."

Many about the fire nodded.

Gudrid said, "You men have spoken of our need for weapons, and for that I should not be surprised. But we also need to build up a store of foods and better shelter. We arrived here in early summer, so none of us know what the winter will be like; it would be wise to plan for it to be long and hard, perhaps worse than in Iceland. It will be a hungry and barren time. If we do not work on gathering stores now, we will starve before we face any skraelings, despite how many weapons we have."

Halla called out her agreement around a mouthful of mutton.

Eskil nodded at his wife, for she raised a good point; it would only be prudent to assume winter would come on strong. "We will winter on the island, in the most sheltered site we can find. We will also have to hunt down the wolf if it stays near, lest it come upon us when we are at our weakest, in the depths of the snow and ice."

He received a chorus of agreement.

"While we prepare for winter, we will also work to build a hall able to handle the worst the gods can throw at us, and one defendable against a great wolf or skraeling attack. At the same time, we will begin looking for food to preserve, whether it be fish for drying or nuts, roots and grains."

Steinarr asked, "That might do for winter, but what of the iron we will need if we live to see spring?"

Eskil smiled, beginning to warm to the plans brewing in his mind. "We will have to go to the mainland and discover what it can offer. For that, we need to build a small boat, and once completed, no one crossing the water will go unaccompanied. We also need to locate a bog for the smelting of iron for the making of blades and tools."

They all agreed, and then their gathering fell silent.

After a pause, Torrador asked, "And what of those still missing? Are they all dead?"

Eskil dipped his head a little before answering, "The sea has taken them. For whatever reason, the gods have seen fit to give only those gathered here this second chance. While we should mourn their loss and honour them for having the courage to make the crossing, we must also respect the opportunity given to us. We will labour to make ourselves safe and to survive the coming winter, but during the depths of that long season, we must also plan for spring and perhaps a move from Godsland, to a better site if one is found on the mainland."

Torrador was downcast at Eskil's words, his gaze going to the fire and thoughts of his missing wife.

Seeing this, Gudrid cleared her throat and said, "We do not know the plans of Asgard, as surely as we cannot say for certain our friends and fellow crew are dead, though it is likely to be true. What we can say is that we need to survive, to build and grow, to create something here to not only honour our gods, but also ourselves, and our lost loved ones."

Torrador raised his gaze to meet Gudrid's sympathetic eyes, a smile of gratitude finding his lips. He was not alone, for all sitting around the fire had lost friends, and many of the men lost their wives.

Eskil let Gudrid's words sink in before he added, "Let us give thanks to our gods, all of them, but particularly Odin and Thor, for they have both had a strong hand in giving us this chance at life in this new world. Let us also give thanks to each other, that we are here, and remember those who are missing from our fireside."

Together they called their thanks into the night, not toasting it with drink, but celebrating with juicy mutton.

***

The next days passed as they finished checking over the island for any better sites for their winter home. They also gathered wood for the making of spears and fuelling the cooking fires. At the same time, discussions ran amongst the men on how best to create a small boat that could take them across the chilly waters of the sound. After Manni's mortal wounding, none were in a hurry to chance the dark waters without a vessel.

While all this went on, they watched for the giant wolf and its lair. The island may not have been huge, but it was large enough that they were not able to check every gully or grove. But they did find more signs of it, including numerous seal bones around shallow caves on the island's rugged northern coast.

Halla and Gudrid, meanwhile, planned what they needed for winter, and Ballr and Erik worked on what was left of the larger timbers from the shipwreck, preparing them for reuse. Soon, they decided to winter where they were because they found no better site. So Eskil, Torrador, Steinarr and Samr began cutting turf to build a wall that would enclose the stone overhang and small caves of the gully at their current campsite.

Everyone worked on the hall.

As the turf walls rose, built like so many halls in Iceland and Greenland, differences in the building emerged.

A single door would open at one end, into the main hall, and a long hall, similar to those they had left behind in Iceland, would be centred around a warming fire pit.

Eskil pushed for the biggest difference: to make the most of the natural overhang since it was strong and would save them much labour and time. Enclosing the space, but including the caves at its back, gave them a large main hall, with a chamber stepping up, and the two smaller caves that ran off that and could be used for stores.

Amidst such toil came a great discovery by way of Samr and Torrador:

Back near the runestone, while constructing a raft using their preciously salvaged rope and larger pieces of seasoned timber, they had discovered hoof prints.

They were both convinced the prints belonged to sheep.

Excited, the two men followed the meandering trail until they also found fresh droppings.

Had some sheep survived the shipwreck?

Forgetting their raft, they immediately switched to tracking the animals, knowing life might be much easier for their people if they could count on such things as sheep's milk and wool – and perhaps, one day, another feast of fresh mutton.

With little caution, the two men hastily followed the trail.

Samr called out to Torrador, "Come! I can hear her bleating from here!"

It was a joke of course, for the only sound about them, so often the case on Godsland, was the wail of the wind and rhythm of the sea's swell.

THE LANDING

Torrador answered, "And what if it is not only one sheep, but two!"

They followed the tracks, meandering through the pastures along the shoreline, before climbing a hillside, moving away from the runestone but back towards the new camp about half a morning's walk away.

The path put them amongst the hills behind the eastern coast of the island, a place not as rugged as its northern shore, but more barren because whatever tried to grow there – whether pasture, brush, stunted trees or hills – had to contend with the constant winds of the sea and the fury of its squalls. This was a landscape with little shelter, and as the two men followed the trail, they realised it was also no place for sheep.

But they continued the chase, occasionally coming to a stop where the tracks would cross a stream or pass over rock, leaving them to search for where the tracks began again.

On their sea crossing, like so many others who had come before to settle new lands, whether Iceland, Greenland or the Faroes, they brought not just themselves, but seed, livestock, and the tools to build a new world. Fourteen sheep and three cattle were on the ship. So far, similar to the way it been with their lost fellow settlers, they had accounted for well less than half their number. The sea had given up the bodies of three sheep, but still others were out there, most likely dead, but perhaps alive, as these tracks suggested, and that gave the men hope.

Following the trail as it cut along a gully, Samr grinned and yelled out to Torrador, "You are not thinking of milk or cheese, or wool or mutton!"

Torrador laughed. "What else could I be thinking of?"

"That you are about to meet your new wife!"

They both laughed, but the comment also struck at something deep inside each of them. Samr, for all his humour, had lost his wife in the landing squall, as had Torrador, and while they said little about the loss, they both still ached from it.

What hope did either of them have of finding a woman to marry in Markland?

Such a thing would not happen, not until they had a ship to take them to Greenland.

Torrador called back with a grin, "I would take the wolf as a wife, not some old sheep. Then perhaps Gudrid would have some fiery company!" as they came to a bend in the gully,

Samr laughed. "She already had one argument with your wolf-wife and she won, remember?"

"Indeed she did."

Both men then froze when they heard the bleat of a lone sheep.

"She is near!" Samr exclaimed as he launched forward.

They rounded a bend in the gully, where the land again spread wider across a rock-studded pasture divided by a stream. On the far side of the flowing water stood the sheep, its coat black and bedraggled. The miserable creature unfortunately was not part of a herd, but it seemed uninjured and moved freely when it stepped back up towards some large boulders looming behind it.

The two men slowed, Torrador holding out a hand to warn Samr, for he was the first to see it; the wolf was also there.

Samr cursed, "By Thor, we have to get her!"

But as he spoke, the great wolf launched itself towards its shaggy prey, the beast's snarl filling the rock-strewn vale.

"Come!" Torrador called as they both charged.

The two ran straight for the lunging wolf, knowing they would not get there before it reached the sheep, yet they had to try. They yelled as they charged, thundering through the cool waters of the stream, barely distracting the wolf in its attack and only confusing the terrified sheep. Instead of trying to escape the wolf, the startled sheep turned to face the men, leaving itself backed up against the rock face.

Samr rushed forward, barrelling straight for the wolf, planning to give it a mighty kick in the ribs. As he moved, the beast flew towards the sheep, flashing long, yellowed teeth in its mighty jaw.

Torrador reached down for a rock as he ran, aiming to come alongside Samr and smash in the beast's head. Yet, as Torrador rose from his rushed stoop, with a good rock in hand, he still had several paces to cross as the wolf reached the sheep, its jaws snapping shut on the poor thing's neck.

The sheep cried out in terror.

The wolf used its momentum to follow through with the attack. With not enough room to turn, the wild creature cruelly wrenched its victim's body by folding it back around, as together they crashed into the boulder behind the sheep. With a great thump and crack, and a renewed rumble from deep within the beast's throat, the wolf rose to all fours, with the now limp sheep still held in its jaws.

Torrador arrived a pace ahead of Samr, his rock clutched in hand. He swung it down hard, aiming for the beast's head.

The wolf held the sheep in front of itself, as if a shield, and prepared to duck back and spring away with its prize. It faced Torrador more than Samr because of the man's speed, leaving the beast's side open to Samr. The creature unsuccessfully tried to dodge the kiss of the rock, yet its movements were so quick that Torrador only managed to graze the side of its skull and ear. Blood ran from the wound, but the raw scrape was quickly lost under the creature's ragged coat.

Samr then came in and put all his weight and power into a mighty kick. His old, worn-yet-heavy boot came swinging in to seek the wolf's ribs.

It was too late for the beast to react to the threat, the boot hitting home with a crack.

The impact shocked the wolf and caused it to open the bloody jaws clamped around the limp sheep. When its grip was broken, the sheep sprang back to life and scurried away from the two men and the wolf, stumbling towards the stream.

The two men stepped back, both uncomfortably close to the great wolf that was now not only bloody and injured but also snarling furiously.

Torrador yelled at it, cursing the beast.

Warily, the wolf kept low, and then backed away along the side of the boulder.

The three watched each other, none focused on the sheep. Soon the wolf drew further back.

Torrador said to Samr, "I shall watch the beast, but I think we have hurt it enough for now. Check on the sheep."

Samr agreed and began to move.

The wolf continued to back up to the boulders, and then circled around behind the rocks. As it moved, it favored the side Samr kicked, showing that his great boot had caused injury.

Torrador called to Samr, "Is it there? Is it alright?"

"She is here, but her wounds are grievous."

"The wolf is also hurt. The beast is limping, with blood running from its head."

"Should we finish it?"

As if understanding the words, the wolf padded off across the hillside.

"Too late; it is gone."

Chapter 4

'

The Wolf

The days passed, and each new dawn brought satisfaction as the men and women of Godsland thanked Asgard for providing them with another chance. Summer's peak came and went, and the toil of the Godslanders continued as they raced the waning days in preparations for winter.

Some finished the walls of the hall to enclose the overhang and small caves while others completed other tasks. Gudrid prepared a small garden and planted some of the seeds they had been able to recover from one of the salvaged chests. They caught and dried fish for food, and cut and stored wood for winter fires. They scoured the island for anything useful for getting through winter's long and bleak season, including leaves and grasses for feeding their healed, but lame sheep.

Finally, as summer passed into autumn, their world became a home to more than fog and frequent rain. The winds rose and the air chilled, followed by the first snow-charged squalls of grey.

Soon after the weather changed, expectant Gudrid was ready to deliver her babe.

It was a night not long after they started living in their mostly-finished hall, the rough structure finally enclosed and preferable to the turning weather. The tents, erected in the gully, were no match for the storms that increasingly came off the sea, the tempests woven of gales, sleet and snow.

Gudrid was tending a fire at the very back of the overhang, in an alcove she named Gods' Hall. She set up the wooden chest to serve as an altar for the carved statuettes, and put a small fire pit in front of it. As she made to rise, a pain stabbed at her, making her gasp aloud before she cried out, "Eskil!"

He was there in a moment.

Ballr and Halla were also only steps behind.

The two men aided Gudrid as others came to offer what help they could.

Some of the few sounds in their new home were the crack of the main fire pit in the long hall and the bleat of their crippled, lone sheep settled by the altar. But the moan of a rising wind outside, as a huge squall came ashore to blast the island, could also be heard.

Halla decided to settle Gudrid in one of the mostly empty caves, giving the labour some privacy. The chamber opened into the space of Gods' Hall, which in turn looked over the long hall.

Once he and Ballr settled Gudrid in the cave lit by the flickering light of the Gods' Hall fire pit, Eskil made to follow the Icelander and leave. He wanted nothing more to do with the birthing than he must, not because he lacked love for his wife, but because it seemed a woman's task and no place for a man.

Yet Halla had other ideas. "Stay. I attended a cousin's birthing back in Iceland, but never midwifed such a thing alone."

Eskil complained, "I cannot help; this is no task for a man! What do I know of a woman's birthing?"

Gudrid, recovering from the cramping pain of a contraction, moaned, "Eskil, you knew enough about it to put a babe in me!"

Halla, in no mood for discussion, worried about the task before her. "Would you prefer I go fetch one of the other men who might be more willing to swallow their pride, in return for the chance of handling your wife while her body leers open and naked at them?"

That silenced his protests.

Gudrid, reclining as comfortably as she could on scraps of material from the re-cut sailcloth, was propped up against the rock of the wall. She looked out through the cave's opening into the Gods' Hall. The entry framed a view of the chest and statuettes, the fire, and the lame sheep.

With each contraction, she moaned and gritted her teeth, her eyes locked onto the idols.

The others of their group left them to it, doing little more than delivering water, rags and wood for the small fire burning before the statuettes.

Gudrid lay with her legs spread and her dress well-hitched. Eskil knelt beside her, with concern and great bewilderment on his face.

Halla, meanwhile, knelt on the other side of Gudrid, allowing the firelight to illuminate her expectant charge's opened legs, as she worked at checking her and tried to remember all she had learned back in Iceland.

So they began their birthing campaign, while the worst of the turning season's squalls came to coat the land outside in snow and ice. The wind increased its blustering wail and turned harsher, more primal, roaring as though it had been forged in the underworld.

Back in the makeshift birthing room, Gudrid's intermittent calls overwhelmed the increasing snarls of the storm outside. Each gasp, grunt or scream was followed by the urgent instructions of Halla. Eskil, forgetting his earlier awkwardness, eventually found his voice and worked to reassure Gudrid as best he could, his concerns blooming for his unborn child and beloved wife.

The labour drew on, running into the night, as, likewise, the storm deepened outside. When the gales shifted, they heard movement several times from the piles of cut firewood and salvaged timber that lay stacked outside against the walls.

Their lone sheep added to the sounds of the birth. The beast called out from where it had now settled between the altar and entrance to the birthing room, sitting awkwardly because of its crippled, improperly healed leg.

The storm raged on, and the wind howled.

Gudrid again yelled out and gritted her teeth.

At the same moment, the sheep struggled to stand unevenly on its legs and called out.

Eskil said to his sweat-soaked, pale wife, "See Gudda, the sheep waits for the chance to feed milk to our babe. Do not keep her waiting!"

Halla almost smiled at the comment, while Gudrid looked lost. Finally, with a sigh, she gasped. "Simply deliver this thing before it kills me!"

"I think the child is ready. Soon enough you will be a family of three."

Eskil smiled and took Gudrid's hand, holding it tight.

It was then that sounds of commotion came from the main hall. The roar of the wind grew louder and more brutal, a sudden draft blustered to suck away the hall's heat and stir the light. Timbers groaned, and the door rattled against the rough frame. Outside, a sharp and loud crack sounded, followed by a heavy thump and crash that reverberated throughout the entire hall.

Eskil wondered if the wall was collapsing.

Voices cried out in alarm, followed by the sounds of panicked movement, as the men of the hall rushed out into the storm to deal with the damage it had done.

Eskil yelled, "What is happening out there?"

Halla snapped, "Forget them; you are needed here!"

A taste of the furied storm came to them as the door blew in, unleashing elemental anger throughout the hall, even finding them in the birthing room. The fire of the main hall, buffeted by the wind,

THE LANDING

flared and surged. The light danced – dim one moment, bright the next – accompanied by sprinting sparks and a billowing haze of smoke. The Gods' Hall fire mimicked the display.

The sheep cried out.

Despite Halla's words, the chaos of the main hall drew the eyes of all in the birthing room. Nothing was visible but the sheep turning to face the hall with wide eyes.

At that moment, Gudrid called out again as another contraction wracked her body.

Halla turned back to her and hissed, "Push!"

And Eskil lost all care of what was happening elsewhere as his focus locked on to his wife.

Halla whispered, "I can see the babe's head!"

Eskil's jaw dropped as his eyes went wide, for he could also see the crown of their child coming into the world.

Gudrid groaned, pushed and did as told. Her eyes locked on the sheep standing in the opening, as the fire's flickering light, flaring sparks and smoke swirled behind it.

She growled in pain, sweat running from her brow.

A dark figure slunk into Gods' Hall, mostly lost between the dancing shadows and chaotic light. It headed for the altar before turning towards the birthing room and the lone sheep.

In the large hall, amidst whatever disaster had unfolded, calls of confusion rang out, punctuating the roar of the storm.

Ignoring the chaos, Halla hissed again, "Push!"

Eskil held Gudrid's hand tightly and begged her to deliver their child. Nearby, the sheep began to retreat into the birthing room, through the opening, before bleating once loudly.

The figure moved quickly and quietly, like a shadow, and came into the opening.

It was then Gudrid gave a loud curse that fell into a groan, as at last, the babe slid free.

Halla sighed with relief.

Gudrid turned to Eskil as she gripped his hand and gave it a furious squeeze. But her gaze only lingered before she gestured with a nod towards the shape stepping forward to come up beside Halla. A figure that now blocked the wind-tormented light.

Seeing the wide-eyed stare of Gudrid and her gesture, both Halla and Eskil turned. Their noses also filled with a new odour that joined the smells of the birth; the stench of an animal, wet-haired, with the sickly sweet-stink of corruption.

There, standing at the entry to the birthing room, threatened the great wolf, its fur dusted with snow. One side of its body, by its back leg, was swollen, and the hair was matted with a wound gone bad. On its other side, by an eye, its head likewise sported a bloating, swelling and discoloured wound.

All three of them understood what had happened in the main hall: the wolf came in through a blown-in door, or perhaps through another way, as part of the wall, buffeted by gales, collapsed. Either way, at that moment, none of that mattered. What mattered now was Gudrid lay prone and Halla cradled a young babe.

Eskil sprung up and took a step forward as he threw his shoulders back and spread his arms, prepared to throw himself at the beast if need be. To him, the most important things in the world lay behind him. He yelled, "By Odin, I will kill you!"

The great beast lowered its head and began a deep and rumbling growl. But, unable to keep its head level or still, it kept shifting it to the side.

Eskil said, "The beast is sick, the side of its head unclean!"

A great and ugly scar sat between the wolf's left eye and ear. At the centre of the pink and horrid tissue rose a weeping lump of yellowed infection. The eye closest to the injury was swollen half shut.

Eskil took another step forward, spreading his arms and flexing his fingers before clenching them into fists. He bellowed, "No wolf is welcome in this hall! I will tear you apart if I have to, even if I must use my teeth!"

The men of Godsland, in their own storm of noise and fury, then came charging back into the main hall with the axe, the hall's blades, fire-hardened spears and burning brands.

The wolf swung around and snarled, snapping its yellow teeth ferociously, but was overwhelmed by so many foes.

Ballr, Steinarr, Erik and Torrador fell upon the great beast with their weapons, stabbing and carving, kicking and punching.

The wolf was pinned down, blood leaking from its wounds to darken its matted coat. The great beast struggled against them, lashing out with claw and maw, but it seemed unable to find flesh. Realising the futility of attack, the creature tried to escape, but quickly losing its strength, it could not rise, but rather slipped on its own lifeblood.

Within a few more heartbeats, it was over.

Eskil advanced on the tangle of dying wolf and men with their crude and bloody weapons. "What happened?"

Ballr shook his head. "It must have been outside when the worst of the storm came. We were checking the old tent after the door blew in, since some of the old timbers hit the top of the hall's wall and damaged it and the door frame."

With the wolf dead, Steinarr rushed to help his brother, who was struggling against the storm to close the damaged door.

"What did it?"

"The tent frame collapsed, the supporting timbers fell down to hit the corner of the hall. When we went out to check on what happened, the wolf must have made its way inside."

The swirling wind died down.

With a glance, Eskil could see that Steinarr and Samr had forced the door closed against the storm, and shoved two salvaged oars in place to hold it.

Eskil turned back to Gudrid and his newborn son. "No matter, the wolf is no longer a threat."

Steinarr grinned. "Not to the Hall of Ravens!"

THE LANDING

COLIN TABER

Part II

Wolf Sign

Chapter 5

-

Smoke

Winter came and went, a dark time of meagre food. Storms battered Godsland and buried it under heavy snows, while the waters of the fjord froze over. The long and tedious season consisted primarily of being holed up in the hall and waiting for better weather to come. Together, they all suffered through it, working on what they might, while shut away from the worst of Markland's cold and gloom.

During that first winter, young Ulfarr grew, feeding from his mother's teat. In time, like the hopes of their settlement, he began to blossom as the cool waned and spring neared.

When the weather eased, the people of Godsland escaped the confines of their warm but smoke-filled hall. They emerged leaner, but more than relieved, dreaming of the more varied foods the previous summer provided: birds and their eggs, fresh fish, crab, hares and even berries. Their bland winter diet had kept them alive, but they all craved the variety and the tastes spring and summer would eventually deliver.

They talked during the winter of many things and agreed they needed more iron and would work long and hard towards that goal.

The few haphazard trips to the mainland, on the raft constructed by Steinarr and Torrador, would need to be bested, including the working of a promising nearby bog they discovered as a source of bog iron. Along with such efforts, they also needed to replace the raft with a proper boat.

While all worked on those tasks, along with repairs to the hall, Gudrid was determined to expand her small garden, to grow more of their seed, along with trying some of the new plants she had seen, hoping they would be good eating. She and Halla knew they needed to improve storing foods for next winter, and most especially to improve on their stores of feed for the sheep, which had barely lasted the season. Again, they also spoke of watching for a better farm site, closer to good timber, plant stock, meat, furs and any other treasures Markland offered.

Mixed feelings haunted the group at any talk of moving, for most had grown attached to the Godsland Hall, while others felt it their duty – a divine duty – to stay. There was also, despite them not yet being sighted, the matter of the skraelings.

Where were they?

Despite the hardship, during that first taste of spring, as the sun grew in strength and the snow and ice started to melt, they celebrated their survival. Adding to the excitement was Halla's announcement that she was expecting. Her husband, Ballr, was doubly thrilled.

Gudrid insisted on taking some time during one of those first fine days after the snow and ice had well and truly begun to melt. She wanted to lead Eskil back to the runestone, along with young Ulfarr. She felt the runestone was the site of their new beginning in Markland, and that as such, it was the place the infant should be presented to the carved stone, Markland and the gods.

Eskil could not refuse her.

It was then, as they walked along the shore, with the runestone just ahead, that Eskil turned to notice a distant column of smoke rising from across the water, and not far from where the bog iron works should be. "Gudda, look!" he pointed.

Peering into the morning, she saw the thin, grey mark as it climbed and broadened into the sky. "A fire."

His face was grim. "Yes, a fire."

"Skraelings?"

"I suppose. We best be quick with our purpose, for we will need to return to the others and then investigate."

As Gudrid looked towards the smoke, her jaw tensed. "I cannot believe the gods brought us here only to meet beasts who would kill us. We will survive what the smoke signifies, just as we did the wreck, the wolf, and winter, too."

Eskil smiled as he put an arm about her waist and began to get them moving again. "Come, the runestone is near."

***

By the light of the midmorning sun, Gudrid and Eskil placed Ulfarr, wrapped in a square of sailcloth and a sheepskin, at the foot of the stone. A small swell behind them, dotted with sea ice, accompanied their thoughts with the rhythms of the world.

Gudrid spoke, raising her voice, "To our gods we present Ulfarr, son of Eskil, the first of our kind to be born in this land. For him we ask your favour, and that you grant him a long life filled with courage and strength, as this is Godsland of Markland, and here we plan to build the greatest of all our kin's realms."

Eskil nodded before finding some of his own words. "May we Marklanders be the ones to fill the grand halls of Valhalla in the days to come, with the might we breed here. Yet what we send will be only a fraction of what resides in these fjords, valleys and islands, as we build a land stronger than what we left behind."

Gudrid whispered, "So may it be."

They stood for a moment, deep in their thoughts, while taking in the frail warmth of the sun. Little Ulfarr lay swaddled at the foot of the stone, only to cry out once. With wide eyes, he looked up at the runestone towering over him.

Gudrid turned to look down the coast at the cairns of stone marking the graves of Drifa and Manni. Both cairns were battered by the worst of the winter storms. It seemed that when stirred, the sea's anger could reach up onto the pasture and still have the strength to move rock, though she could only guess how much of it had been caused by surging water or shifting ice. She knew in time they would have to return and repair them so they had a better chance of surviving the winters to come.

Her thoughts led her to consider the runestone, for it also faced exposure from the rage of winter's squalls. It was a sign of their landing place, where they had first camped, the place where the gods had revealed Markland to them. The Landing Stone also needed protection.

With her gaze upon it, she whispered, "Like us, it should never be let to fall."

Eskil thought on her words, but then cleared his throat and prompted. "There is smoke on the horizon."

His wife reluctantly nodded before collecting Ulfarr.

They made their way back along the shore and then cut across the hills as swift as they could, while watching for signs of smoke from across the water. The telltale column of light grey had faded, perhaps blown away by the rising breeze, or perhaps the fire that had caused it now burnt more cleanly. Regardless, they still needed to investigate.

***

When they returned to the hall, they found the others had also seen the smoke and had begun to prepare. The iron knives and axe were sharpened, as were the stone and bone blades they had begun to make and use, along with their fire-hardened spears.

THE LANDING

The iron represented some of their settlement's greatest treasures.

Eskil spoke as they gathered at the ice-caked shoreline, gathering around Steinarr and Torrador's beached raft. "I would rather take twenty men, but we do not have them."

Ballr offered, "All six of us should go. Skraelings are said to be fierce if but short wretches."

Steinarr countered, "Perhaps we will meet a different type of skraeling to what has been faced before?"

"We lack knowledge to make any decision with certainty. We must be cautious," Eskil observed. "While we are close to both Greenland and Vinland, we are also far enough away that we might face a different kind of people."

Torrador agreed. "The raft can only take five. If things do not go well and we need to get away, do we draw lots to decide which of us stays behind and waits to be collected after the others are all safe?"

Eskil gave a nod. "A good point."

Torrador grinned.

"We will send five, and I know who will remain behind, for he has something to attend to in a season's time." His gaze fell on Ballr.

"Me? I will not stay! I will go across to fight these skraelings! Besides, I am the lightest. We should leave the heaviest behind in case the swell rises to swamp the raft!"

Steinarr turned on him and gave him a shove. "I will not be staying! I have only blooded myself on a wolf, a seal and a bellyful of fish. I will be going to gut some skraelings!"

Gudrid stood watching at the edge of the men's argument, while Ballr got back his balance after Steinarr's push. His face was red with anger as he looked to both his tormentor and Eskil. He snapped, "I will not be staying!"

But it was Gudrid who answered him, "You will be staying, as Halla is due in a season or so, and if any should stay, it should be you to see the birth."

Halla came to stand beside Gudrid, her eyes downcast. Her pregnancy had been a point of great joy between her and Ballr, yet now it was opening a vein of resentment.

"You will stay, Ballr," Eskil said in a firm tone, "You will stay to protect the women and also little Ulfarr."

"I wish to go."

"Of course you do, but Torrador is right that we can only take one load. There is also wisdom in leaving at least one of us with the women."

With a spiteful look at Steinarr, Ballr took a metal blade out from where he'd tucked it into his belt and threw it down on the stones of the beach. With a curse, he turned and stalked off towards the hall.

Halla moved to follow him.

Gudrid looked to her husband and said, "You will not be taking all the blades with you. You need to leave at least some sharpened bone or stone."

"You will have some blades."

"Good luck then, my husband. May the gods aid you."

"They have had a hand in our fate so far, so I do not doubt they will come if we have need." He walked across to her, and kissed her, and then little Ulfarr in her arms. "We will go now before Ballr decides to return and argue."

She nodded.

He turned to the other men and said, "Let us discover the source of the smoke and, if possible, return by sunset so we might make our plans. If it is opportune, we will stay and do what we must. But we will not take needless risks. There are too few of us to join a fight we cannot win."

Most of the men nodded, but Steinarr flexed his arms and grumbled.

THE LANDING

***

They landed on the other side of the sound after midday. They used two oars from their long-sunken ship to paddle across, poling in the shallows of the foreign shoreline. From there, they immediately began to climb the rising, scrub-covered side of the fjord, seeking the source of the smoke that had seemed to come from a valley one or two ridges beyond.

While they paddled across, Eskil decided it best to come at the smoke from the cover of land and not from the exposed waters of the sea. They expected groves of trees deeper in, the same as were on the fjord's steep slopes, or perhaps even small woodlands. Such a landscape would give some cover and might give up signs of other inhabitants before the Godslanders encountered them.

They climbed the steeply rising land and kept quiet and close. Eventually, after following the hard trail past rocks and through shrubs and stunted trees, they approached the top of the ridge.

Puffing, Steinarr whispered to Samr, "We better not get into a fight. Ballr will never forgive us!"

Samr chuckled at his brother's words. Taking the opportunity to stop and catch his breath, he turned and looked back, the view stilling his laughter.

Steinarr also stopped, making the others stop and turn.

Before them lay the waters of the sound, flat and smooth, but still speckled with ice in many places. Looking across what seemed a narrow passage of calm, they then looked down at the green and white spread of Godsland, the island's hollows still caked with snow.

Torrador spoke first, breaking the spell, "Look, there is our hall." He pointed to where their settlement lay, half hidden by the hill.

Erik asked, "Do you think Ballr is watching us?"

Eskil looked about, stroking his blonde beard. He shook his head and instead said, "And who else has watched us - or perhaps watches us even now? We are too exposed. We need to put more effort into exploring what lays about us, making sure we cannot be surprised by unknown neighbours or other rogue beasts."

"By the strength of Thor," murmured Torrador, seeking divine protection.

"If we have seen the smoke of another fire, I think there exists a good chance someone has also seen our own. We must be more careful."

The others agreed.

"We have not seen anyone yet, not in any of our expeditions," Erik offered.

"Not yet, but we will see someone soon enough." And, with that, Eskil turned and continued the climb.

***

They finally came to the ridge's crest, the lichen covered rocks showing amidst a mix of tired grasses, brush and the odd bit of stubborn snow. Stunted pines grew in some places, but most trees stuck to the sheltered gullies or the base of the fjord where a variety such as birch and willows crowded the ground.

Eskil made them all crouch down as they approached the crest, preparing to look on more of Markland than most had previously seen.

Over the ridge, to one side, a small cove opened off the sea. On the other side rose another ridgeline, and beyond that appeared to be an even deeper fjord. Above the cove stretched a small valley, the land stepping up to some height. At the back of that higher valley, nursed between two snow-capped bluffs, a wood crowded beside a small lake. The lake spread mostly on the far side of the trees, where a stream ran down a series of foaming white falls, into the cove to find the sea.

THE LANDING

Torrador whispered, "That looks to be a grand place."

Eskil nodded, while the others murmured agreement.

"There is much timber, that is certain, and it looks to be sheltered from the winds off the sea," answered Steinarr.

Eskil mused, "I do not see any sign of a camp from here."

Samr answered him. "No, but it is hard to be certain. In truth, I cannot be sure of where I think the smoke rose, but if I had to guess, I would say it was from that valley and not the next."

Steinarr agreed with his brother.

Eskil also was uncertain of whether this was from where the smoke had risen, as he and Gudrid had seen its sky-climbing trail from much farther off. "Let us back down our side of the ridge and follow it along. Then we will try to cross over and get down into those woods. We need to try and remain unseen."

It had been mid-afternoon when they first reached the ridge top. Now, as they made their way along, checking for signs of movement from the vale below, the afternoon waned. Eventually, when they found a good spot for crossing and making their way down to the woods, they could see they would not reach the lakeside until sunset.

Though the skies remained mostly clear, Eskil wondered if they should risk spending the night in the wild, exposed as they were to the early spring elements. Finally, he said, "Let us stop and wait for the coming of dusk. We will then make our way down, using the night to aid us. It will work to double our numbers and perhaps we will even see a fire light to help give our foe away."

So they sat up on the ridge, taking in the view, not only of the vale they were to enter, but of their own fjord. From where they sat, they could see other vales in the landscape, some crammed with trees, others not. The heights around them still wore tattered shrouds of snow, but the lowlands held such stores only in shadowed gullies.

The thaw was well underway.

As they waited, Steinarr said, "It is a good land, if harsh, and its winters long and cruel."

Eskil smiled at his friend's words. "Yes, a harsh land, and one we will need to master if we are to survive. I suspect it also hides great riches for us to uncover, but first we must make ourselves safe."

When the sun finally slipped below the snow-capped mountains to the west, the meagre heat of the day died.

"Let us continue," Eskil said.

They got up and readied their weapons. As quickly as they could, and with much care, they crossed the ridge's peak and started down the hillside. They headed for the closest edge of the woodland.

Torrador whispered to Eskil as they neared the end of their descent, "I smell smoke."

He was right.

A light breeze had come in off the sea late in the morning and scattered the smoke before it could rise and be seen, but the scent lingered.

Before long, they were at the edge of the wood. After a quick check that they were all down, they dove into the maze of branches and trunks, passing swiftly through a thick leaf litter of rich rot, some of it still frozen or caked in snow.

The night settled cold and dark about them, while the wind picked up strength. Scattered, heavy clouds started to come in from the east, though it seemed they would be safe from any rain or sleet for a while yet. But such a thing, this close to winter's last gasp, would be uncomfortable to bear, and perhaps, at its worst, even deadly.

Soon, they were at the edge of the lake, looking across the waters, taking what cover they could from the trees around them, many only now coming into leaf.

Steinarr turned to Eskil and asked, "Which way?" He was asking if they should follow the lakeshore seaward or inland, yet the answer came from elsewhere.

THE LANDING

Out of the cool night and the whisper of the rising wind came the sudden and stark bleat of a sheep.

The Godslanders quieted in an instant.

"Sheep?" Torrador finally gasped.

Eskil smiled. "Perhaps our own, once lost, but now found?"

Another sheep sounded.

Steinarr pointed in the direction of the bleats. "Two of them! The call is coming from across the lake. That puts them at the base of the bluff, the place best sheltered."

"But are they living wild or tethered in a skraeling camp?" Samr asked.

Eskil tightened his grip around his spear. "We did smell smoke, after all, and it is what brought us here. There must be a camp."

The men agreed.

Eskil continued, "We approach in the dark, slow and quiet." He then turned to lead the way, heading seaward, following the lake's edge.

They made their way amidst shrubs that gave way in places to last autumn's dead reeds. They continued to pass along the edge of the mostly leafless wood, some of the trees yet to awaken from winter's sleep.

Again the sheep called, their bleats coming to them on a slow but smoke-scented breeze.

After some time spent following the lake around, they reached the base of the bluff, a place where more trees and rocks crowded as the cliff face stepped down steeply into the vale. Once there, they caught a glimpse of light ahead.

Flames!

It was the soft, yellow glow of a campfire.

The nearer they approached by dusk's dying light, the more they realised that what they saw was the stirring of a fire pit as they looked through a doorway into a hall. The detail of the building was lost to gloom, but the structure was clear enough.

For a moment the light died, blocked by a figure passing through the doorway and into the night. The sound of the sheep came a moment later, them calling out as they were led inside. With that, the door shut and only the barest of golden lines from the fire was visible.

Eskil slowed his men by holding out his arms as they neared the camp. He whispered, "Let us take great care in this. While we could do with those sheep, there is something here that unsettles me."

"What is that?" asked Steinarr.

"It seems too familiar, so unlike what I would expect of skraelings."

"What do you mean?"

"I know dark is upon us, but look at what we can see of that hall." They all peered through the night, taking in what they could from the escaped glow of fire light, or from what the night shared of the silhouette. "It looks to be a hall, a hall of our own kind, not a hut or tent roped together by wretches of no consequence."

As they looked at it in the dark, weighing Eskil's words, a great gale of laughter erupted from within the hall, one borne of several strong voices. Amidst the roar, one voice declared, "By Thor, I am surprised she has not had twins yet!"

Eskil swore, "By all the gods!"

His fellows exchanged glances and cursed in surprise.

Steinarr whispered, "What in all of Valhalla is this?"

Eskil was smiling. "Kin! Our kin, I think. Was that Thrainn's voice?"

Torrador whispered, "It might be, but how could such a thing come to pass?"

"Perhaps they survived their own ship's wreck as well, but landed over here."

Steinarr eagerly stepped forward, with Samr and Erik at his back, the three almost pushing past Eskil. "Let us get in there!"

Eskil stayed him. "Stop! If you barge in, you will end up with a knife in your gut or an axe in your face."

Steinarr relented.

"I will call out to them and see what we might learn. Even if it is not our lost brothers, at least they are our own kind."

The others agreed.

Eskil strode forward, out of the cover of the trees. He waved his men forward, indicating for them to stand arrayed behind him just before the thicket. With a whisper, he said, "I alone will speak until we know all there is to know. Keep your weapons down."

The others agreed.

Eskil took a deep breath and called out into the night, "By Odin's grace, Thrainn, is that you, survivor of the sea?"

The fading laughter coming from the hall now died.

A deep silence settled as they listened to the last of Eskil's voice echo into the night.

The door opened, but no one stood there revealed. The light within dimmed, as someone in the hall worked to smother the fire.

Finally, a silhouette came to stand in the doorway.

After only a brief pause, the silhouette stepped fully into the night, with an axe in one hand. By the light of the stars, the Godslanders could see it was indeed the big Swede, Thrainn.

Eskil stood still and silent, despite his excitement at finding survivors from the other ship. While the Godslanders might be eager, he knew that to Thrainn, the night's newcomers would seem to be more likely phantoms of the dead.

They would need to be careful.

Thrainn did not address Eskil or his fellows directly, although he gazed at them. He spoke instead to his own in the hall at his back. His voice came deep and rough, just as his hard and long years had made it. "Five figures by the trees; they look to be Norsemen."

Movement of shifting silhouettes in the doorway revealed at least three more survivors, perhaps four, within the dim hall. Their hissing voices questioned Thrainn, who stood with his bulk blocking the way. They also made observations as they stole glances over his high and broad shoulders:

"Nothing good arrives cloaked in the dark of night."

"Could there be more of them?"

"Is that an evil sea mist lingering around them?"

"Can you tell in this gloom if you know any of them?"

Thrainn continued to ignore Eskil as he studied him and the other Godslanders, speaking only to answer the questions coming from those behind him. "Five of them, not wreathed in fog or seaweed, and yes, I know their faces."

Steinarr shifted with impatience, although he did nothing more than move his weight.

Thrainn glared at him.

Eskil moved his hand ever so slightly to Steinarr as he quietly let out a disapproving hiss.

Meanwhile, more questions came to Thrainn from his fellows:

"Who is it?"

"Who do you know?"

Thrainn cleared his throat and loudly announced, "They look to be our fellow travellers, or at least their long missing bodies."

Eskil recognised the voice asking many of the questions as that of Thoromr, Thrainn's own son, now a man himself. Thrainn, a Swede, had married in Iceland twenty years before and had raised a family, bringing them west to seek fresh opportunities and claim land. He had been one of the oldest men on their voyage, near on forty, and one with a big temper. He and his like-minded son had made enough enemies back in Iceland to make trying their luck elsewhere a wise choice.

Thoromr asked, "Who is there, who can you see?"

"Eskil, Torrador, Steinarr, Samr and Erik, so it seems.

"Be wary."

Thrainn snorted in irritation, and then hissed, "Be quiet! You are acting like a frightened girl." He then stepped forward two more paces and called out, "Eskil, if it be you, come forward a few steps and let me see what the night dares deliver to the Lakeland Hall." He lifted his axe as he spoke, adding with menace, "And if you are a shade come crawling from the sea, or a dark spirit that has taken his sodden corpse, also come forward so I can put an end to you."

Eskil whispered to his fellows, "Stay back." He then slowly and steadily stepped forward, stopping when he stood halfway between the two groups.

Thrainn watched him closely and then demanded, "Speak, tell me what brings you here tonight?"

Choosing his words carefully, Eskil answered, "We saw smoke this morning; it was rising from across the water, so we set out to see who made such a thing."

"From across the water?"

"Yes, our own hall is on an island. That is where we wintered."

"You have a hall?"

"Yes."

Thrainn did not ask anything more. He merely stood there for a time, looking over Eskil, while his own people passed through the doorway and spread out behind him.

The Godslanders recognised both Thrainn's son, Thoromr, and his nephew, Trion, as well as the farming cousins Alfvin and Ari, not of

Thrainn's kin.

Thrainn frowned and then strode forward, axe in hand. He walked up to stand a pace from Eskil, stared him in the eye, and then walked around the Godsland leader, examining him, while also keeping note of what the others were doing. He clutched his axe tightly the whole time. After circling around again to face Eskil, he said, "You survived?"

"Yes, but we lost many to the storm."

The words hung heavily over the meeting, as all had lost family and friends.

Thrainn stepped forward, bringing his free hand up to grab Eskil's shoulder and brush his fingers along his neck. The big man could feel flesh. Eskil was warm and real. With a sigh, Thrainn said, "I had given up on you and the others, believing you were all dead. But you are not made of mist or a spirit of the sea or shrouded in a grave's stink." He began to shake his head, but stopped himself. "Or so it seems. Come, and bring your men into our hall and let us see you by the light of our fire pit."

Chapter 6

-

Lakeland

Eskil and his men stayed the night in the hall, not just reunited with five men from the other ship, but also, it felt, the wider Norse world.

Thrainn led them, the Lakelanders, as they called themselves. The big Swede, the oldest survivor from both halls, stood both tall and broad, with blonde hair verging on red, a colour obvious in his beard, although grey had begun to touch its edges. A strong man, he was also known for his cunning and pride-fired anger. His son, Thoromr, was a young, hulking man in his own right, who shared those attributes, both in appearance and temper. Three others were also in the group: Thrainn's nephew, Trion, and the two farmers, Alfvin and Ari.

The men all held broad skills. Ari knew a good deal about hunting and of the labour of a woodsman, and both Alfvin and Trion held skills in farming and working iron. Thoromr, young as he was, had learned much in the ways of a warrior from his father, as well as farming. Together they had made the trip from Iceland with two dozen others, their own vessel following alongside Eskil's ship. Inspired by

Eskil's vision, they had hoped to claim their own land in the west and start afresh in a settlement dedicated to honouring the true gods.

That is until the great storm came.

They were an intense group, more so now for the hardships they had endured, and knew they had been lucky to find an abandoned hall. The finish of the structure was rough, but no doubt raised by Norse hands. It seemed to be a hall for seasonal use, perhaps built by Greenlanders, who some said visited Markland to explore and harvest the natural treasures, particularly the furs and timbers.

The luck of finding the hall was supported by the discovery of a nearby swamp showing signs of being worked for bog iron.

Whether it was someone's summer camp or not, one thing was certain – it had been built by Norse hands. That alone gave the place a comfortable feel.

Eskil and his fellows were invited into the hall, although the Lakelanders continued to watch them in case they were malicious spirits labouring in deceit. The Godslanders gratefully embraced its warmth, but they soon discovered that not only the five Norseman lived there; along the back, skulking away from the men, shone the timid and dark eyes of four skraeling women.

The women were rugged up in furs, and, Eskil noted, at least two of them sported heavy bruises to the face.

As the Godslanders were brought closer to the re-stoked fire pit and were encouraged to sit, Eskil asked of Thrainn, "Tell us of your escape from the storm."

Steinarr added, "And of these womenfolk, please tell us of them."

Eskil frowned and gently reprimanded Steinarr for speaking out of turn, for he could see all his men were taking an interest in the female skraelings. "Steinarr, let Thrainn answer my question first. I'm sure it will lead to the women here."

Thrainn, busy studying the faces of the guests in his hall, barely turned to look at the women. "Sit and we will tell you our tale. First though, tell us of your own camp. Did you also find a hall?"

THE LANDING

Eskil shook his head. "We came ashore amidst the ruin of our own ship. With its timbers, ropes and sail, we were able to get up a roof that first day, and then the only thing we had to worry about was food."

Torrador added, "And the wolf."

"The wolf?" Thrainn asked.

Eskil nodded. "A great wolf, one of the biggest I have ever seen. It came on our camp, just after dusk on our first night, when only Gudrid and Halla were there."

Steinarr laughed. "The women went to face it, but we beat them to the fight. Most of us returned from our various dusk wanderings just as the wolf was about to attack."

"You came ashore with weapons?"

"Not at the time – only the one blade. We also recovered a small wood axe and some other knives in the following days as we scoured the beaches for more salvage. We chased the wolf off that night with our numbers and by raining down rocks upon it."

"So Gudrid and Halla went to face the wolf?"

"Yes, but they are safe." Eskil smiled. "And Gudrid has given birth to a son, Ulfarr, while Halla is now expecting."

"Expecting?" Thrainn looked about. "Did Ballr survive or is she widowed and remarried to one of you?"

"Ballr lives. He is back at our hall with the women and young Ulfarr."

Thrainn burst out laughing. "At home with the women!"

Many of the men laughed at the charge, but Eskil answered Thrainn. "Our raft, as small as it is, can only fit five."

"You have a raft?"

"Small and solid, yet not worthy of the sea."

"So, with Ulfarr, there are nine of you?"

"Yes." Eskil looked about the small hall, particularly at the skraeling women. "And of yours?"

"Only what you see."

Eskil sighed with disappointment, and he was not alone. "I had hoped to see your women, and also Leif."

Thrainn frowned. "No," he said, then shook his head. "No, none of them."

"What happened?"

He began the tale, looking at his men as his first words flew. "We struggled ashore, the five of us. We found some others, including Katla and Herdis, but they did not last the night. They died with water in their lungs, the chill of the dark finishing them."

At his words, Alfvin and Ari looked down at the glowing coals in the fire pit, their troubled thoughts lost to memories of their dead wives.

Eskil studied the two men before turning back to Thrainn. "I am sorry to hear of it. Many good men and women have been lost. It is also a shame Leif did not make it ashore. The big Dane knew a lot about working wood and shipbuilding. He would have been a handy man to have."

Thrainn's men all turned to their leader as he glanced down at the flames and frowned anew. He finally met Eskil's gaze and said, "Leif did make it ashore, but he was in a bad way, as all of us were. He did not survive."

Eskil and his men nodded their understanding.

Thrainn continued on, "We had little in the way of salvage from the ship, so we needed to look for shelter as the day waned. That was when we stumbled upon this hall, but it was not empty." And he tilted his head towards the skraeling women. "We discovered this family, sisters I think. They were passing through the area, for they had little with them and were simply using its roof to shelter from the storm."

Thrainn shook his head before glancing at his fellows again. "They were here with their old father, a man weak and sick. There were also some younger men who tried to stop us." With a dark smile, he added, "I slaughtered them."

Thoromr gave a hard laugh. "Do not forget I helped."

Thrainn raised an eyebrow, but gave a single nod. "And Trion. Do not forget the part your cousin played."

Thoromr grimaced, while Trion smiled in appreciation.

Eskil asked, "Slaughtered? Do you have weapons other than your axe?"

"No, no others besides a blade. My axe came ashore with me, still strapped to my back. We surprised them and took the hall in moments, the fight over quickly. The women cowered, while the old man died not long after. We then took the women as our own, bringing them into thraldom."

His men nodded, staring into the flames as they recalled that fateful night.

Eskil asked, "Sisters?"

Thrainn gave a shrug. "In truth, we are not certain. I think at least some of them are, the others perhaps cousins. Either way, they now are ours."

Eskil noted that several of his own men turned to look at them, appraising the idea. To take people into thraldom was nothing new to the Norse. Such enslavement was accepted.

Thrainn also noticed the interest of Eskil's men with a frown that deepened amidst his red beard. "Thralls, I suppose, is the word for it, or perhaps even wives. Having been with them through winter, the truth of it is we probably owe them our lives for the knowledge they shared of where and how to gather food in this harsh and strange land."

Eskil looked to the dark haired women again, observing more than anything how fearful and withdrawn they were. "Wives you say?" But it was indeed thralls, or maybe prisoners of a sort, that he saw.

"Yes, and now all four of them are expecting our sons."

Eskil's men laughed aloud at that, offering smiles and well wishes. "So, there is five of you, four women and now the coming of four babes?"

"Yes, a brood of thirteen, I suppose."

"Have you seen any other skraelings?"

All eyes turned back to Thrainn.

Eskil noticed how Thrainn's own men waited for the answer as much as the Godslanders, as if they did not know what he might say.

A grim smile cracked the big man's features, built of blood and satisfaction, as he squared his shoulders and leaned back. "There was some sign at the end of summer, of three sets of visitors, I think. We found two of them; one of two skraeling men, the other of a lone man, though it would be fairer to call him a boy."

"What happened?

Thrainn lifted his axe from where it sat beside him by the fire, moving it in his hand as he felt its weight. "I killed them."

All the Norse stirred to hear such a thing; Eskil's men to hear of battle, Thrainn's because of the memory.

Eskil asked, "And how did it come to that? Did they start the fight or come to trade or try and talk?"

Thrainn glanced at the women sitting alongside the wall.

At his gaze, they shrank back further into the shadows.

"I think they came looking for the women, but we never let them get close enough to know."

"What makes you think they came looking for them?"

"In truth, I am only guessing, but they were geared to move, not to hunt. They had some weapons, but for the most part travelled light. They carried no game with them, so I think they were not out hunting animals in the woods, but instead, seeking their lost kin."

"I see."

"They tried to talk, but I would have none of it."

"So you killed them?"

"Yes, while they were distracted in trying to make themselves understood. My axe took them both; one in the neck – I nearly got his head clean off – the other in the ribs. What we did understand from them, before I ended our conversation, was that they were looking for someone or something. I did not want to give up our thralls or even the knowledge that we had them."

"And that was the two of them?"

"Yes. Later, quite a while later, we saw a lone skraeling, a young man in the woods. He was more a boy, I suppose. It took some doing to catch him, but eventually we realised he was coming back to check on us, so we set up a trap for him one night."

"And did you capture him?"

"Yes."

"And what was he after? Searching for the other missing skraelings?"

"Yes, I think so, for the men. We will never know. He did not survive his catching."

"You mentioned a third sign of skraelings?"

"We found more tracks, but never caught sight of who made them. We did find a campsite a good day's trek away. It looked to have been used by two or three men. They had stayed the night there and had a fire. We do not know if they got close enough to see our hall, but we caught signs of their passing on the beach of the cove. In truth, having seen it, the camp told us nothing other than they had been near."

"And you have had no other visitors since?"

"Not that we know of. Perhaps more will come with the melting of the snow?"

Silence fell for a moment, a heavy moment Thrainn eventually broke when he ran his fingers along the head of his axe. "They were dressed to keep warm, but had little in the way of weapons, using sharpened stone, bone and wood."

"What do you mean? What were they armed with?"

"Spears. They also had knives and axes, but with stone blades. We kept them, but not in here." He nodded towards the thralls. "I think the women worked out that we met some of their kin and fought them. I am certain they have heard enough of our talk and seen the blood on our clothes. But I thought it best to keep them from seeing the bodies or belongings, in case they recognised any of them. Besides, the weapons were so poor that while we might use them outside of the hall, we do not need them in here."

Steinarr wore a grim smile. "Worried you might wake up with a skraeling axe in your throat?"

Thrainn did not try to hide his scowl. "They are timid enough, but with five of us and four of them, having extra weapons about to tempt them, particularly if they feel the need to avenge kin, is not something I would see happen."

Steinarr ventured through a smirk, "You fear them?"

Thrainn growled, his tone threatening as he used his axe to point. "No, we are being smart with our numbers. Five versus four, as it stands, weighs in our favour, even more so because of our weapons. But give them blades or axes also, the sight of their dead kin to fire them on, and maybe then one of us will have an accident. Suddenly it will be four versus four, and then maybe three versus four. In truth, I am of half a mind to simply slit their throats and be done with them."

With such harsh words ringing in the air, Thrainn's kin, Thoromr and Trion, did nothing but glare at Steinarr. Contempt radiated from the young men, the feeling as menacing as the way their leader gripped and pointed with his axe.

The other two men, Ari and Alfvin, were more subdued. They stole glances at two of the thralls before dragging their gazes back to the fire pit.

THE LANDING

Eskil knew the look; they did not like to hear such talk about their thralls, wives or women.

But which was it?

Eskil knew he needed to get the conversation to other matters and away from the fires of argument, despite feeling he needed to know more about what seemed to be a hidden division. So he asked, "Nothing more has been seen of their people?"

Thrainn broke his gaze away from Steinarr, turning to Eskil. "I expect we will see them soon enough, as the snow melts and the days grow longer."

"Are they a threat?"

Thrainn exchanged glances with his fellows. "No, I think not. I think they are cowardly and easy to scare. They are a tall and big folk, like us, but timid in their own way. They do not match the skraelings in the tales we heard back in Iceland, of what they found in Greenland or even Vinland, for that matter."

"What do you mean...in their fierceness?"

"That, and in how they were described, and spoken of." He turned to the women and growled, "Here!"

One of the women rose, hesitating for a heartbeat as she did. Urged on by the others, she wrapped her furs about herself and quickly scurried across until she stood a pace away from Thrainn, at a break in the Norsemen's circle about the fire pit.

Her eyes went to the axe.

Thrainn nodded that he was pleased, and then rose to stand beside her.

She shrank away a half step.

He chuckled at her fear, and then reached out and yanked open her furs.

She winced at his rough hands, but stood mostly still, trembling before the fire and the staring eyes of the men. Her body was tall and long, her hips broad, and her belly swelling with Thrainn's child. Her ruddy skin was smooth, but sported the occasional scar, as did her face, with a great bruise sitting on one of her cheeks. She had black hair and dark eyes that glittered as she tried to hold back tears.

Thrainn put a hand to the back of her neck to hold her still, her own hands cupping to cover her exposed sex. "This is my thrall, not my wife, though I do use her." And with his other hand, he reached across and rubbed her belly. "But what we had heard of skraelings was that they did not bleed when you cut them and that their wounds went white as if edged by frost. I assure you; they bleed red. The rumours also said they were a much smaller people and of slighter build, but you can see she is of a similar height and bulk to us. We may call them skraelings, but they are not. They are something different...another breed of this land's people."

Eskil asked, "Are the tales completely wrong?"

"Perhaps, but I think those stories talked of the skraelings in Greenland on fields of snow and ice, living by the sea, and of others in Vinland, too. I do not think either of them spoke of the skraelings to be found here, who seem to be more at home in the woodlands."

Eskil's men were staring at her round breasts, full and caressed by the dancing light of the flames.

Irritated by the show and worried it would not end until one of his men gave into temptation and tried to touch the woman, Eskil said, "Thrainn, cover her against the cold; she is with child."

Thrainn smirked. "She is warm by the fire and mine to do with as I wish." He leered and added, "Besides, I know how to warm her if she is cold."

Eskil knew there was no point in pushing the matter. Besides, he had other questions to ask. "As you will."

Thrainn grinned and then slapped the woman on the thigh before pointing back to the wall where the others watched from the gloom.

She did not hesitate in her retreat.

Thrainn soon sat back down.

Steinarr laughed, breaking the tension.

Eskil asked, "What of the future? Would you stay here in your own hall with your thralls and coming kin, or should we all band together, either in Godsland or at any better site we discover this summer?"

Thrainn shrugged, falling into a more thoughtful mood. "It is a good question and one to consider. Living together to best defend ourselves from what may come does make sense."

"Wise words," Eskil said.

The lingering tension in the hall faded.

Thrainn nodded. "Whether a joined settlement should be here in Lakeland, in your Godsland, or somewhere else, I do not know. We cannot answer that tonight."

Eskil agreed. "Let us celebrate finding each other for now. In coming days we can talk of other matters such as Godsland, our hall there, and the space beside it for another."

There were many murmurs of agreement.

Chapter 7

-

Welcomed

Gudrid had not slept well. She missed Eskil and a fear that he had crossed the water and entered a place of anger and blood nagged at her. She knew smoke on the horizon was not likely to be a good sign.

Little Ulfarr had also noticed his father's absence.

She had gotten up well before dawn, letting Ballr sleep, for, as agreed, the three of them, including the expecting Halla, had taken a watch to look for any sign of their hall-fellows' return.

Ballr overcame his anger at being left behind, courtesy of his fatigue after a long, middle watch. Like Gudrid and his wife–Halla had taken the first watch–he found the hall, despite its space and warmth, to be too empty and quiet. He merely wanted to see the others return safely.

The previous, tense afternoon gave way to a chilly and restless night, only to stumble into an awkward morning, as each of the hall-dwellers tried to busy themselves with tasks. Ballr fished, Halla watched over Ulfarr while weaving a basket from willow canes, the infant boy wrapped in a skin at her feet, as Gudrid worked to clear an area for a garden bed. They toiled half-heartedly, none of them focussed on his or her work, but on the distant shore.

Such is the way the bulk of the morning passed.

Finally, they sighted the raft across the water, crewed and returning, with a crowd behind it on the sound's stone beach.

Ballr saw it first. "Gudrid, take the sheep and put it in the hall." As he spoke, he gathered up his gear and catch, and put it into a willow basket.

Gudrid asked, "What is wrong?" But as the words came, she also saw the raft on the sound's waters and the others left behind on shore.

Halla picked up Ulfarr and stood. "The raft!"

Ballr walked past her as he went to put the fish and basket in the hall while also fetching the stone and bone blades they had been left with. He called out behind him, "When they are closer, we will know what is happening and who is with them."

Gudrid nodded and led the crippled sheep across the gully and into the hall.

Ballr came back to Halla and looked down at young Ulfarr in her arms.

His wife asked, "Skraelings?"

"I do not think so. They would be coming at us by themselves if they knew we were here. I am hoping Eskil and the others are bringing guests. We will just have to see, and be careful."

She agreed.

They watched as the raft slowly crossed the waters, the ramshackle craft half-way through the trip when Gudrid returned. Halla offered her Ulfarr back, but she shook her head, looking to her babe and Halla's growing belly. "No, you keep him until we know we are safe." She reached out to Ballr for one of the stone blades and clasped it behind her back.

Ballr nodded.

Soon they could see Eskil at the front of the raft, waving. Behind him was another man, though they did not recognise him from such a distance, as well as others, including some people wrapped in dark furs.

Before long, with an awed curse, Ballr said, "By Thor, it is Thrainn!"

Halla and Gudrid both watched in surprise. They realised Ballr was right; it was Thrainn, although he looked thinner and worn after a long winter.

Despite such wear, the big man grinned from the raft, and also began to wave.

Ballr said, "They must have found survivors who came ashore elsewhere."

"I hope Leif is amongst them, his high spirits and lore are sorely missed," Gudrid said.

Halla nodded, growing excited, as she asked, "And the others?"

Ballr answered, "I do not know, but they are not Norse."

Gudrid looked to both Halla and Ballr, meeting their gaze, as they considered such a thing. "We will know more soon enough."

"Yes," Halla whispered.

And, with each word, the raft drew closer.

The raft closed the last fifty paces, making the situation much clearer: Thrainn was indeed on board with Eskil and Torrador, and with them a sheep and two people who were quite obviously not Norse. Judging from their darker skin, hair and furs, they could only be skraelings.

Eskil called out, "We found Thrainn and others and they have four skraeling thralls and two sheep!"

The raft moved through the shallows as Eskil and Torrador used the oars to get them to the beach.

Ballr and Gudrid came forward as Eskil and Thrainn stepped

ashore. Torrador helped the skraeling women and sheep off the raft as they looked about at the Godsland settlement, taking in the size of the new hall built into the gully-side.

When both women were on shore, Eskil pushed the raft back out, letting Torrador return to the other side of the sound to collect the rest of their party.

The Norse were excited to be reunited, and Ballr, Halla and Gudrid could not help but stare with curiosity at the skraelings. The thralls, in turn, looked wide-eyed at what lay about them.

Thrainn announced, "So this is Godsland, and with Gudrid, Halla and young Ulfarr, too. Ah, and I see Ballr, also here at home with the women!"

Ballr's smile faltered at such words, but he held himself.

Into the awkward silence, Eskil said, "Our home and hall, and families, too. We are making a start, as the gods have willed it."

Gudrid asked, "And who else is with you? Was it your smoke we spotted yesterday morning?"

"Yes, it would have been smoke from our fires. We were smoking fish, although I can barely stomach such food after such a long and bleak winter. More importantly, we also set again to work at smelting bog iron."

"And who else?"

Thrainn's smile faltered. "Only five: me, Thoromr and Trion, and also Ari and Alfvin. We did have Katla and Herdis, but they did not survive the first night after our landing. It was the cold and all the seawater they swallowed that finally took them. We do not speak of the others."

News was swapped as the raft reached the other shore.

Torrador reloaded, and then returned with Steinarr and Erik, a sheep, and two more skraeling thralls.

Gudrid noted that all the women were pregnant.

Grinning at all the use the raft he had built was getting, Torrador took it back across before returning, this time with the remainder of the Norse.

And then, in Godsland, they were all finally reunited.

While it might have been spring, the air still had a chill to it, and the horizon a threat of worse weather to come. After a long afternoon of talk in the meagre warmth of the sun, they retreated into the hall, well before dusk.

Their guests marvelled at what they had built over the previous year's summer and autumn. For the Godsland Norse, it had been a time of promise and rising happiness, with just enough eager hands to see their work through. That and their belief in what they were doing.

Thrainn looked over the Godsland hall, inspecting it with a critical eye; the stone of the hill's over hang, the cut turf making up the main wall, the timbers and style of build. He also checked over anything else of interest, whether it be salvage, such as the raven banner hanging by the inside of the door, or anything forged anew.

After showing their guests the hall, the Godslanders led them to sit around the fire pit.

Thrainn sat opposite Eskil, the low flames between them, the Lakelander beside a cut log the Godslanders used as a chopping block. The timber held the small and only axe the hall had, the tool more suited for cutting kindling and dwarfed by the much heavier axe Thrainn carried. Needless to say, the quaint chopper caught his eye. Looking upon it, the big man laughed. "That is no axe for a hall!"

Eskil smiled at the comment, as the axe was indeed a small thing. He offered, "The axe may be small, but when wielded with determination, we were able to use it more than anything else to not only build our hall, but to finish the woodwork within. Only our muscles have been worked harder."

Thrainn chuckled, shaking his head. "Your axe might be good for chopping wood, but I would bet you need four blows to cleave a skraeling's neck!"

THE LANDING

Thoromr laughed at his father's comment, and then said, "Tell them again of how we took our hall, as they have not all heard the tale of our bloody conquest."

Trion smirked and agreed, as he looked at the small axe. He seemed to be contemplating how many blows might indeed be needed to separate a head from its neck. "Yes, speak of our hall-taking!"

Eskil listened patiently again to the tale of the Lakeland landing and the hardships faced. As a group, he knew the Lakelanders had done well to survive, but he now also sat with them in growing discomfort, suspecting Thrainn did not tell the whole truth.

The longer the tale went on, the more certain Eskil was that there was more to the story than merely the luck of winning the hall and the skraeling women after a quick fight. He watched as Alfvin and Ari grew restless at the retelling, as if it threatened to turn their guts to water.

Eskil only watched and listened, for now.

Of the Lakelanders, only Thrainn's kin, Thoromr and Trion, offered their leader loud backing for the tale being told, a tale that seemed to be growing more dramatic and bloody with its retelling. It was as if the story was coming into a life of its own.

Eskil pondered things as Thrainn's tale droned on.

The Lakelanders had not seen anyone else in Markland, aside from a few skraelings, although it seemed Greenlanders came often enough to have bothered with the carving of the runestone and the building of a hall. That Norse had been to Markland was plain. But what of it? Did that mean there were other workings about, halls or places for smelting bog iron perhaps, or maybe even a permanent settlement deeper in the fjord, where the land should be better and more sheltered from the fury of the sea?

It was a possibility, one that led to others.

Eskil asked, "Thrainn, how did you survive the winter? When did you begin to store foods?"

"Not long after we found our hall. In truth, if we had not found it, I think we would have died. But having it and its shelter and warmth–

89

and also the gaining of our thralls–left us so few other things to worry about that we were able to concentrate on gathering food for the winter. It was a great gift."

Eskil nodded, as did the others. They could all see the truth in that, in the labour such a discovery saved. As Thrainn had suggested, it was probably a great enough thing to have been the difference between surviving winter or not.

The newcomer continued, "We will survive the next winters to come. I know I can say that now, after having just come through one, but I have no wish to do it in the same style. I am sick to death of dried fish and stewed roots. I wish to make sure we have not only more variety in what we take into our winter larder, but that there is also much more of it."

Eskil's own also agreed with such a thing, most sharing wry smiles and a rueful laugh. "We were lucky to survive, but it was only barely, and more through good fortune and the wishes of the gods. I also hope for a much better prepared larder, and I am sure this time we will manage such a thing."

Steinarr moaned as he dramatically clutched his stomach. "Let us hope so!"

Gudrid laughed. "You could have tried wolf stew for a change?"

"Ah, the same wolf I heard you faced off on the beach?" Thrainn asked.

"Yes, though it met its fate when it came to watch Ulfarr's birth. The beast broke into our hall during the first bad winter storm and was killed by our menfolk."

Steinarr laughed. "Not Eskil, though, for he was helping with the birthing!"

Eskil smiled at the memory, for taking part in such a thing had opened his eyes to a great wonder.

Thrainn cursed with wide eyes. "By Thor, that is of women, not that of a man!"

Ballr offered, "Halla did what she could as a midwife, but needed aid. In truth, I do not think Eskil regrets it. In fact, I think he would do it again without the need for asking."

Thrainn shook his head and grimaced. "It is no work for a man, that is certain. When it comes time for our thralls to give birth, I will be having no part of it. I am not even sure I will be allowing them to keep what they will be birthing."

Gudrid shifted uncomfortably at his words. "They will be your kin nonetheless, and half-Norse at that. I think you should keep them if Freya sees fit to deliver them alive and healthy to you. Besides, think of the work you will be able to put them to."

Thrainn grimaced as he leaned back. "Eskil, your woman has always had things to say, but I cannot help but notice how much more she wishes to offer them up now!"

Eskil forced a smile at that, for they all knew it to be true. "She has wisdom in her words, and I would advise you to listen."

"Only my wife can try and tell me what to do, but the sea stole her away," he then added with a hiss, "May Odin take better care of her dead than he did when she lived."

"Without Gudrid's counsel and preparations for winter, we would all be dead. The gods favour her."

"I shall not be taking orders from any woman - your wife or a thrall - regardless of whether you think she is an instrument of the gods."

Gudrid, unable to stay quiet, spoke up, "Whether you want to listen or not, I would suggest you do so. If any of us makes a bad decision in the coming year, it could well mean doom for all of us. We came to this new world to start again, maybe not heading for this exact shore, but here we are in Markland, building the world we want, as it should be. We need to make the right decisions in the choices that lay ahead. Until we number in the hundreds, we will not be safe, either from something as simple as a bad winter or from the skraelings."

"They are no threat; look at the sad bitches here. They are nothing to me, and neither were their men, from what we saw." He gestured to the skraelings, who all sat cowering along the back wall.

Gudrid bristled, and though she answered him, she kept her cool, "You were lucky, that is all. You would be a fool to expect to be so lucky again. This is their land, and yes, we will be taking it, but they start with the advantage."

"They are nothing but wretches!"

"But they no doubt outnumber us in the hills and vales about, and they also know what is good to eat and where best to hunt. We stand in peril, not them. We must settle ourselves and learn how best to farm this land so it can feed us, while also raising defences and increasing our numbers."

"You talk not only of a lifetime's work, but that of my children—and their children!" contended Thrainn.

Thoromr frowned and shifted uncomfortably as he sat by his father's side.

"And that is the truth of it. We came to claim the land for Odin and his kin, and the price was always going to be a lifetime enslaved to the task. We all knew that. Even some of your own, such as Leif, spoke of it."

The Lakelanders froze at the mention of the dead man's name, Alfvin going as far as to wince.

Eskil noticed the expression.

Thrainn frowned before his eyes half-closed and he fell into a sneer. "Now the truth of it comes; thraldom for all! And you, the witch-queen of Markland, will be the slave master over us!"

Gasps sounded from around the fire pit. Even the thralls shrank back, perhaps not understanding the words spoken, but hearing the hostile edge.

Eskil got to his feet and hissed, "Look at you, Thrainn, coming into our hall as a guest, yet spewing nothing but evil and lies. You worried last night that we were the returned-dead coming to deceive you, but that is a charge more fitting for you!"

THE LANDING

On the other side of the fire pit, Thrainn also stood, his extra height taking him almost half-a-head over Eskil, despite the Godslander's own solid build. "You defend your wife as though bewitched! How do we know she did not pull you all from the sea as corpses and then fill you with malicious spirits? You are gutless after being blooded not by war or battle, but by the birthing bed!"

Others got up from the fire pit now, stepping back to keep clear of the violence sure to come.

Eskil shook his head. "Thrainn, after listening to your tale, I can say there is only one person here who is possessed. You show signs of madness, have inflicted bloody violence, and raged with a cruel lust since your landing. You! When your ship wrecked, I bet you were at your worst, as your body clawed its way free of the sea, powered not by the man we all knew in Iceland, but by a malevolent shade come to wreak havoc. You stink of lies, rape, blood and murder!"

Around the circle of faces, Eskil was not alone in noticing that Ari, one of Thrainn's own men, nodded.

With a curse, Thrainn pulled his axe and bellowed as he leapt over the fire pit's flames, swinging for Eskil's neck.

Eskil was not afraid to fight, but he was no fan of needless blood. He had been preparing himself for a confrontation with Thrainn since the big brute had begun to sow doubts in his mind with the changing tales of the Lakelanders' landing.

The Godslander kicked out to knock Thrainn off balance, landing his boot on the big man's thigh. Eskil hit the side of his adversary's body, opposite to that holding the axe, the brute already swinging it down.

Once Eskil's boot connected, the Godslander threw himself out of the way, using Thrainn's own bulk to kick himself out of reach. He landed at the head of the fire pit, while Thrainn turned with the impact of the kick, landing off balance on the edge of the fire near where Eskil had earlier been sitting. The axe sliced down harmlessly, cutting through the air.

Eskil started his defence off good, but he needed a weapon better than his small blade. He reached out and grabbed at a long piece of wood, a branch longer than his arm and two-thirds aflame.

Thrainn quickly stepped away from the fire pit's edge, his boots uncomfortably close to the flames. He then spun about to face his enemy, cursing under his breath, "Gods, do not dare desert me again!"

Eskil despised fights. For him they were the resort of animals, the desperate and fools, but he did not fear them. Grunting dourly to himself, he went after Thrainn, striding toward the turning giant, already swinging the burning length of wood.

Thrainn turned just as Eskil closed. He tried to step back to give himself space, but with the fire pit on one side, Eskil in front, and his balance still not settled, he could not. Cursing, he raised his axe, its previous swing spent, and moved to get the weapon in position.

Eskil's burning branch, aglow in yellow and amber, came in hard from the side as it cut through the last of the space between them, leaving a trail of smoke.

Thrainn, unable to dodge out of the way, tried to shift the axe to deflect the blow.

Eskil let out a roar of satisfaction as the burning timber hit the Lakelander in the side of the head, sizzling as it did, sparks flying and flames billowing. He poured his strength into the swing, hoping to force Thrainn to the side and into the fire pit.

Those around them called out.

Thrainn realised too late that he could not avoid the blow, his reaction too slow. The branch had already landed against the side of his head, flames flaring and sparks flashing before his eyes. His nostrils filled with the scent of his burning skin and singeing hair. Amidst the burst of pain, he gritted his teeth and tightened his grip on his axe, as he went with the momentum and clumsily leapt back across the fire pit.

He landed again at the edge, kicking embers and burning wood across the hall, the sparks and swirling smoke adding to the chaos. He jumped clear, one of his boots smouldering, as he worked on gathering himself and regaining his balance.

Eskil knew he needed to press the advantage, so he was already in the air, flying over the fire pit, flaming branch in hand.

Thrainn steadied and brought up his axe, ready this time. With a roar, he swung at Eskil.

The Godslander brought the branch up in front of him, knowing it was not enough for either a killing blow or for deflecting the axe if it hit. But his motivation for leaping across the fire pit was not to continue the fight, but rather to get to the wood axe sticking in the chopping block.

Thrainn's axe landed, biting so closely to the branch near Eskil's hand that Gudrid, Halla and some of the men cried out.

But the axe had not merely come close; it hit him, striking the edge of his hand.

Eskil hissed but, even injured, he managed to keep the lethal weapon's passage away from his chest as the branch broke, sending sparks and embers flying.

Blood began to pepper the floor in the firelight around Eskil, earning a cheer from Thoromr and Trion, but the Godslander had already moved on. His leap meant he also crashed into Thrainn, forcing the bigger man back a step. While Thrainn regained his footing, Eskil grabbed the wood axe and then spun back around, already swinging with it. As he did so, a trail of blood spots followed his progress, dropping on the dirt floor.

Thrainn glowered. "You bleed!"

Eskil, coming to a halt, stood long enough in the firelight for all to see he had lost his little finger. He clasped the axe tight, his blood running along the handle and dripping into the dirt. "A wound, but nothing compared to your burnt and blistered head."

Thoromr growled, "Finish him father!"

Thrainn nodded and stepped forward, his own axe raised.

Gudrid held little Ulfarr close and said, "End him like the wolf!"

Eskil stepped forward, the two men glaring at each other and studying the other's wounds.

Their own people watched in tense silence, occasionally shifting to get out of the way, and the skraelings watched in horrid fascination. The violence of these strange people stunned them, but at the same time, every one of them wanted Thrainn dead.

Eskil stepped in and lunged once, feinting a swinging with the axe.

Thrainn stepped back, moving awkwardly on the foot wearing the smoking boot.

Eskil feinted again, advancing on Thrainn, trying to force the Lakelander back into the ruins of the burning branch, hoping Thrainn would be distracted enough to provide an advantage.

Thrainn stepped back, hissing at Eskil and his latest lunge.

He backed into the field of smoking embers and sparks. The Lakelander did not notice them until he stepped on a section of Eskil's discarded branch and slipped, setting his already-smouldering boot to smoke more.

The big man glanced down to check his footing.

Eskil grabbed the chance and charged in, axe up, eyeing Thrainn's ribs.

Thrainn reacted to the movement, bringing his own axe up and around. He cried out in a strangled gasp of pain as Eskil's small axe got through and briefly tasted flesh, before the bigger axe knocked it away.

Eskil backed up to evade Thrainn's lethal swing.

He was frustrated that he had gotten so close and blooded his weapon but not been able to make the most out of the attack. But as he stood there, he noticed the dirt under Thrainn begin to darken from the speckled blood running from the fresh wound to his side.

Eskil charged in again.

Grimacing, Thrainn ignored his pain and swung wide with his axe.

Eskil dodged the blow, but failed to land another.

Thrainn followed through when Eskil was exposed, but luckily for the Godslander, it was not his axe that he had let swing. A solid shove sent Eskil off balance and wheeling, causing him to fall backwards into the dirt.

Thrainn stepped forward, roaring, as he brought up his axe.

The giant Lakelander loomed over Eskil, stumbling closer as blood continued to run from his side. He glared as he looked down on him. "I will enjoy this far too much!"

Eskil took a deep breath and tensed, ready to scramble out of the way.

Thrainn frowned and lifted his axe high, but groaned as he did, a flow of blood raining down onto the dirt floor.

Eskil kicked out with his legs and struck one of Thrainn's knees.

The Lakelander fell back, while Eskil jumped up.

Eskil, axe in hand, shook his head. He then shoved Thrainn over and onto his back. He was soon astride Thrainn's chest, his knees and legs pinning his foe's arms and axe to the ground. He hissed, "It did not have to be this way!"

Thrainn, angry, his face burnt and blistered, with blood running from his nose and his side, spat at Eskil. "A curse on you and your hall...may winter come one day and never let go!"

Eskil raised his axe.

Trion watched, his eyes focused on the small wood axe. He whispered under his breath, "How many blows?"

Eskil, grim-faced, brought the axe down to end the matter.

Blood sprayed up to coat Eskil, running down his neck and cheek. The wound was deep across Thrainn's neck, causing the Lakelander to spasm and gurgle, but that soon ended.

Steinarr said, "You have to remove the head in case he is draugr or some other accursed dead."

Eskil gave an exhausted nod and brought the axe down again. Another blow followed, spattering more blood over the weary Godslander, and then Thrainn's head finally rolled free.

It was over.

He got up and glanced for the first time at his missing finger, but he did not stop, instead turning to seek out Thoromr.

Thoromr stood still and silent, his face pale, Trion by his side.

Eskil crossed to him, with his bloody axe in his wounded hand, held down by his side. Behind him, surrounded by glowing embers and a circle of swirling smoke, Thrainn's body and head lay, as a pool of blood spread to darken the ground.

Thoromr took a step forward to meet Eskil.

Eskil locked his gaze onto him, Thrainn's blood evidenced on his cheek and neck. "Your father was possessed. It was not your fault."

Thoromr was pale, and started to shake his head. "He was my father."

Trion stood nearby, watching,

Eskil nodded. "Choices become difficult. Kin cannot turn on their own, let alone a son against a father, particularly when matters are blurred after a shipwreck and so much death."

Thoromr stilled and then swallowed. Finally, he gave a slow nod, willing to grab at the absolution Eskil offered.

The Godslander continued, "We need to work together to keep ourselves safe. All of us. It is the only way we will survive the trials of the winters to come and any skraeling threat."

Eskil's people, as well as Alfvin and Ari, nodded in agreement.

Thoromr began to frown, an expression typical of his father's face. "I serve Thor, it is true, and I agreed to come west with my father in search of new lands to devote to the creed. But after arriving and surviving its long winter, I have come to the conclusion that this is a frigid waste of barren wilderness." He sneered. "And worse than that, one filled with cowards and fools who let themselves be ruled over by..." he paused for a moment as he carefully chose his next word, "...women!"

Gudrid said, "We have spoken of nothing but caution and planning!"

With words sounding like his father's, Thoromr snapped, "You have silenced your own men in this!"

Eskil sighed, while beside him, Steinarr shook his head. Yet Ballr was the one to speak. "Working together is the best way for us to survive in Markland."

"It is nonsense." Thoromr turned to look for the skraeling women at the back of the hall, as far away from their Lakelanders as they could be. The three sheep lay near them. "I will go and take any with me who wish a life free of this nonsense!"

"Come now, Thoromr," Eskil replied. "Please reconsider. It will be better for all to work together."

"I shall have nothing to do with any of you." And he then turned away, striding across to his thrall.

The skraelings shrank away from Thoromr as he neared, but he ignored their chatter and whines, and reached down for a handful of his thrall's long, black hair. With a sharp tug, he brought her to her feet and then turned back to face the Norse. "I will take your raft, and in return, you will be rid of me. I will also take whoever wishes to go, as well as my sheep." His hand went to the rough hilt of a knife he wore tucked into his belt.

Many of the others saw the move and followed suit by reaching for their own blades whether stone, bone or iron.

Halla stepped forward between the groups, a hand resting on her swelling belly. "Have you lost your senses? We are all to be found of our own kind in Markland, and that means we need to work together!"

Straightening up to face her, Thoromr cursed and then turned to Eskil. "What is it with your women? Is it that they all dare to speak with the supposed voice of the gods or that they have taken your balls while you slept?"

Eskil stepped forward. "They are entitled to speak."

"To their husbands and children, perhaps, and also to your lame sheep...but not to me."

"They have earned our respect with not just their actions and labour, but also their words. We would not have survived without them."

Thoromr mocked, "I thought you said the gods brought you here?"

"They did, but not to lay about in sloth while awaiting their favour. They brought us here to work for them and to make the most of what we have been given."

"Enough! I shall be leaving!"

"If you wish."

Thoromr turned to face his three fellow Lakelanders, standing with his trembling thrall, who slowly dropped down to squat by his feet. "Come, this is no place for us."

Until now, his men had said little, but their faces spoke a range of emotions.

Alfvin was the first to break the silence. "They are right, Thoromr. We need to stay together. It is the only way we will survive in this new land."

Ari then spoke up, and anger laced his tone. "Together they say; it is nothing but wisdom. They have a message to heed, not spurn!"

Thoromr's anger grew, just as his father's would have. "Spurn! They are being enslaved!"

Ari answered, "You have become bitter like your father, almost poisoned against the gods and this land. Your anger is not fired by being told what to do by women, but rather that your mother is not doing the bidding!"

Alfvin held up his hands in an effort to silence the growing fury and soothe the heat. But Trion broke the brief calm, stoking the fire once again. "Hold, Ari and Alfvin; Thoromr is right about malady being in this place. Yes, it would be wiser for us to work together, but that does not mean it has to be. Besides, maybe we are unable to work together. Perhaps we should live separate lives and build our own farms and futures. We came here not only to be free of the agents of the White Christ, but also free from the rise of new kings."

Thoromr smiled at Trion's words, turning toward Alfvin and Ari – particularly the latter – his fellow's harsh tone still ringing in his ears. "You can stay here if you will, but I intend to return to Lakeland and take my sheep."

Eskil said, "You will be going nowhere without our raft, and about that we have yet to agree."

Thoromr pushed his chest out and widened his stance, his one free hand now well and truly settled on the hilt of his knife. "Are you coming with me, Trion?"

The Lakelander looked first to his fellows and then to Gudrid and Halla before striding to join Thoromr. Turning back to face the others, he looked to the remaining skraeling women and barked for Thrainn's thrall, "Huncha, here!"

One of the women rose and scurried across to Trion, swapping worried glances with Thoromr's thrall and the two left behind.

Thoromr said, "And what of you others? Who will go with me to live in Lakeland?"

Ari shook his head angrily, still fuming, while Alfvin looked on in grim silence.

"Then this is the breaking of our fellowship."

"It was long broken, long ago," Alfvin agreed darkly.

Eskil spoke again, eager to calm the tension in his hall. "If you must go in this manner, we still offer our friendship, as there may yet be times ahead when we need to talk or seek each other's aid."

"I want none of yours!"

"So you say, but who is to know what may yet befall any or all of us."

"Bah, you sound like the Christians' priests!"

Eskil's eyes blazed at the comparison, but he withheld his anger. "That will do for now. Go."

"I will take the raft and the sheep."

"We will trade the raft for one of your sheep."

"They are my sheep and you will not have any of them!"

"If you want our raft, and half your people are staying behind in Godsland, then this is the way it will be. I will even let you take your father's axe."

Thoromr cursed, "The sheep are mine, and not yours to take!"

"As the raft is ours. I think your own men would argue for some portion of ownership of the sheep. If they wish to stay here with us, as they are welcomed to do, that means two of the thralls will remain as well. Alfvin and Ari cannot come empty handed to our hall."

"That is a quarrel for you to have with them, if indeed they are not coming with me."

Eskil lost some of his calm as the exchange continued. "You will not leave here without our blessing–unless you mean to swim the frigid waters of the fjord. I offer you the raft as the means to go in peace and to even take a sheep, but you will return my token by leaving the other animal, as you will also be leaving behind a great many mouths to feed."

Alfvin spoke up, "It is a fair trade and a kind enough offer after the hard words Thrainn and you have used in soiling this hall."

Thoromr sneered. "And who are you to judge such a thing?"

"A man once of Lakeland, now welcomed into Godsland, with his thrall and sheep. You shall not take that away from me."

Ari also spoke, "Look about you, Thoromr. Look at all they have built and done! The tales they tell; of landing as the storm died about them to reveal a world of green touched by golden light at the foot of a runestone!"

"It is merely a tale!"

"This is where we should be, working together so all survive. Why do you not see?"

"I will have none of it. If it is so important to you, I will trade a sheep only so I can journey from here."

Eskil relaxed. "Good."

Torrador supported him. "A fair trade."

"Then carry it for me." And he made for the door, dragging his woman behind.

From there he stopped and turned, looking to the raven banner hanging on the wall. With a sneer, he hissed, "This hall of ravens may have slaughtered a wolf, but I shall build up a hall across the water that will house nothing but wolves fed on fury, who shall one day return to repay you and your sour hospitality."

Eskil shook his head. "Go, Thoromr, return to your hall with no more bitter words."

It was dusk when they left – Thoromr and Trion, with Thrainn's body, two thralls and a lone sheep. Few words were spoken as they poled off into the deepening night. The only sound to come back across the water was that of harsh laughter as the two Norsemen exchanged a joke of ill temper.

COLIN TABER

Part III

The Rift

COLIN TABER

Chapter 8

-

Spring

The last of the snows melted, revealing the land springing into green life. While the thaw might have come and gone, the bitterness of the opening disagreement between ravens and wolves lingered. The Godsland Norse tried to put the sour events behind them, setting themselves to work, but Eskil feared the quarrel would haunt them for a long time to come.

The skraeling women responded well to a gentler hall. The first tentative bonds of trust grew as they worked alongside Gudrid and Halla, reinforced by softer dealings with their men, Alfvin and Ari. The two former Lakelanders seemed relieved they were free of Thrainn and his bloodstained hall.

While Ari and Alfvin initially spoke little of life with Thrainn, Thoromr and Trion, they were more than full partners in their labours as they worked to ensure a place in the Godsland hall. One of the first things they did outside their daily chores of fishing and gathering firewood was help Torrador and Steinarr build a small boat. They fashioned the craft out of salvaged timber planks to replace the raft traded to Thoromr as part of their move between halls.

Before long, spring moved into early summer, and the hall welcomed more babes into the world, this time from the thralls. Alfvin became the proud father to a boy, while brooding Ari was presented only days later with the surprise of twins, a boy and a girl, although he seemed, as he often did, to take the news quietly.

The new arrivals looked neither Norse nor of their mothers' stock. They were born with a skin of a hue in-between the two groups, and with lighter hair. All the adults suspected that such looks, along with their blue eyes, would drift as the babes grew. Neither could say what such issue would eventually resemble, whether it favour Markland's newcomers, those long of its cool vales, or that the babes would be the first of a new people.

The initial strands of trust built between the skraeling women and Gudrid and Halla strengthened as each thrall went through her own labour, aided by the Norse. Eventually, even the men noted the rise of this new sisterhood, including the newcomers, Alfvin and Ari.

As the weather continued to improve, so did the range of foods gathered from the island, the sound and the journeys farther afield along the fjord, in the new boat. One of the skraelings would often accompany the expeditions across the cool waters, helping to identify what could be eaten and showing the uses of various plants new to the Godslanders. Such voyages, usually led by Eskil, had several goals: explore their surroundings, find better sites for settlement and discover what treasures the land had yet to give up, be it timber, food or bog iron.

They also watched for any sign of neighbouring settlements, be they Norse or skraeling.

Eskil and Gudrid had discussed the thralls at length, particularly on the morning after the twins' birth, as they walked the shores of Godsland, looking for driftwood or anything of use given up by the sea. He asked, "Can they be trusted?"

"Do you mean are they looking to grab a blade one night and slit our throats?"

"I suppose that is part of the question, but what also of running away and leaving us?"

"Where would they go?"

"Well, not back to Thoromr, but their people must be somewhere near."

She nodded in agreement. "Yes, I suppose."

"I admit that when I take them to the mainland, I only take one of them, and we travel to places we have already seen and know."

"You are wise to be careful."

"I do not want to run into their own kind, not when we have no idea what the two women would tell them."

Gudrid walked on, thinking, her eyes watching the gravel of the beach. "I do not think they would slit our throats, not when they have children and are so outnumbered. Having said that, I cannot be certain they want to remain with us either."

Eskil nodded. "They seem more settled, even speaking words of Norse."

"Yes."

"We need them."

Gudrid stopped to pick up a branch lying on the beach before she answered. "They know this land, certainly better than we do. I hope to learn from them, as to what we can grow and eat. There must be grains and root crops we can rear."

Eskil nodded, pleased to hear such a thought. "And are they thralls or wives? By Odin, sometimes I cannot tell the difference with how Alfvin treats his woman, although Ari is a colder sort."

"You pose a good question."

"I imagine the other men would also like to know. I suspect more than one of them would be quick, given the chance, to wed either of them. I pity them and feel responsible for their loneliness."

Gudrid saddened. "If the Greenland Norse return to Lakeland, we may yet meet more of our own kind."

"Perhaps."

"Frae and Seta have been good for us."

"Yes...their names...I suppose it would not hurt for us to use them instead of referring to them as skraeling or thrall."

"No, particularly when Alfvin and Ari both use their names when you and the other men are not around," she grinned.

Eskil chuckled. "Do they?"

"Yes, and they seem to also be confused as to whether they are wives or thralls."

"The thralls..." he paused for a moment before trying again, "Frae and Seta,"

Gudrid gave a pleased nod.

"They have already given us valuable knowledge, particularly of local foods and materials from the woodlands, pastures and fjord. I would simply prefer to know they can be trusted."

"While we need them, perhaps we should offer them their freedom to come and go. Let them decide if they want to stay."

Eskil looked to her with wide eyes, startled by the very idea. "They might leave!"

"Yes, and there lies your answer as to if they can be trusted. But what if they chose to stay?"

"Why would they?" Eskil asked.

"For their children, and perhaps our hall is not as bad as their other choices."

"You mean Lakeland. But what of their own kind?"

"They would choose us over Lakeland's hall, of that I am certain. But who knows what is left of their own people?"

"What do you mean by that?"

"As you have stated before - something bloody happened when Thrainn stumbled into their world. We know this, yet perhaps we have only half the truth."

Eskil grimaced. "I need to talk to Ari and Alfvin. I have tried before, without pushing, as neither desires to dwell on what happened with Thrainn. We also need to discover their feelings on other matters."

"Like?"

"The thralls are theirs, even if we deem it wise to set them free. I need to convince both of them."

Gudrid gave a nod. "The women have already had chances to run off. In any case, if they were going to do such a thing, I would think they would do so in the summer - certainly not in spring when the weather can turn - or as we head into autumn. They know, better than us, that they need be ready with food and shelter for winter."

"Do they talk to you, I mean in the way of conversation?"

"They were quiet at first, but when we brought them into our duties, they spoke a little more. I think they already knew some Norse from Lakeland. In particular, after the birthings, they have become more trusting. Alfvin and Ari have helped by treating them better. I have not seen either strike them since they joined us."

"Do they fear their men?"

"They watch and obey them, listening for commands. I doubt Frae fears Alfvin, although I am not certain of Seta, in regards to Ari."

"Feelings are growing between Frae and Alfvin; I have noticed hints of it. Such a thing is harder to say about Ari and Seta, since he is a quieter man."

Gudrid offered a smile at Eskil's comment and raised her eyebrows to emphasise her words. "That is not unlike Seta herself, do you not think?"

Eskil chuckled again. "I have hardly spoken to her - not like you - but she does seem a little distant and frostbitten."

She laughed at that. "I think she is much happier here, despite not showing it. I think all of them are."

"I shall try and talk to the men, one-on-one, to see what their thoughts might be. I will ask Ballr to help as he spends much time collecting timber with Ari. Can you talk to the women and see if you can draw out their intentions?"

"Yes."

"And we need to know more about their people since there must be some still around. We need to know if they are nearby, in what direction, and how many. One day we will run into them and, in truth, I would rather do so with Frae and Seta by my side–and wanting to be–instead of them being tempted to turn on us."

***

Eskil and Torrador were on the boat along with Ballr, Alfvin and Seta. They were heading up the calm waters of fjord in the early morning to check sites ahead, including marshes suitable for bog iron, and a series of spring-green glades for settlement.

They needed a new bog iron site, as the existing marsh they had been trying only produced poor quality ore. Upon examining it, Alfvin had declared that better marshes must be about, for they certainly were to be found in Lakeland, so why not elsewhere. Having announced the search on, he was keen to get it underway.

While the search for bog iron was a driver, so too was the matter of food and furs. On a previous trip, as spring took hold of the land, Torrador and Steinarr discovered a wide variety of green life across a string of glades. Upon hearing this, Gudrid suggested taking Seta along to see if she could identify any plants that might be good eating. If they found any, the plants could be uprooted and brought back for the garden she was establishing. Eskil agreed, also liking the idea of being able to spend some time with the enigmatic thrall.

The morning was peaceful on the fjord, the sun shining much of the time. Yet despite the light, beauty and space about them, a rising tension came to settle over them. They were passing alongside the shoreline that would bring them close to Lakeland.

Little chance existed that Thoromr would be there, as the man, no doubt, had a lot to do, particularly now that the settlement had only the two Norsemen and their thralls. Regardless, the Godslanders drifted past the shore, and even though no one raised the subject, all eyed the woodland that climbed from the fjord-side ridge up above, beyond which lay Lakeland.

All five travellers sought some sign of their hostile neighbour.

Was Thoromr there?

Eskil noted that the pace of their rowing slowed, and he was as much to blame as anyone else. Annoyed at this haunting by Thoromr, Eskil grumbled, "Let us keep moving."

Torrador grunted, but did what Eskil bid.

Ballr whispered, as if somehow Thoromr might over hear, "Even if he was there, you would not see him; the trees grow too thick."

Eskil caught himself nodding, and then became annoyed that he had even acknowledged the shadow of the man hanging over them. Still, having done so, he ventured, "It would be so much smarter for us to work together, but if we cannot, then that is the way it must be."

Torrador answered, "He is an arrogant brute, like his father, but also good with his axe. In a fight, I would rather him on my side than be against me. Thrainn trained him well."

Ballr agreed, but Seta and Alfvin remained quiet.

They continued along the shoreline, scanning the woods for any sign of Thoromr, eventually passing far enough that they felt they were out of Lakeland's domain. The shore itself broke up in places, shadowed by a few long, thin, well-wooded islands.

They soon passed a slight bend, where Ballr pointed out a heavily wooded gully backing onto yet another steep slope. He said, "See, this was the spot I was telling you about, that Ari and I had spied before: A place of good, tall and varied timber, also close to Godsland. You could merely float the logs down the channel with the tide and current."

Eskil could only agree. Many of the trees climbed tall and straight, making the gully their closest stock of not only good timber, but of the kind of logs they would eventually need for roof beams or perhaps a ship's mast. The trees certainly were much better than the smaller and softer birch and willow they had on Godsland. "Yes, Ballr, but perhaps it is still too close to Lakeland. You would probably not run into Thoromr while going ashore, but the sounds of you felling trees might bring him on. I do not care to see any of us go up against him if armed with his father's axe, for he is strong and fast."

Torrador offered, "You could best him, as you did his father."

Eskil shook his head. "Maybe not, not with our battered, old axe. Thoromr is as strong as his father was, and almost as big, but now also has more to prove. I think he might have the advantage."

Ballr frowned, but tried his luck. "Maybe later we could try for some timber there, when it is more opportune?"

Eskil grimaced.

"Perhaps when we are at peace?"

Alfvin muttered, "Peace? Thoromr is too much like Thrainn; I would not wait for it."

Torrador smirked, "Or when Alfvin can get enough iron together to make some real axes." He turned to the former Lakelander and asked, "Have you not already gathered a good amount from salvaging nails from our ship's ruin?"

Alfvin gave a nod. "I have some, but not quite enough."

Ballr grinned. "Axes! What a day that shall be!"

The Icelander's fellows all smiled to hear his enthusiasm, but did

114

not comment further. They did not want to encourage Ballr, since they all had heard of the jarred hands and elbows, of blistered palms and fingers too often over the past season.

They briefly travelled in silence, the oar strokes the only thing to sound as they drifted past the promising shore.

Eskil turned to look up the fjord, to where they were headed, but his attention stopped as a call came to them from the shoreline.

"Eskil, keep your filthy Ravens off my land!"

It was unmistakably Thoromr.

They all turned to search the distant woods, trying to spy him out.

Eskil stopped himself from shaking his head or offering some ill-considered rebuke. He raised his voice instead and yelled, "We only pass by the free lands of Markland!"

Thoromr stepped out from amongst the trees near the shoreline, his father's axe in hand. "These are my lands...Lakeland!"

Eskil despaired at the stubbornness of the young man. So much like his father, he was perhaps even destined to be worse. Their boat had already drifted past, yet Thoromr persisted in his challenge, "Get away from here, all of you!"

Eskil answered him, "It would be fair to say your border would come in at the islands we have only passed, not here. You cannot claim all of Markland. You are no king!"

"I shall claim what I want, even if it be all of this side of the fjord!"

"Let it go, Thoromr, as you can see we are not stopping."

The big man, face red, raised his axe and shook it. "A good thing too, for I will bloody any of you who try!"

Eskil glanced at his fellows. Ballr wanted to reply, but was held in check by Eskil's presence. Torrador was bemused by the young man and his impotent anger. Meanwhile, Alfvin watched impassively, as Seta sat next to him and glared, not hiding her hate for the Lakelander.

Eskil wondered aloud, "If there is only him and Trion, and one of them must watch over the women, they can not get much done."

Seta frowned. "Him bad man."

Ballr said, "They will starve this winter if they do not get enough food stored."

Eskil agreed, "Yes, and guess where they will come when they get desperate?"

Thoromr could see them talking, but could not hear their words. He shook his axe and cursed, "By Thor, Ballr, why are you not at home with the women! That skraeling beside you has bigger balls than you!"

Ballr tensed and took in a breath, about to hurl a retort.

Eskil went to put a hand to his shoulder to stop him, but they were silenced by Seta, who stood up, making the boat rock, as she yelled, "Thoromr stink bad, worse than sheep!"

Her voice rang out across the fjord and then echoed back over the water.

Thoromr stood stunned, his raised and shaking axe stilled.

She added, "Or is sheep dead? Have you put axe in it, too?"

The Godsland men all burst out laughing, doubly silencing the Lakelander, who flushed redder than his beard.

Eskil tried to gather himself, indicating for Torrador to keep on the oars. "Come now, let us move on."

Ballr and Torrador nodded, but could not quiet their mirth. The latter glanced back at Seta, admiration in his eyes.

Seta looked to Eskil, embarrassed.

Alfvin chuckled, while announcing. "I cannot wait to tell your sister!"

Eskil smiled, trying to reassure her. "Are you alright?"

"Thoromr bad."

"Merely angry."

"Full of angry."

"Yes, it blinds him, but maybe one day he will calm down."

"Blind?"

"He cannot see." Eskil used his spare hand to cover his eyes.

She gave a quick nod of understanding. "No," she said, before shaking her head. "He die blind."

They continued on, Thoromr disappearing back into the woods behind them as he cursed loudly and worked his anger out hitting his axe to the trees.

Eskil said to Torrador, "I do not want them coming to Godsland in winter if they lack food. We shall have to watch their preparations. We may have to help them or even destroy their raft so they cannot get across unexpectedly."

"Wise words. Upsetting the raft would be easy; we would simply need to cut the binding ropes. They could still try and cross the ice, but it would be a dangerous journey, and one undertaken when fully exposed to winter."

"We shall see how they are going when autumn comes around."

Torrador, Alfvin and Ballr nodded. Even Seta seemed to understand enough of what was said to quietly agree.

They continued for a long way, reaching the glades and the variety of plants they held. Seta confirmed some of them were edible, particularly a low-growing and long-leafed root with bitter tubers that stored well over winter. Eskil and Torrador helped her dig those up while also collecting some other plants, including various shooting berry bush canes.

Meanwhile, Alfvin stood at the shoreline, looking farther down the sound to where he could see low hills around the entrance to a larger vale, all framed by bluffs and peaks.

Torrador asked him, "Can you see something?"

Alfvin smiled. "Yes." He turned and raised his voice so Eskil could hear. "You may as well not hurry. I can see an area we need to check for bog iron. But it is too far away for us to spend real time there today."

Eskil got up, brushing his dirty hands on his pants. "What is it?"

"A place of promise. Looking down there, I can see something that reminds me of the land back home."

Eskil smiled, and he was not alone. "When we finish here, we will go a little closer, to see what we can, then head back so we still make Godsland by dusk."

Alfvin looked to Seta, a grin on his face. "I hope Thoromr will be waiting on the shoreline so we can give him another rousing."

Her face lit up at his words.

***

Gudrid looked at Frae; the woman kneeled in the dirt, only paces away, using a stripped branch, with a sharpened end, to break the soil. With strong hands, the skraeling lifted the wood high and then, with a grunt, brought its point down, stabbing into the stubborn earth. The work was hard, but broken up by other tasks as they loosened the soil and prepared the garden bed.

They worked where the turf had originally been removed and used to build their hall's walls almost a year ago. In that naked earth, after stripping out the worst of the rocks, Gudrid had established a small garden for cropping. They now worked to expand it.

This year, with the last of the salvaged seed brought from Iceland, they needed a good harvest, but not just of roots and vegetables. No, this summer Eskil wanted her to grow her crops not only for food, but also to replenish their seed stocks.

The plot lay at the centre of the gully, beside the stream that drained it, in front of the birch grove, and well back from the seashore. The spot received good sun, and the shoulder of the hill that curved around to form the hall, amidst the rock outcroppings and overhangs, sheltered it from the wind. The other side of the gully likewise offered shelter from the worst of the seaborne winds.

The soil they worked was as much gravel as dirt, yet Gudrid had been adding manures to it from both the sheep and the hall - a farmer's trick learned from her mother many years ago - to provide depth. Now, turning the soil mixed up what they added, and also kept it loose. They would plant the bulbous roots that Seta harvested during their expedition up the fjord.

Frae knew the tubers and said they were good for winter eating, though she also indicated they did not possess a pleasant taste.

Lost in her thoughts, Gudrid stabbed at the stubborn earth with her own sharpened stake, which had become blunt after a long morning of use. She did not notice she had uncovered a rock, an upward thrust of stone that lay in wait for her fingers, as she again brought her tool rushing down.

The pain came suddenly, a kind of burning, as the skin tore open and blood flowed.

Gudrid gasped and then hissed out a curse.

Frae looked up to see blood on Gudrid's hand. She cried out and got up to hurry over, then dropped down to kneel beside her.

Gudrid let go of the stake and held out her hand, palm downwards, spreading the fingers to examine the hurt. Blood ran freely from grazed knuckles and a cut running across three fingers. She cursed again and moved to wipe away the dirt.

Frae reached across for a water skin and brought it to Gudrid's wound. With a quick look to the Godslander for approval, she then began to pour the cool liquid over the wound.

Gudrid let out a pained hiss.

The skraeling continued, using her darker fingers to carefully clean the dirt away so they could better see the extent of the wound.

119

Frae's touch was firm, the water numbingly cold.

With a sigh, Gudrid sat back on her legs and turned to look at their work. They had done enough digging for the day; it was time to focus on planting. Besides, she thought to herself, she would then have a chance to rest her hand so it could scab over and dry.

The water revealed the wound to be shallow, more of a graze and a bruise.

Once the water skin was empty, Frae gave a grunt of satisfaction and looked to Gudrid before saying in her broken Norse, "Not bad."

Gudrid gave a weak smile, despite the rising sting coming from the wound now that the icy water had stopped. "Thank you. The rock got me."

Frae looked into the hole being dug, spying the stone's tip. She frowned, reached for the stake and used it to ram the pointed rock, knocking it loose. She pulled it out and tossed it to the pile of others they were building beside the garden. "Bad rock."

Gudrid's smile broadened, and she even chuckled. "Yes, Frae, bad rock." She sighed, but then added, "Let us do some planting."

The skraeling woman smiled and nodded.

Gudrid stood, followed by Frae. Together they went to the small pile of rootstock.

Frae gathered up several roots, being careful of any green leaves, as Gudrid watched.

The Godsland woman stood there holding her bloody hand. The flow had all but stopped, but it was still wet. She was about to bend down and pick up some of the roots when Seta came out of the hall with Halla, the two women carrying all four babes. Ballr's wife was the only one of them still expecting.

Frae called out, "Gudrid hurt!"

Halla frowned and looked to Gudrid standing there, still holding her hand. She walked over, followed by Seta. "What happened?"

Frae offered up, "Bad rock."

Gudrid laughed, glancing at the smiling Frae, before turning back to Halla and Seta. "Yes, a bad rock. I caught my hand."

The women all gathered to look at the wound, which was now beginning to dry.

Seta said something to Frae, but her words were in their own tongue.

Halla tensed and took half a step back.

Frae chuckled as the two Norsewomen turned to look at her. After a moment she said, "Seta say roots good winter food, but taste bad, worse than bad rock."

Gudrid began to laugh again.

Frae, Seta and a surprised Halla joined her. The sound, not a complete stranger, but one not heard enough, rolled through the gully. Afterwards, under the sun, the late spring greens of the gully looked that much greener.

***

By the shore near the hall, Halla checked over the rock pools with Seta, wading carefully through the cool shallows the low tide had almost finished leaving behind. The daily search often turned up trapped fish, crabs and other sea creatures. The haul gave them more variety in their eating and often a small surplus of fish to be dried and stored for winter.

While Halla liked the hunt, and Seta also seemed to enjoy it, they did not often speak. If the skraeling woman did talk, she used a broken Norse that could be confusing when she tried to communicate anything more complicated than a simple question or to point something out, yet Halla persevered.

Gudrid had asked her to spend time with Seta, to get a sense of what the woman was thinking in relation to the Godsland Norse. Between them, Gudrid quietly confided that she wanted to see both of the thralls freed.

Halla was at first surprised by the idea, perhaps even shocked. Gudrid explained she wanted the women to choose to stay at the hall – and to do so freely. As the two Norsewomen discussed the idea, Halla began to understand that Gudrid hoped if the skraelings chose to commit to Godsland, they would all benefit from Frae and Seta's local knowledge – of plants, animals, the weather and sea, and of neighbouring skraeling bands. Gudrid suggested the women might offer the information more quickly and willingly if they wanted to see the Godsland settlement thrive. She insisted such a generous sharing of knowledge was unlikely to happen if the women lived as thralls, in a world of fear.

Halla was not convinced.

Gudrid asked Halla to watch Seta, in the time they spent working together, to see if she could get a feel for the woman's deeper thoughts.

She did.

The work was not hard, despite Halla nearing her own birthing time – at most another season away – yet being with Seta made her uncomfortable. The skraeling was aloof and quiet, often not showing any type of emotion. In fact, it was only after the joke made a few days before about how bitter the roots would taste that Halla had finally seen Seta not only open up a little, but also try to speak more Norse.

The change tempted Halla to warm to her.

Yet, she was still so distant and unreadable.

Over the past half-season, as they'd settled into a routine of checking the few pools near the hall, Seta had begun asking about ranging further away to find new and better spots.

Halla liked the idea, but was also concerned at going any distance away from the hall, with only the skraeling. She often felt the woman was lonely and sad unless she was with Frae or her twin babes. Unlike Frae and Alfvin, who had some warmth in their relationship, Seta and

THE LANDING

Ari seemed to hold a colder, more practical understanding.

This left Halla with reservations.

She not only did not trust her, she also felt that if she took her eyes off Seta, the skraeling woman might run off, even though that would mean leaving her twins behind.

Yet, on this day, as they stepped into the second pool, having finished searching the first and tossing their finds into a willow basket, Seta again spoke of heading further along the coast. "Should check other pools?"

Halla was inclined to agree, but she was still uncomfortable at the thought of wandering off alone with Seta. Thinking on it, she turned and watched as Seta waded past her, towards a dip in the rocks, where the low tide drained the pool and ran through a shallow channel, giving the trapped fish and other sea creatures their last chance of freedom. The skraeling was searching the area again, which seemed odd, as they had already gone over it.

The Norsewoman went to take a step forward, curious at what Seta was doing, but got distracted as she heard a splash and felt something shoot through the water and past one of her bare feet.

She turned to see a fish, one that had somehow escaped discovery, swim into a deeper basin behind her. The fish was not big, but long enough to offer good eating. With Seta forgotten, Halla turned and stepped down onto a submerged ledge, preparing to try to catch it.

The fish was aware of her and tried to slip into a long crack in the fractured rocks of the pool.

Halla took another step, one that landed on a misleading slope. She reached out as she lost her balance, managing to control her fall, her heart pounding as she slumped into the chilly water that rose up to cover her belly.

Now steady, she turned back to see if Seta witnessed her mishap. As she did, she saw the woman standing only two paces behind her, with legs spread, her face in an ugly grimace, as she hefted up a big rock.

Halla's heart stopped and her jaw dropped as she froze. She lay still

123

for a moment, half lost in the water. The skraeling stepped forward with her murderous rock, eyes squeezed tight, and she lifted the heavy thing, water running off it like blood.

Seta took a half step and then began to turn, but Halla had already pushed herself off the slimy rocks and into the deepest part of pool, putting the depths between them.

Seta turned again with another half step, this one away from Halla, and then dropped the rock in the low lip of the channel where a trickle of water still ran. A small sea creature lay in the way. The rock landed with a crunch, shattering the shell of the thumbnail-sized critter, and plugged the outflow by damming it.

Halla let go of her breath, only now realising she had been holding it all this time.

Seta stood, straightened her back and then turned to see Halla, up to her neck in the pool. With widening brown eyes, she asked, "You fall?"

Halla tried to find her footing, the fish forgotten. "Yes, I was chasing a fish."

"Fish faster?"

Halla could not help but smile.

Seta went on, pointing to her rock. "We block and make pool bigger. Catch more fish, even fast ones."

Before Halla could answer, the woman began wading towards her. She then stood at the edge of the deeper pool and reached out a hand. Seta smiled, a rare thing, and said, "Halla, I help."

The Norsewoman reached across and took the thrall's hand.

Chapter 9

◆

Alfvin

Eskil and Alfvin looked back as they strode up the gentle slope of a scrub-covered shoreline hill. They checked on the boat, yet again, to make sure it lay beached and secure. To have the precious craft stolen away by a rising tide would not only be an indignity, but akin to a crime for a Norseman.

On this particular trip, Eskil and Alfvin went deeper into the fjord than before. They passed the shoreline where they had last seen Thoromr, and journeyed on a fair distance, putting three islands between them and Godsland. The cost of this longer trip was that they certainly would not be going back to the hall tonight. For now though, with a half an afternoon's light ahead of them, under scattered clouds, they wanted to see what this vale held before they returned to the safety of a small, nearby island to camp for the night.

They came to check the area because they noticed good signs from afar. The steeper heights beyond the shoreline hills, looked as though they nursed a broad and long vale, hopefully one with a wider range of woodlands. Eskil also hoped the land might be better protected from the ravages of the sea, not solely by the bulk of distant Godsland, but also by the other islands.

They had passed the vale on the boat once before, but did not have time to land. Now, before camping overnight, the two men had very definite goals of exploring what lay ahead, looking for good farmland, timber and marshes with potential for bog iron.

The gravel beach hosted several streams that ran from amongst the low hills. A wider flow, large enough to be called a river by those with a romantic heart, was also farther up the shore.

But the beach was at their backs. Now they headed into the hills, intent on exploring.

They crossed a few low hills covered in grasses, clovers and small stubborn shrubs, and they headed for an entry into the vale. They had only glimpsed the wide valley from afar, since much of its lower detail was lost behind the shore-side hills and the curving terrain as it turned and headed deeper into Markland's interior.

But soon the land would be unveiled.

Without a word, both men stopped when they crested the tallest of the shoreline hills. The vale straight ahead, struck by the occasional shaft of sunlight, opened wide, with a broad plain as its base. In the foreground, the plain spread, cut in two by the river's meandering flow. The reed-edged riverbank hosted thickets of trees and shrubs, and clumps of woodlands also dotted the bottom of the vale before thickly climbing the gently rising sides.

The variety of colours and shapes told of a broad range of trees. Eskil could already recognise pine and fir, and of course more birch and willow. But there were also other shapes and colours that looked new to him. Compared to Godsland, the trees were not just better, bigger and healthier, but also more plentiful.

The heights cupping the vale were of steeper slopes and starker bluffs.

The timber held great promise, but what lay closer to hand excited Alfvin more, as he looked to a series of marshes nestled between the smaller hills upon which they stood.

Alfvin said, "We will need to check here for bog iron, but I would say there should be some."

Eskil nodded and looked back to the depths of the vale that stretched off well into the distant haze. Where they stood was not that high up, but it gave him enough clearance to see the glimmer of a lake ahead that seemed to feed the river. "And wood, pasture and water. This is a good sight."

Alfvin gave a satisfied smile.

They climbed down the hill, heading forward. As they did, they also searched for any sign the vale was already home to skraelings or other Norse they were yet to encounter.

The land seemed empty.

Eskil took the opportunity to ask, "How are you doing now that you have settled amongst us?"

Alfvin glanced at Eskil as they continued on, veering towards a ridge that would keep their worn boots dry as they crossed a stretch of bogs, quiet water and reeds. A rising buzz told them the area was also home to a good number of insects.

With half a smile, the former Lakelander said, "Thrainn was a hard man and easy to anger. He was furious at what befell our ships, particularly after what seemed like such a good start after leaving Iceland. That first afternoon on the beach was..." his words trailed off, while his walking slowed and he examined the ground around them. Something caught his eye. He turned towards it and carefully stepped down into the wetter soil. He knelt and looked at the dirt, putting a hand to it.

"Have you found something?"

Alfvin nodded. "I think we have."

"Is it good for bog iron?"

"Perhaps. I would say this looks as promising as the works at

Lakeland."

Eskil lifted his gaze, looking about at the maze of bogs that sat cradled between the low hills behind the shoreline. "It certainly spreads farther than the bogs at Lakeland."

Alfvin smiled. "Yes, more extensive, and also a good distance away. Getting bog iron from land like this is a slow process, as you know, but even so, this looks worth trying." He gave a laugh. "We all might get axes yet."

"And knives and nails, plus a hundred other things we need to make a go of it here."

Alfvin chuckled. "Is Gudrid working on a list?"

Eskil laughed. "She has not said anything, but I am sure she is."

Alfvin stood and stepped back up to firmer land. "Eskil, I am grateful that Ari and I were able to join you and your people. Thrainn was a furious man who was angry with the gods, blaming them for the loss of his wife and the rest of his family. What we did that first night does not make me proud, even if it was needed to survive."

"What really happened?"

Alfvin met his gaze, thoughtful for a moment. Finally, he gave a nod and said, "Let us continue on to the vale ahead while the light is good. I will tell you as we go, but you must not speak of this until I can talk to Ari and see if he is also willing to admit to the truth, for it is also his shame. You must also understand that the two of us had little choice in matters as we were outnumbered by Thrainn and his kin."

Eskil said, "An alliance of blood is hard to go against."

"The big brute made us swear we would never speak of it, and I do not take breaking an oath lightly. But such a thing, built on vile deeds and a lie is, to my thinking, already broken."

Eskil agreed as they again began to trek through the low hills, heading for the vale.

"Thrainn gathered us together, the six men and two women, but both Herdis and Katla were barely alive."

"Six men?"

"Leif survived."

Eskil thought about it. "Yes, but Thrainn said he was in a bad way and died."

Alfvin shook his head. "Leif dragged most of us from the surf. In truth he saved us."

"By the gods!"

"It was Thrainn who was in a bad way, overcome by grief for his missing wife, and slipping into a mad rage."

"Go on with your tale."

"Our two women had swallowed half the sea. We knew that, as the afternoon started to dim, we needed to find shelter for them. That was all Ari and I cared about, the lives of our wives faltering in front of us. Thrainn, at that point, had spent most of his time searching the surf for his own wife, while chopping at waves with his axe and cursing the gods. He was wild and oblivious. Even his son and nephew begged him to stop and tried to drag him from the breaking surf."

"What happened?"

"Leif had climbed a path that led off the cove's beach and up the hillside, following a stream. I think he initially hoped to simply get a better vantage point, but he found an unexpected scene."

"Lakeland?"

"Yes. As the sun began to set, he came rushing down, saying he had found a hall, one that looked occupied. He had not gone in, but instead, he came back so we could carry the women up and then make our approach. He knew if we did not get the women to some kind of shelter quickly that, as the heat of the day faded, they would also pass on."

"Leif was a wise man."

Alfvin nodded, troubled by what he was revealing, continued as he said, "His death was a crime, but now that I started the tale, please let me finish it."

Eskil nodded, the two walking on through the low hills, skirting yet more marshes.

"Leif told us all to pick up the women and follow him up the path. But Thrainn would not. He remained standing, amidst the foam of the breakers, cursing the sea.

"Leif went to him and grabbed him, trying to get him to focus, but the big brute spun around and swung his axe."

Eskil was horrified.

"Leif dodged the swing, throwing himself back and ending up in the surf. Thrainn went after him, roaring like an animal. We ran from the women's sides to stop him, arriving just as he strode over, grabbed Leif's head by the hair, and raised his axe." Alfvin shook his head with the memory.

Eskil was dumbfounded by the murderous turn of events.

"We got there in time, all of us grabbing at Thrainn's arms, trying to stay his weapon...even Thoromr and Trion. Pinned as he was, he eventually gathered his senses. Finally, he let go of Leif, who got up, leaving us all to stand in the tensest situation I have ever witnessed.

"Thrainn slowly relaxed. We could feel his muscles calm and hear his breathing slow. The wild look in his eyes faded, yet we still held him. Soon Leif, now recovered, told us in a hoarse voice to let him go.

"We stepped back from Thrainn, watching. He fell to his knees in the surf and began to mourn.

"Leif called to us as the sun continued to set. He told us we had to get moving or the women would die. We knew he was right, so we went to them. Meanwhile, Leif strode back into the surf and dropped to his knees, face-to-face with Thrainn.

"He told him it was a tragedy that the sea had stolen both of their wives away and not even left their bodies behind for them to mourn.

But, he said, they needed to get the others to shelter or all of them would die."

Eskil was mesmerised by the telling of the tale that rang of truth. There had been too much death at the end of the crossing that had touched both halls–and neither place gently.

Alfvin continued, "Ari and I were eager to get our wives to the hall, as we could see both of them, barely alive, were weakening. With the sky colouring with sunset, the shadows deepening and the warmth seeping out of the day, we knew it was urgent."

"Leif left Thrainn kneeling in the surf and came to help, calling Trion and Thoromr to assist. Between the five of us, we carried the women up the steep trail and off the beach."

Eskil asked, "What of Thrainn?"

Alfvin shook his head. "Leif told us to leave him since he would eventually follow. He said we needed to worry about the women.

"The path climbed the hillside out of the cove, the beach closed off by bluffs at each end. The trail followed a stream that stepped down in a series of waterfalls until it found the sea. We climbed it, knowing we needed to find a better place for the women, but were mindful that path was not an animal trail, instead worn by boots and feet. The more we gathered our senses and focussed on our plight, as we carried our women, the more we steadied our advance and moved with care, for we knew a great unknown awaited us in the hall ahead.

"Eventually the path rose into a higher vale – a small one – where we saw woods along one side of a lake, and a cliff face on the other side of the water, with a grassy bank along its foot, amidst a scattering of trees. It ran away, inland from us, but it was hard to see any detail as the sun had almost set, leaving most of the vale lost to shadow. Before long, we spied the silhouette of the small hall at the base of the cliff between a few thickets of birch. In the deepening gloom, we advanced.

"The women were both unconscious as we closed on the hall. We were desperate. Even more, the wind swung about and we smelled smoke from the hall's fire. As dusk settled in, we saw the first flickers of firelight through gaps in the hall's doorway."

Eskil slowed his steps as Alfvin's telling began to intensify, the two of them coming to the last of the low hills around the bogs. He wanted to hear the end of the tale before they had to deal with whatever lay beyond.

Alfvin stopped and looked to him. "We put the women down in one of the thickets, side-by-side, to share each other's warmth. Leaving them, we then crept further ahead. That is when Thrainn joined us, silently catching up as we crossed the clear ground before the hall. We were glad of it as the sight of the big man and his axe gave us more confidence.

"We could hear voices in the hall, that of women and a man. They were not speaking Norse. Leif looked to us and gave a reassuring nod. He whispered that we would try to befriend them.

"Thrainn stepped forward, no longer lost or cowed. He tapped Thoromr and Trion on the shoulder when he walked up to face Leif. He said we should merely take the hall. His words, hissed and crisp, were powered by his seething fury.

"Leif told him we were ill-equipped and in no state to fight. He said we needed help, not enemies."

Eskil asked, "What did Thrainn do?"

"He shook his axe – the only weapon of note we had with us, aside from a few blades – and then, cursing Leif, turned and charged the hall. His kin, Thoromr and Trion, joined him. There was nothing for the rest of us to do but follow."

Eskil shook his head, picturing the tension and ruin of such a bleak day.

Alfvin sighed, swallowed and then continued, "Thrainn charged into the hall while bellowing a battle cry to vent his rage. Thoromr and Trion were right behind him. Ari and I followed Leif, ready to do whatever was needed, with no real idea of what we would face.

"By the time we entered, Thrainn had already put his axe in the chest of a skraeling man, and Thoromr had pushed another into the fire pit's flames. The hall was in an uproar. Sparks, burning coals and smoke were getting scattered about, while at the back, the women we took as thralls cowered and screamed beside a sick old man."

"It was over before Leif, Ari and I even got into the hall. The skraeling hit by Thrainn's axe died in moments, gurgling his last breath while his blood sprayed about. The other one, knocked into the fire pit, died in terrible pain, and sadly was not a man, but little more than a boy. The four women were terrified, and cowered and screamed until Thrainn advanced on them."

"Leif called out to Thrainn to stop, but he was covered in blood and overcome by his rage. The murderous warrior spun about to face Leif, who hurried up behind him, but instead of talking, Thrainn simply planted his axe in Leif's neck."

Eskil was stunned. "Thrainn killed Leif?"

Alfvin shook his head, pale and still troubled by the tale. "It all happened so quickly: One moment we were outside the hall, the next, inside, surrounded by blood, screams and sparks. Thrainn's kin were also stunned, but quickly moved to back him, leaving us little choice but to accept events. Remember – all Ari and I wanted was to get our wives to some warmth and shelter."

Eskil asked, "And that is when you took the women into thraldom?"

"Yes, but first Thrainn used his axe to cut the old man's throat in front of them, despite them begging in their strange tongue for him to be spared."

Eskil winced and shook his head.

Alfvin grimaced as he remembered what he had been part of. "It was a bloody business with great dishonour, but we needed the shelter. Our women were dying, or so we thought."

"What do you mean?"

"Aris and I hurried back to our women to bring them in and lay them by the fire, but when we got back to them, they were already dead."

Eskil despaired to hear such a thing, picturing the anguish and ruin in the Lakeland men's hearts.

Alfvin turned from Eskil and looked to the vale that beckoned just beyond the side of the next low hill. "Enough of that. Come, we are nearly at a new land. Let us go and see what it holds, for I long to leave the bitterness of Lakeland behind me.

Eskil nodded.

After a few steps made in silence, Alfvin looked up to the clouded sky that currently had them in shadow, and said, "We should have brought Gudrid."

"Why?"

"For whenever you are in need of the thing some might call luck, or others deem divine favour, you have had her by your side."

Eskil smiled at the observation. "We have had our trials, but it is fair to say they have not been as bloody as yours. Yes, it is true that Gudrid seems to be a beacon for Asgard's favour, but we have also worked hard to create much of our good fortune."

"What do you mean?"

"We talk about and plan what we want to do, considering how things might play out. Having said that, as I struggled out of the surf on the shores of Godsland, to watch the rain fade away, golden, in the mid-afternoon sun, to reveal a green land ahead, I swore it was by the grace of none other than the Allfather, not of luck or planning."

They were rounding the side of the last low hill, the green plain of the vale already opening ahead.

Alfvin, almost giddy, chuckled, and like Eskil beside him, had the sense that something good lay beyond. "But Gudrid was there with you, even if you did not know it." They continued forward, the greens of the vale revealing a winding river and thickets of trees along its banks. "And I think only saying her name is likely to invite Odin's favour."

The vale opened up before them as they continued on, the bottom of the valley covered in pastures on either side of the river and dotted with groves of trees. Then, it slowly rose into steeper slopes, where the woods thickened. The area was wide and open, and farther on was the glint of more water. At the sides, in some places, the hillsides gave way to bluffs that would offer shelter and good visibility to the lands around it.

Alfvin put a hand to Eskil's shoulder as they emerged from the maze of the low hills nursing the bogs. "Say her name with me."

Eskil looked to his fellow's hand, to Alfvin, and then turned to the land beyond.

"Say it, Eskil."

Eskil gave a single nod, and then, together, they whispered, "Gudrid."

And, in front of them, the clouds parted to bathe the vale in shafts of golden light.

***

That night, Eskil and Alfvin, wrapped in furs, lay in a sheltered spot on an island opposite the vale. They ate a simple meal of dried fish and spoke excitedly, particularly Alfvin, of the land they discovered. "Even if the marshes lack much bog iron, with the number of them, I would think they must be worth working. Of course, the best way to work them well would be to live closer. It would be a great waste of time to travel so far to labour for a day or two, only to return to Godsland."

Eskil nodded. He had been thinking the same thing.

They had also walked into the vale, only over the plain and to the edge of the lake they had seen. Even so, by the time they got back past the bog hills and to their boat on the beach, dusk was setting in.

Eskil admitted, "The land looks fit for farming and many things."

"Yes, it does."

"I do not want us to be spread too thin, but it looks like we need to consider setting up a separate hall for those willing to come here, or perhaps to even relocating all of us from Godsland."

Alfvin was pleased Eskil appreciated the site, but grimaced at the last suggestion. "Gudrid will never leave the island. You know that."

"Perhaps not, but maybe she will not need to. Perhaps we should keep people there, but move the bulk of us here. Godsland is limited, and we have already nearly stripped the island of timber."

"And our numbers grow."

"Yes, they do, and they will only grow more."

Halla was likely to deliver any day, much to Ballr's joy.

Alfvin observed, "It is the way of things."

Eskil grinned. "Particularly if Ari and Seta provide the hall with more twins."

Alfvin laughed.

With the man now at ease, Eskil dared to ask a personal question, "And you, Alfvin, what of you and Frae?"

Alfvin lost his enthusiasm, and became guarded. "What do you mean?"

"This is your business and I do not wish to talk of things that do not concern me. But I wonder if she is only your thrall or perhaps something more. What I mean is if we talk of splitting our group to people two halls, one here and one in Godsland, do we need to talk of such things as you and Frae staying together. Is that what you would wish?"

Alfvin was quiet for a moment, the silence awkward, but it passed when he finally spoke, "Frae is my thrall; that is the way of things after Lakeland, but she has also become a wife, of sorts. We talk. We have a child. We are together. I want us to stay that way."

Eskil nodded. "I am glad to hear it; that she gives you some joy and comfort after all that has happened."

"She does."

"Do you mind speaking of this?"

"It is not what I would normally talk of, but if you have another question, go on. I can always tell you to stop."

"Would you go as far as giving her back her freedom from thraldom or taking her as a wife?"

"To what end?"

"So she would be an equal, of sorts, and have a proper place amongst us."

"Why?"

"So she can choose to stay with us and work to make Godsland thrive. So we can trust her."

Alfvin looked out across the fjord's dark waters. "I would need to think on that, but perhaps."

"Perhaps which?"

"Both. I think I would give her back her freedom and take her as my wife. She is foreign, and we do not understand all that is said between us, but she is warm and sincere."

"I am pleased you would consider marrying her."

"Now that you have said what you want to achieve, I will add that I think she is already trustworthy."

"Good. I think you may be right."

Alfvin was quiet for a moment as he turned over his thoughts. "Yes, I think I would take her as a wife, not only because I would be without a woman if I gave her freedom, or because one of the other men might marry her, but because I have grown fond of her."

"Think on it and tell me if you can make a decision."

"I will."

They sat in silence for a long, awkward moment. Finally, Alfvin asked, "There's more, I can feel it; ask your question."

"What of Ari? If I asked him the same question, what answer would he give?"

Alfvin laughed aloud. "You have been able to get away with this conversation with me, but I do not think Ari would have it. He would see it too much as prying."

Eskil chuckled, because he was right.

"He has treated Seta well since Lakeland, but they are both distant people. I do not know if any real warmth exists between them, or if they are merely doing what they must and making the most of their situations."

"I see."

"Let me think on my own answer and then talk to him. Whatever I do will also affect him."

***

Frae looked to the pile of pelts in the corner of the hall, a mix of grey, brown and black, some solid in colour, others mottled. They came in all sizes, but most were small. All had their time drying in the sun on one of the summer racks after the brothers Steinarr and Samr had brought them in. The first two frames, now emptied, the furs and skins ready for working. Frae glanced at Seta, who stood by her side, looking at their future toil. In her own tongue, she said, "What do we need most; rugs or clothes?"

Seta did not smile, but then, she rarely did. Instead, she stepped forward to check a few off the top of the pile as she lifted them. "Leave the bigger ones. First, we need boots and then clothes. If we have warm clothes, we can sleep in them if we must."

Frae gave a nod, a smile coming to her face, as predictably as Seta's remained cold. "Yes, boots."

"Ari needs boots."

Frae's smile widened. "Alfvin, too." She stepped forward and started sorting the pelts into piles, based on size and thickness.

Seta joined her.

They worked a while, without talking, until Seta mumbled in their own tongue, "Ari needs good boots but all the men will need them."

Frae asked, "How is Ari?"

"What do you mean?"

"Alfvin is kind, more so since we left Lakeland."

"Ari is also kind, but he was always more gentle than the giant."

"Thrainn was an animal; he deserved death." Frae hissed. "But I worry for our cousins."

"I worry, too. Soon enough the snows will return and they will be stuck in that hall with those men, all through winter."

Frae said, "I still remember when they burst in; Thrainn yelling, and then putting that axe into your husband's chest."

Seta nodded, her eyes softening with the memory. "Thoromr and Trion followed behind and shoved young Dorek into the fire," her words trailed off for a moment, tears interrupting her, but she continued, "Dorek's screams still haunt me."

Frae put a hand to her arm. "Dorek is gone now. Thoromr is not only an animal, as Thrainn was, but also something worse. He is a monster like a wild bear. How anyone could not only throw someone into a fire, but then hold them down against the embers, is beyond cruel."

Seta put down the fur she was holding and wiped at her tears. "And Trion simply stood there and laughed at Dorek's suffering. Both Thoromr and Trion are monsters. We are lucky to have escaped that hall and to be treated much better here, but I still want to be free to go."

"Back to our own people?"

"If we could find them, but we know most of our family is dead, the men by Thrainn's and Thoromr's own hands. And we will never know what happened out in the woods before our first winter at the hall; we can only guess. Thrainn came home with his axe and clothes coated in blood too many times."

"Yes, and we never saw meat, so whatever he killed was not for eating."

Seta nodded, her face grim.

"Have you ever asked Ari?"

"No, we talk now, but not much, and never about what happened at the other hall."

Frae frowned. "I will ask Alfvin. He might not like the question, but he will not hit me for asking."

"Do you talk to him about when they first came to us?"

"We never talk of those first few days. I think he is ashamed."

"They would have died without us, even if they had found the hall empty."

Frae agreed. "I think that is what hurts them most of all, knowing that without us, they would have perished."

"Lakeland is a very different hall to here. At least here I feel safe."

Frae agreed. "Eskil leads, but with a gentle hand."

The hall door creaked behind them, having already been open to let the daylight and breeze in. The women turned.

Little Ulfarr stood there, steadying himself. Ulfarr turned and looked to the women, his face lighting up as he saw them. After a moment, he pushed off the door and walked with unsteady steps towards them.

THE LANDING

Frae smiled and was glad to see Seta's face also soften.

Shadows appeared in the doorway behind Ulfarr, quickly replaced by Gudrid and Halla, who came in after the infant. Gudrid held Seta's two young, one in each arm, the babes wrapped in furs. Halla carried her own fur-wrapped, days-old newborn – the hall's most recent – as well as Frae's.

Frae stepped forward and knelt to meet Ulfarr as his unsteady progress forward slowed.

Gudrid smiled and asked, "It seems like a lot of furs and skins, but we shall never have enough, as we will always need new clothes against the cold, and rugs against the night. What do you think we need most of all?"

Frae and Seta answered at the same time, "Boots."

Ulfarr giggled at the sudden sound.

All the women laughed, even Seta.

Chapter 10

-

Ari

Ballr travelled with Eskil and Torrador on several of the original rafting trips, as they explored their immediate surrounds on the fjord. One thing the lean Icelander noted on those first ponderous journeys, in a time before they discovered Lakeland and built Godsland's small boat, was that the water's currents delivered a good amount of driftwood along certain channels and shores.

The most favoured shoreline, as fate would have it, was the long one opposite Godsland, located on the other side of the ridge from Lakeland, on the same shore where Thoromr had stood, challenging them as they passed.

Regardless of being on the same side of the fjord as Lakeland, the shoreline was a long way out and not an easy trek to Thoromr's own hall. This made it a tempting target, particularly farther in, where the gravel beaches, woods and steep slopes seemed an even greater distance from Lakeland.

Besides, Ballr had long ago begun to reason that a piece of driftwood was not like a standing tree. The wood could come from anywhere, wash up on a beach, to then be taken away by the next tide or storm. Driftwood did not belong to anyone aside from the man who could grab it.

Ballr eventually fell into handling much of their needs for timber, for he enjoyed working with wood and confronting the challenge of trying to build whatever Godsland required. Through his efforts, their hall and its fittings were completed, and a shed, fences, drying racks and several armfuls of tools were constructed. The arrival of Ari in spring meant Ballr had readymade help because the Lakelander previously felled timber in the homeland and was no stranger to carpentry. So, during the last part of spring and through much of summer, the two men took to searching the fjord's shoreline for usable driftwood, seeking out the best logs and other worthwhile timber that could easily be bundled and then floated back down the fjord.

Due to their shapes, certain pieces became tools, while the larger pieces converted into frames, beams, planks and posts for new buildings or drying racks. Torrador and Steinarr wanted timber suitable for not only making another small boat, but also wood they could use when they tried their hands at constructing a proper ship. Anything left over was destined for the hall's ever-hungry fire pit, which would eat through any woodstack, regardless of how large, during the next winter.

Over the busy summer, Ballr also became a father to a young boy they named Brandr. Halla had endured a difficult delivery, but Mother and babe were well now. The episode was the only time he had been idle, waiting for her to recover and escape the birthing bed. Once she declared herself fit, he went back to his toil.

Summer waned, and the weather finally began to turn. The new babe and coming winter made Ballr more determined than ever to gather what timber they could, providing plenty to keep the hall warm when the deep snows came.

His work was never ending, for the hall would always need more. They had cleared the barren and wind-blasted island of Godsland of its best timber by the end of the previous winter, so a constant and broader wood harvest was necessary.

By the end of summer, they had also exhausted the easy timber to put to water and float down to Godsland hall. Ari and Ballr increasingly needed to trek farther into the fjord for fallen timber, seeking to harvest the standing trees that suited their needs. They used the one small, iron-headed hand axe they had and the smaller stone axes.

The work was not easy.

Good timber, in lengths thick and long, were a rarity in Godsland, even before their arrival, so all of the people considered Ballr's work as important as fishing or the efforts at the bog iron works. Only the women's tending of the gardens and preparation of winter stores trumped the toil of others in importance.

By the time the colours of fall had found the trees of Markland, Alfvin had smelted enough iron to forge a few small axes and issued a knife to each of the men. Word also spread that his next work was almost done, but what it was had been shrouded in secrecy.

That is until one autumn night, when the first snows were due.

In a rare moment outside of winter, all the Godslanders gathered in the hall to feast on fresh hare. Because the weather was beginning to turn, the men stayed closer to home; those trapping and hunting for meat and furs no longer ranged so far to camp overnight, similar to those searching for timber or seeking bog iron. So on that night, Alfvin stood before the group, holding his hands behind his back.

Silencing the room, Eskil asked, "Alfvin, what do you hold behind your back?"

Alfvin presented an object wrapped in the raven banner. "I have a gift of iron for two of our men."

All cheered, for while the object was not huge, it clearly was bigger than a blade, and came at the end of a long handle.

Eskil knew something of what lay under the banner, having asked Alfvin if he could make such a thing. Despite that knowledge, he was still surprised at how quickly Alfvin had been able to forge the item.

Expectant, they all looked to Alfvin, including Frae and Seta, who had long ago begun eating alongside the Norse.

With a flourish, Alfvin pulled the banner away to reveal a wooden handle that ended in a rough, but more-than-workable large axe head. "For our woodsmen!"

Both Ari's and Ballr's eyes widened with surprise as their friends cheered, although Eskil did not miss Seta flinch at the sight of the axe.

Halla, nursing their son, sat beside Ballr and leaned over to whisper in his ear before urging him to stand with Ari and accept the axe.

Neither of the men needed much encouragement.

Ballr rose and wiped his food-greased hands on his pants as he stepped over to Alfvin, nodding for Ari to join him as he called out, "By Thor, I could fell a giant with it, but for now, tall timber will simply have to do!"

They all laughed when Alfvin placed it into Ballr's hands, Ari beaming a rare smile as he stood beside his grinning friend.

Ballr marvelled at it, admiring his fellow's efforts to make such a thing.

Eskil said, "The giants will have to wait, but not the trees. I hope we can now expect too much wood to burn this coming winter!"

And all those about them called out their agreement.

***

Ari and Ballr went out the next day, both eager to use the new axe, hoping to retire some of the rougher tools they had been forced to use. Alfvin waved them off, along with Gudrid, Halla, Seta and Frae, as they set out on their boat, wrapped in new furs for warmth against the cooling weather and fog.

Leaving Godsland behind, they turned their focus to the journey ahead, continuing across the waters of the fjord. The sky was not to be seen, except for when the grey mist briefly parted before again moving to smother the day in overcast gloom.

The weather was turning and all knew that one of the coming nights would soon deliver the first snows, just as the rain and sleet at this time of year frequently plagued the days. Preparations for winter were well underway, but much still needed to be done. Stores of dried fish and cured meat were ample, but Ballr worried they needed more wood. The hall held more bodies now, including the babes, and warming the large space required a good stockpile of cut fuel. In truth, they had barely had enough over the previous winter. Ballr badly wanted this coming bleak season to be different.

They headed out and crossed the fjord, following the opposite shoreline, seeking the best woods. The journey took them past Lakeland's territory, but Thoromr's hall and vale were a good distance away, hidden behind the steep ridge that made up the fjord's looming side and acted as a wall.

A flock of waterbirds near the shore quieted as they watched the men pass near-by. Many of the local birds learned the Norse were happy enough to ignore them one day, or to kill them or take their eggs the next. Some of them anxious, they gave into caution and took to their wings, flying farther down the channel.

Ari watched the wooded shoreline with a frown.

Ballr asked, "What is wrong?"

"Nothing. I am simply thinking back on our dark beginnings back there." With a flick of his head, he indicated the area over the ridge.

Ballr shrugged. "We all struggled at the beginning, full of worry and fear. You are with Godsland now."

Ari gave a slight nod with the dip of his head, a smile almost daring to mark his stoic face, yet his eyes never left the thickening woodlands along the shore. "Those first days were bloody and dire."

"It cannot have been good."

"No. Sorry, I should not have begun talking about it."

146

"It is alright."

Ari nodded thanks for his friend's understanding.

Ballr changed the subject. "This will likely be our last trip out this season, but I do not think we should go too far. The weather is chilled and changeable, and the fog disagreeable."

Ari met Ballr's gaze. "This shore is the closest for good timber."

The Icelander choked off a nervous laugh, not certain what Ari was suggesting; did the woodsman really want to tempt fate and go ashore this close to Lakeland?

Ballr answered with a shake of his head, and said, "We will go a little farther on before we land. Soon enough, we will be outside Lakeland's borders, beyond the island and point, as Eskil told Thoromr."

"On the day Seta accused the brute of being a sheep murderer?"

Ballr laughed, relaxing.

Ari chuckled. "I wish I had seen it. I asked her about that day when I heard the tale. She was very pleased with herself."

"She should have been."

Ari grinned.

Ballr continued, "Eskil wants us to keep well away from Lakeland's lands, but their timber stands well, and their shores seem to catch the best driftwood."

"It is an injustice!"

Ballr agreed with a nod, but said, "We will continue on to where Eskil told him he could not claim. If it looks to be quiet, we can land there."

Ari showed no reluctance. "We only need one more good load. Once done, we will not be back until spring, as we will be spending the rest of the season helping with other chores closer to the hall and cutting up what we have already brought back to Godsland."

They rowed on in silence for a short time, the thinning fog rolling over them.

Then, with his gaze still focused on the mist-shrouded trees, Ari said, "I hated that hall. If I did not worry about the slumbering beast of Thrainn's anger, I worried the thralls would cut our throats at night, if the one of us on guard fell asleep."

Ballr did not have an answer for such a confession.

"I was glad to get out of there, and in truth, could not have found a better hall, with more honest people, to come to; people who have also made me most welcome."

"You are welcome." Ballr answered, meaning the words.

Ari took his eye off the shoreline for a moment to meet Ballr's gaze. For once his voice was soft and thoughtful, "And Seta."

"She is also welcome, as is Frae and Alfvin, and all the children. The sisters are good for our hall; they know this land."

Ari nodded.

They rowed on in silence, but as they did, Ballr noticed Ari's search of the nearby shoreline never stopped.

The mist continued to thin, improving visibility, but never completely cleared. They moved further along the shoreline, passing the thin islands and the point where Thoromr had once challenged Eskil. Eventually they came ashore, beaching the boat where two different thickets came close to the water's edge. While both men were eager to try out the new axe, they would mainly be going for driftwood, or perhaps felling one or two tall, but young, trees if they found something suitable. Of course, any tree to be cut needed to be close to the water, as they would have to haul the timber into the fjord before floating it to Godsland.

Looking about, the hillside came right down to the shoreline, the slope steep and its rise high. All wooded, initially by birch and other trees, but eventually by pine and fir as the hillside climbed.

Ari and Ballr quickly collected and floated the best driftwood lying on the ground by the shore. They used the new axe on occasion to free any entangled or snagged logs; the work was hard.

After collecting the easy wood, they stopped and checked over the surrounding standing trees. The hall needed long and straight trunks for beams, building frames and drying wracks. Older saplings were ideal. Felling such trees did not take long, even with a stone axe, and neither did their stripping, in preparation for rafting them back to Godsland.

Ari pointed out a group of young pines not far up the steep slope that stood at the right angle to fall down and reach the fjord. "We should take some of those."

Ballr looked at the timber and then the mist-haunted hillside. No one else was about, the sounds of water birds the only thing to disturb the peace. "The axe will make a lot of noise."

"By the time someone in Lakeland hears our chopping, if they can, and sets out to investigate, we will be on our way."

Ballr was unsure, but the fog, even if thinning, would help stifle some of the noise.

Ari grabbed the new axe. "Come, we have to try this thing out on standing greenwood. We are not in Lakeland; we passed that boundary long ago."

Ballr gave in and nodded.

Ari smiled and put the axe on his shoulder as he turned and headed up the slope. "I shall bring a tree down, and I shall do it for Godsland."

"Let us just do it quickly."

They did not have far to go. The young pines were near a much larger and ancient pine that had fallen and lay down the slope, its thick trunk and dying foliage running like a wall.

They struggled up the steep slope, the ground slippery in places with wet soil and fallen leaves. Shrubs and moss covered much of the hillside, all of it shaded by the trees they passed under. All would soon be lost under snow.

They reached the young pines, the trunks straight and tall.

Ballr said. "Yes, let us take one. We shall then head home."

Ari stepped across to Ballr and offered him the new axe handle first. "You should break it in."

Ballr smiled. "Thank you, but I thought you wanted the honour?"

"You do one, the first, and I will take another. With an axe like this, it should not take long."

Ballr looked around the woods and the breaking mist. Birds were down in the waters of the sound, only forty paces away. Visibility was increasing, and no one was about. "Alright...but quickly."

Ari gave a nod and stepped back, out of the way.

The Icelander sized up the closest tree's trunk, the straight and textured shaft just over a hand-span in width. He spread his legs and checked his footing before drawing the axe back, and then swung it hard to give the trunk a taste of Alfvin's iron.

The axe bit into the trunk, the smell of resin rising in the air as green wood was revealed.

Ari smirked, his arms folded across his chest.

Ballr chuckled and his smile broadened.

They were both pleased.

Ballr swung again, the sharp chop of the impact ringing out to echo down the fjord.

Ari's smirk grew into a broad smile that fell into laughter.

Chips of wood flew with each swing. The rhythmic sound of it became both pleasing and hypnotic.

After working up a sweat, Ballr watched the tree begin to lean, a movement accompanied a heartbeat later by a sharp crack as the trunk began to fall. He stepped to the side to watch.

150

Ari also moved back.

The trunk teetered for a moment before falling with gathering momentum, all of it announced by a chorus of cracks and snaps that gave way to a rising whoosh as the branches brushed against their neighbours and rushed for the ground. The noise ended quickly, with the crash and crunch of the trunk, the cool autumn morning suddenly full of falling twigs and pine needles.

A few moments later, the woods were again mostly quiet. With the tree down on the hillside, the only sound to punctuate the morning was the call of birds from down on the water.

Ballr let the head of the axe rest on the ground between his feet as he steadied it by the handle. With a grin, he looked to Ari and asked, "Are you ready for your turn?"

Ari nodded and stepped forward.

Ballr handed him the axe. "It feels good, certainly better than the old axes." He then stepped back to get out of the way. "I will go down and get it stripped and ready for rafting."

Ari nodded and waited for him to start down the steep slope and get out of harm's way. He then began to swing, the strikes sharp and hard. Ari knew how to handle an axe; he was a fine woodsman.

Ari worked to bring the pine down, as Ballr descended the last of the steep slope.

The hillside was slippery, the footing treacherous – certainly much harder to descend than to climb – forcing Ballr to slow. No matter how careful, the Icelander lost his footing, slipped, and then slid down the rest of the way on mud and wet moss. After barrelling through a shrub, he finally tumbled over to land in the dying needles and branches of the huge fallen pine.

Ballr lay there for a moment, startled by the fall. After he gathered his senses and began to rise, he noticed the nearby birds had all taken flight, flapping and calling as they cleared the water.

He watched them go, their calls fading and leaving him in silence on the edge of the gravel beach. In the settling quiet, he realised he could not hear the rhythmic chop of the axe.

He turned to look up the slope and, with a shiver, realised he could not see Ari.

They had stayed too long.

Ballr was about to begin to climb the slope and seek out Ari when he paused, thinking he needed to take more care. Something did not feel right. He did not even hear the sounds of Ari's breathing or movement through the undergrowth.

He backed up and around the end of the ancient pine, and began to use it as cover as he carefully climbed the hillside. He tried to get a little higher before trying to sneak a look through the branches. He looked uphill, searching for any sign of Ari or a hint of what had happened.

Ballr would encounter whatever awaited him unarmed, aside from a small blade. The new axe was with Ari. Even the old axes were not nearby, for they were down by the boat, where they had been working on the driftwood earlier.

Compared to the scraggly groves of Iceland, the woods of Markland were thick, but not enough so that he could expect to advance – or fall back – unseen.

Ballr silently cursed his luck.

There was still no sound from Ari.

Above, the fog had thinned enough to reveal an overcast sky that let out a soft roll of thunder, a rumbling that grew to crack and boom.

Thor was here.

Ballr felt emboldened by the thought. He needed allies.

As quietly as he could, he crept amongst the ancient pine's limbs and knelt down by the thick trunk, hoping to see what he could through the withered branches.

Ballr wanted to glimpse what he could of the slope, to see any possible sign of his friend.

Again thunder rumbled.

The sharp snap of a twig came from uphill, near where Ari had been.

Ballr looked, but could not see anything clearly, now that he huddled in the branches of the fallen pine lying covered in struggling growth.

Rain began to fall in drops heavy and hard.

Sounds now rang out as the rain hit leaves, rock and wood.

Thunder rolled again, this time married to lightning that washed over the woodland.

Another crack sounded, of a snapping twig, this one from uphill, but also perhaps to the side. The rain's chorus was making it hard to tell from where such subtle sounds were coming.

Ballr eased closer to the fallen tree, putting his arms out to heave himself up and over the thick trunk, in the best spot he could find. He breathed deep and then prepared to weave through the branches on the other side and move up the hill, closer to where he had last seen Ari.

He took a few steps, trying to keep low, as he wove between the pine's branches, pulling one gently towards him so he could escape the maze of needles, only to reveal Thoromr standing patiently, waiting for him.

The big Norseman looked lean and fit. He stood, with one of his hands clutching his father's bloodied axe, while he stared at the Icelander.

Ballr froze.

Thoromr demanded, "What are you doing here?"

Ballr quickly looked him up and down in a brief glance that gave away terrible detail.

Fresh blood still ran to gather and drop from the axe head, the red made thinner but no less gruesome by the rain. The mess also coated not just Thoromr's hand, but painted his arm and the furs he wore. The Norseman's eyes were wide and wild, as veins stood out on his neck, forehead and temples.

"We came for wood."

Thoromr frowned before curling his lip. After a long pause, he asked, "Ballr, should you not be at home with the women?"

Ballr tried to offer a calm face. Eyeing Thoromr, he asked, "Where is Ari?"

The Lakelander grinned, his staring eyes sparkling. "Dead."

"You killed him?"

Thoromr took one step forward, his fingers tightening about his axe. "He was taking my timber."

Ballr heard another sound behind him, a little uphill, on the other side of the fallen tree.

They were not alone.

Thoromr glanced at someone and gave a nod.

With a quick look over his shoulder, Ballr saw another Norseman, not Trion, but someone else, in much less ragged clothes. Surprised, he asked, "Who is that?"

Thoromr grinned. "A friend from Greenland. Lakeland has had visitors this summer."

Ballr had another quick look. The man nodded. He clutched the new axe forged by Alfvin and stolen from the dead hands of Ari.

Thoromr took another step forward, coming into the branches of the fallen pine, including the one Ballr had pulled back and still tightly gripped.

Slowly, Ballr eased back a step, but kept his grip on the branch, bending it with his withdrawal, its length arching.

His rival watched him, but did not move. He squared his shoulders, and asked, "Are you also here to steal Lakeland's timber?"

154

THE LANDING

"We are a long way from your hall."

"It is only over the ridge and down the vale."

Ballr knew he was running out of time. Thoromr would not let him go, not to carry news of Ari's murder back to Godsland.

He had to get away, yet he was outnumbered.

Lightning flashed with a booming thunder, making the very air shiver. The suddenness of it made them all start.

Ballr did not waste the chance.

He pushed the branch he held so it flicked back to block Thoromr's path, cracking towards the giant Lakelander's face like a whip.

At the same moment, sensing Ballr's imminent escape, Thoromr surged forward.

Ballr did not stop, but turned and dove under the pine's ancient limbs, scrabbling to get away.

Thoromr cried out behind him.

Ballr crawled free of the maze of branches to get back onto the clear slope, using its wetness and mud to aid him in a speedy escape.

The Godslander hurtled down the steep slope. His last sight of Thoromr had been of the bloodied man lunging forward as the branch hit him fast and hard in the face. Now, the fjord rang out with his furious cursing, amidst a chorus of snapping wood and cracking twigs.

Ballr did not stop or even turn to look. He just tried to keep his footing as he charged down the hillside towards the beach.

Thoromr howled as he and the Greenlander followed down the slope, but the outsider was on the wrong side of the tree from Ballr and not as nimble.

Meanwhile, Ballr threw his small frame whichever way he needed while he desperately plunged down the hillside. The Icelander occasionally missed a step and stumbled, but he was able to bounce back up and again find his footing by reaching out and grabbing bushes.

Thoromr cursed anew, but was interrupted by the roll and thud of tumbling as he lost his footing.

Ballr dared to glance over his shoulder to see what was happening.

The Greenlander, on the far side of the fallen tree, continued on, but was a distance away, having trouble finding safe ground. Behind Ballr, on the same side, Thoromr rolled hard and fast down the hill, his limbs flailing as he tried to stop himself.

Ballr stopped and watched, just as Thoromr tumbled over an outcrop of rock half-hidden by foliage. The big Norseman's body passed mostly over it, but his head caught a rough edge, the crack of the impact clear.

Thunder boomed again as lightning flashed.

Thoromr continued to roll down the hill, but his limbs fell about loose and uncontrolled. In that storm of movement, his axe came free, cartwheeling ahead and away.

Ballr looked across to the Greenlander who had only now noticed how heavily Thoromr had gone down. The man steadied his own advance, settling on an unhurried pace, as Thoromr's descent slowed. The newcomer had also come to the end of the fallen tree that had separated them, leaving Ballr feeling vulnerable.

Thoromr's axe slid forward along fallen leaves, coming to rest at Ballr's feet.

The Icelander snatched it up by the bloodied handle and then braced himself as Thoromr rolled toward him, still slowing, but with enough momentum to knock him over. With care, Ballr put a boot forward, planted it firmly in Thoromr's back, and stopped the body.

It came to a stop, yet Thoromr did not react.

The big Norseman lay on his side, with his limbs spread out. His eyes were closed – one of them swollen, bloody, and crusted with leaves, dirt and twigs – while blood covered half his face from a wound under his thick hair.

Ballr looked to the axe in his hands and then back to the Lakelander.

Thoromr breathed, blood still flowing from his wounds, but was otherwise motionless.

The Greenlander frowned.

Ballr let the beginning of a smile ride his lips. He reached down and pulled a blade from Thoromr's belt, putting it on his own. Leaning in also gave him a closer view of his foe's wounds.

Thoromr's eye was not only swollen closed and caked in dirt, leaves and twigs. Ballr realised that the end of the branch he had pushed into the big man during his escape had gouged large gashes along the man's cheek, with some of the pine digging into the flesh about his eye. Twigs and loose leaves did not surround his eye, but rather the end of the branch stuck right through the closed and swollen lid.

Thoromr had lost an eye.

Ballr's smile became grim as he turned to face the Greenlander. "You have found poor company."

"He was in my hall, although welcoming enough."

"How many of you are there?"

"Two score. Enough to take either of your halls."

"Friend, Thoromr is the one with anger and hate, not me or mine, certainly not against you and yours."

"He said you are nearby, at Godsland he called it, across the water."

"Yes."

"We are harvesting timber and furs, but will soon leave for home to winter."

"You would be welcome to visit our hall if you come in peace, but not Thoromr or Trion, although their thralls we would be glad to see."

"The skraeling?"

Ballr frowned. "There are two, sisters."

"One died, Trion's, he killed her in a rage. Only one now remains; pregnant, and with two babes to care for."

Ballr shook his head. "I'm sad to hear of it."

"Why, what do you care?"

"Their cousins, two sisters, also live with us."

"Skraelings?"

"They are good people."

The Greenlander thought on that a moment. "We may visit to see what you have built. If we do, it will be only for the day, before we head on to our own home, as we are already late in leaving and winter here is a vicious beast."

"If you come as friends, you would be welcomed."

The Greenlander nodded. "It is a new world. In such a place, our kind needs friends."

Ballr agreed.

The Greenlander slowly stepped closer, keeping his hands in view, including the new axe taken from Ari. "What of Thoromr? Will you kill him?"

"No, our leader is not one for blood or revenge. He thinks we need to work together to make this place a land fit for Odin's people."

"A wise man."

"Your name, friend?"

"Faraldr of Greenland."

"And Ari is dead?"

"Thoromr put his axe into the back of his skull. I doubt your friend would have felt the blow. I followed Thoromr here; he heard your axe. I saw, from a distance, his attack on Ari. We were checking snares down in the next vale."

Ballr was saddened to hear of such a cowardly attack. He looked down at Thoromr and pondered running the axe along the bastard's throat.

Faraldr dropped the new axe Alfvin had forged into the leaves between them and folded his arms. "You could do it; I would not stop you. You were right when you said he is an angry man."

Ballr shook his head. "Our landings were hard; the sea stole his mother and dreams away; what came next cost him his father, Thrainn. That loss fires Thoromr's anger. I will not kill him in cold blood, but I doubt he will survive his wounds."

Faraldr stepped closer, but stopped short, making sure Ballr was comfortable with his approach. He peered at Thoromr; the big man had not moved. He noticed the blood on his face and in his hair.

Ballr stepped back, letting Faraldr get closer. The Greenlander knelt beside the fallen man. "He has lost an eye."

"It looks so."

Faraldr turned to Ballr. "If he survives, he will not be the same threat."

"That is what I was thinking."

"Leave him then. I will get him back to our hall. For now though, let me help you with the body of your friend."

"That would be good of you."

Faraldr nodded, rose, and then turned his back on Ballr as he began to climb the hillside, heading back to the body of Ari.

***

Ballr brought his boat to the gravel beach by the Godsland hall. He had left the load of timber behind, after Faraldr had waved him off, instead carrying Ari's body as his only cargo.

Wearing two axes and an extra blade on his belt, his arrival, as the lone figure in a boat that should have carried two, caused a stir. By the time he reached the shore, Gudrid, Frae and Halla had gathered with Steinarr and Alfvin. Ballr scanned the pale faces, the closest having already seen that Ari was not down injured, but bloodied and dead.

Movement by the hall caught his gaze.

Seta.

She came walking out from where they had been stockpiling cut firewood. She saw the gathering at the beach and began to slow, searching amongst those who stood there. As soon as the boat was beached, Gudrid ducked down to check on Ari, drawing Seta's eyes to his still form.

She began to run.

Frae let out a stifled cry as she took in the truth of what Ballr had brought home. She then turned to see her sister running down the worn path to the shore.

Seta began to wail. A moment later, she arrived to push past the others and dropped to the gravel beside the boat, looking to Ari's waxen face that sat over the bloody ruin of the back of his head. Her arms stretched out across his chest.

She called out loudly, before falling into deep sobs.

Gudrid and Halla looked to Ballr. Frae also sought some kind of explanation as she dropped to her knees beside her sister and put her arms around her.

Ballr gazed on the shocked faces around him as mourning took root. He cleared his throat and said, "Thoromr killed him."

Alfvin frowned, his fury firing to burn deep. "What happened?"

"We were taking turns using the new axe, so while Ari worked to bring down a young pine, I was going to get another we had already felled to the water so we could bring them back. The sound of axe-work stopped, so I wondered what had happened. Fearing things were amiss, I tried to make my way, unseen, back up the slope. That was when I walked into Thoromr. He had been coming down the hill, with a bloody axe, to find me. He accused us of stealing his timber."

"Did you fight him?" Gudrid asked, her face pale, her eyes glistening with held-back tears.

"No, he was not alone. He had a Greenlander with him. I was cornered, so when a great crack of thunder sounded to startle us, I pushed a branch into him and fled downhill."

Halla clasped her hands to her heart. "Thanks be to Freya! Then what happened?"

"I ran. The way was so steep that it almost became a fall. The Greenlander slowed, not holding his footing well, but Thoromr lost it, tumbled down the hill and cracked his head on a rock. I went to him and took his axe."

Seta looked up, suddenly fierce, "Did you take his head?"

"No."

Seta glared at him.

Ballr could not hold her gaze, but went on. "The branch I pushed into him tore up his face and put out one of his eyes."

Seta was not pleased, but turned her attention back to Ari.

"The Greenlander and I spoke; he then helped me with Ari's body so I could bring him home."

Gudrid shook her head. "We will need to bury him."

Alfvin stepped up behind Frae and put a gentle hand on her shoulder as she worked to comfort her sister. He looked down with sympathy in his eyes. "Let us lift Ari free and bring him ashore."

Frae's own tears ran, but something shone in her eyes at his open and comforting touch. The others noticed the gesture.

She, Gudrid and Halla helped Seta up while the men lifted Ari off the boat and brought him onto the autumn-faded pastures outside the hall.

***

By the last light of the afternoon, they had raised a cairn over Ari, setting his body to rest in a small gully beyond the hall, on the hill's far side. Not long after, as the women stood by it, comforting Seta, Eskil returned with Torrador on the hall's newest boat.

Alfvin and Ballr went to meet them and tell them what had happened as their fellows put the final touches on the cairn.

Ballr told the tale, as he had been there, and he used the ambiguity of the shore's distance from Lakeland Hall as an excuse to land and claim the driftwood, a timber of unknown source.

Eskil, trying to hide both his frustration and disappointment, had only one answer for Ballr. "Your daring is what placed Ari in harm's way. Although, I suppose, you are not alone in that guilt if he also wanted to test his fate."

"I am sorry Eskil, but the timber was too great a temptation. In truth, it probably lay closer to our hall than Thoromr's."

Eskil frowned and let out a deep sigh. "You knew the land was in dispute. In the end, the result is that Ari is dead and we have no path for justice, because of that dispute."

Ballr looked to the cairn and Seta, who was sullen and marked by tears. "He cannot claim all of Markland on his side of the fjord and farther south."

"I agree that it is a foolish claim, but he has made and now defended it." Eskil shook his head. "Ballr, you are a friend and also a man I trust, but in this you have erred. Thoromr may be a brute like his father, but we cannot blame him for defending what he sees as his, regardless of our disagreement. If we want to challenge his claim, we cannot do it by stealing timber or landing there to take what we will.

We need to either get him to agree to a change in borders or we go to war with him."

"You mean to do nothing?"

"There is nothing we can do, not as the weather turns toward winter. I will not waste any more blood on an unnecessary argument. There are too few of us as it is."

Ballr nodded, sombre.

"Next spring we shall look at the matter, but not tempt fate with rash acts. If we can get Thoromr to agree to a compromise or a deal, we shall pursue that...if he survives the wounds you gave him."

Ballr agreed.

"Come, let us attend Ari's burial."

With Alfvin, the two men turned to go to the cairn.

**

Following the burial, the night began with a subdued meal of hare and nut bread, eaten by all around the fire pit. When most were finished, Alfvin stood, rising from where he sat beside Frae and Seta. In response, all the Godslanders stopped their own eating and conversations.

Lit by the light of the flames and watched by all in the hall, he first looked down at Frae and smiled, before turning self-consciously to face Eskil sitting on the other side of the fire.

Eskil had a hopeful inkling of what might be on Alfvin's mind. He asked him, "Alfvin, do you have something to say?"

Alfvin gave a nod and licked his lips, his skin paling. "I have a question for the head of the Godsland Hall."

Eskil stood. "Ask it then."

"I wish to give voice to a matter long on my mind."

Eskil nodded.

"I wish to free Frae of the thraldom that binds her to me and, with your blessing, I wish to marry her."

Frae's eyes went wide as she looked up to him, her expression falling from surprise to joy.

The hall was silent, aside from the crackle of the fire.

All eyes went to Eskil, the women's gaze intense, almost as much as Alfvin's.

Eskil was silent, his face unreadable, framed by his blonde hair and beard. He stood at the same fire pit where he had founded a hall for his people, nursed newborn babes, slain Thrainn, and welcomed Alfvin and the skraelings, Frae and Seta. He finally smiled. "Her freedom is yours to return to her, and giving my blessing for the two of you to marry is an act I would very much like to do."

Relieved, Alfvin turned to look down at Frae. He offered her his hand.

She took it.

He helped her up and said, "You have your freedom, and if you will marry me, you can have mine."

With tears beginning to run, she said, "Alfvin, I only want to be with you."

He smiled and took her into his arms.

The Godslanders cheered them, the women with great enthusiasm.

After these congratulations, Eskil cleared his throat and made it clear he had more to say. "Alfvin, you arrived in our hall with Frae and Seta, both taken into thraldom in Lakeland. If you are to free Frae, what of Seta, as Ari is no longer here to speak for her?"

Alfvin and Frae turned to look down as Seta, who gazed up at them in surprise.

The former Lakelander nodded and offered her his hand.

Unsure, she reached out hesitantly, but then took it.

Alfvin helped her stand, and Frae reached across to aid him.

"Seta, I give you your freedom and hope you choose to remain with us."

Dumbfounded, she looked about at the Godslanders as they cheered her. A disbelieving but tired smile slowly came to her face, one built on a day of contrasts and emotions.

***

Alfvin and Frae became husband and wife, now in an open and straightforward way. Seta also received her freedom – to her surprise – and elected to stay, at least for the coming winter.

As autumn deepened, the people of Godsland toiled closer to home, gathering and finishing the last of what they would need to survive the snows ahead. They harvested what they could from the gardens and gathered seed from the best plants left to set. They also brought in fodder for the sheep, the bulk of it being hay and leaves. They added to the stores of dried fish and cured meats. And lastly, despite the long and tall stack of firewood built up to line the hall's main wall, they kept adding to it, layer by layer, day by day, as they cut the timber collected into smaller sections.

But one day such labours were interrupted.

Gudrid gazed out into the water of the fjord, looking to the channel before it found the open sea. Something caught her eyes, making her search the vista edged by distant coastal headlands and dotted with the rock and green of the windswept islands.

A bird's wing or a wave's white cap was enough to grab attention, but she was certain she had seen something more. Whatever it was had passed behind some rocks, leaving her to wait to see what emerged from the other side.

She was sure it was bigger than a bird and glimpsed it in white and red.

Had it been a sail?

Gudrid held her breath, watching as the swell moved along the channel and past the rocks that hid her find. She waited, growing anxious.

Where was it?

Halla stepped up beside her, "Did you see something?"

Gudrid glanced at her before turning back to the water. "I thought I saw something behind the rocky islets."

"What?"

"I am not certain, but it was white and red...perhaps a sail?"

The women stood together, watching.

Nothing emerged.

Gudrid began to feel a fool.

And then, as if charging out from behind the rocks, a ship emerged, with oars out, a red and white sail billowing as it caught the breeze.

At first Halla was struck speechless by the sight, despite the news Ballr had recently brought of Greenlanders in Lakeland. Finally, she reached out and grabbed Gudrid's hand.

Gudrid also stood frozen, but, as always, was the first to find her voice, "By all the gods of Asgard, Godsland has visitors!"

Halla gathered herself and turned to call out to Ballr, who worked nearby at chopping wood, cutting logs into pieces that could be better stacked and carried inside the hall through the winter.

He looked up from where he had bent over to stand a log on its end, getting ready to split it. "What?"

THE LANDING

Halla raised her voice so the others around them, lost in their various labours, would hear, "A ship."

Ballr raised his eyebrows and turned. Others heard the words and stopped to look.

A ship.

Ballr turned to Eskil and Alfvin, who toiled nearby. "The Greenlanders?"

Eskil stepped forward towards the beach. He certainly hoped so. They had numbers enough to face Thoromr and Trion, but not a ship holding a score or more, with unknown intentions. "Watch them and look for Faraldr. Let us know if it is he. Gudrid, Halla, take Seta and Frae and the children to the woodshed and wait."

The women began to move. Halla grumbled, "We should stand together in all our numbers."

Eskil looked to Ballr and then to Alfvin. "Perhaps, but do as I say. If we see Faraldr, we will call you back. Also, take the sheep.

The ship was still a way off and coming from the direction of Lakeland's waters, as if it had left the cove leading to their narrow vale.

Ballr stepped up to be beside Eskil.

Eskil asked, "Did you say Faraldr said there was two score of them?"

"Yes."

"Did he say how many ships they brought?"

"No."

"Forty men would be one or two ships."

Ballr nodded. "They came here for timber and furs. They are likely to have two ships so they can also fit a good cargo onboard. Otherwise, it would be a wasted trip."

The ship cut forward through the calm seas, but the waters stirred as if the dark and chilled depths knew winter was not far off.

Only five days had passed since Ari's murder.

Eskil called out to the men about him, "We need friends, but we will defend our hall if need be." He looked in the direction of Ari's recently built cairn, the hill of the hall obscuring it from view. "Taming Markland will demand enough of our blood, so we cannot give it away to pay for squabbles and petty disagreements."

There was more than one nod of agreement amongst them.

The ship was closer now, but the low autumn sun above made the detail of it and its crew hard to see. Clouds overhead occasionally came to soften the light and cut the glare off the water.

The boat continued to near, the sail not quite full, while oars along both sides rhythmically cut into the water.

A voice called out when a dark silhouette appeared at the prow, "Ho, Ballr!"

Ballr grinned, offering up a soft chuckle.

The tension that had settled over the men of Godsland faded.

Ballr put up an arm and waved, "Faraldr?"

"Ballr, this would be Godsland then?"

"Yes, come ashore and be welcome."

Eskil asked, "Can we trust him?"

"I do not know, but he could have killed me back on the hillside. I do not think his fight is with us; Thoromr's might have been, but not the Greenlander's."

Alfvin spoke with a deep voice behind them, one hand clutching a new axe, "No, we have no fight with the Greenlanders. Not yet."

Eskil pondered that. "Remember...it was not these men who killed Ari, but Thoromr. That does not free them from our suspicions though, as we know that the White Christ has reached Greenland, too. Be wary."

The ship was closer now and they could see Faraldr more clearly as he waved afresh. He looked relieved to have found them so easily. Behind him, his men lowered the sail.

Ballr stepped forward to the edge of the water and called out, "I was beginning to think you planned not to visit!"

Faraldr actually laughed, as other Norse faces came into view behind him. They seemed curious and plain, not threatening. "We saw to Thoromr, a man whose anger for now is well and truly quenched, then gathered our timbers and other cargoes before heading out this morning."

"Back to Greenland?"

"Yes, but first we wanted to see what you have built here."

Those on the oars behind him let them drag in the water, holding them there to slow the ship. They also dropped an anchor.

The ship slowed as it cut through the shallows.

The crew began working the oars to bring the ship to a stop, reversing their stroke when the vessel headed straight for the gravel beach.

Ballr and the others stood back to make way for the ship as it closed in. Such ships were often beached, but it looked as though the Greenlanders planned to leave the ship in the water.

The ship was full with cut timber and bulging sacks of furs. The cramped crew, nearly thirty in number, sat or stood around the cargo, watching the beach and taking in the sight of the hall built into the hillside.

Eskil whispered to Torrador, "Fetch the women back."

Torrador turned to do so, but began to laugh instead when he spied them watching from around the corner of the woodshed, barely hidden from the new arrivals. He waved to them, calling them over. Seta led them down the path, causing Torrador to smile. She had fascinated him since she faced off Thoromr, a full season or more ago.

Eskil shook his head, as Ballr grimaced.

Alfvin frowned and hissed a word at Frae when the women returned. It took Eskil a moment to realise that the word was not Norse, but rather of the skraeling's own tongue.

Frae shrugged back at him, ignoring what must have been a scolding, while, beside her, unbelievably, Seta laughed.

The ship's prow came to a stop just short of the beach.

At the same time, Godsland's women arrived, all now gathered to greet the ship.

***

The Greenlanders, led by Faraldr, stayed not only the day, but also the night. They feasted on seafood, in the hall's warmth, and helped build a good-natured chorus of talk, laughter and song.

Some of the Greenlanders seemed surprised at the presence of the skraelings and their treatment, but they respected the ways of the hall. Faraldr himself asked Ballr about Ari's thrall as they ate their fill by the fire pit. Later, Faraldr sat with Eskil and Gudrid, Ballr and Halla, and also Alfvin, Frae and Seta. The Greenlander looked about him while the fire pit's flames lit the main hall, the Godslanders and his own men. "You have a good hall."

Eskil answered, "We are pleased with how it lasted through the winter, and have only made it stronger for what is to come."

"You have room enough, and good stores, I trust." He looked behind him to the altar, statuettes and the small fire burning before it. "I am also glad to see such respect shown to our gods."

Gudrid smiled to hear it. She had taken an instant liking to the Greenlander when he initially toured the hall and saw the fire-lit altar with its carved figures. He had not only been pleased, but also paused to pay his respects.

"Thoromr already told me the tale of how you left the old lands, joined with others of like minds such as he and his father, and then came to be shipwrecked here." His gaze settled on Gudrid. "He also spoke of his father's anger at what he called the unnatural influence of the women."

Gudrid shook her head. "He would have been better to call it common sense."

"I suspect you are right, since he is dead and his son is back in Lakeland, missing an eye"

Frae and Seta both frowned, dragged back to dark and bloody memories.

Faraldr shook his head as he continued, "I swear, things have calmed down in Lakeland since we arrived, but of the three of them, you simply could not know who would be the first one to knife who."

Ballr asked, "Have some of your people stayed behind?"

"Yes, they shall winter there."

"It is a poor hall to winter in."

Faraldr gave a nod. "Our hall, Lakeland as they call it, is good enough for shelter over summer, not well-made for winter's cold, yet it will do. We have left people there to keep not just the peace, but also our claim on it. Besides, if you are here, perhaps we shall look at permanently settling some of our own people. My family has several farms in Greenland and back in Iceland."

Eskil offered, "We would welcome neighbours, certainly some of our own kind, to help with things. I would greatly love to see some women for our lonely men, but above all, we want to keep Markland as a place for our gods, not the followers of the White Christ. That is the vision that delivered us here."

Faraldr considered his host's words and looked about the hall again, his eyes coming to rest on the raven banner hanging by the door. "I also honour the gods. I cannot speak for all who might come, but I can give you my word that all I bring across will be faithful to the Allfather and Asgard. I can dissuade any others with tales of fierce skraelings, weary stories of harsh conditions, fields of stone, and fjords packed with ice."

Those beside him nodded their appreciation.

"While you have done well in establishing yourselves, you must also be short of many things?"

"There is much that we need, and I suspect each of us would give a different list. But my first suggestions would be livestock, seed and people-particularly women."

Faraldr grinned. "Grains for making ale?"

Eskil laughed. "Amongst other things. It has been a dry year."

Alfvin offered, "And iron, but we are working on that."

Gudrid grunted. "We also need cloth and pots."

Ballr laughed. "To be fair, there are too many things for us to name, but we can easily build up a stock of timber and furs ready for you to take back to Greenland in trade."

Faraldr liked the idea. "Greenland has trees, but they are often small or stunted, usually only willow and birch. We can use the wood for many things, but finding good trunks for masts and roof beams is difficult. We have none of the towering pines and firs that are here."

They talked on of things they might trade and do to help each other; Markland had things Greenland could use, while Greenland had more people and thus a broader range of talents and skills.

The night wound on, but was a good one.

***

The Greenlanders made ready to begin their voyage home the next morning.

Eskil considered what they had talked about, particularly in regard to what they could trade or needed of each other. In the end, as

Faraldr and his men had boarded their ship, Eskil repeated those needs for both Godsland and the new vale they planned on opening up.

As they waved off Faraldr and his Greenlanders, Eskil promised to have a load of timber ready for collecting by midsummer. Faraldr nodded, calling out that he would return. He added, "Do not forget...we shall also want some furs!"

Eskil nodded and chuckled. Godsland was going to be busy come next thaw.

He had not said specifically where the fresh valley he had spoken of was located, but he was thinking of the golden vale where Alfvin now sourced their bog iron, a place that held room for scores of farm halls, all of which needed more people.

Faraldr understood.

Then, into the morning, the ship set back to sea, rowing out before setting sail.

Part IV

The Rise of Ravens

COLIN TABER

Chapter 11

-

The Lonely Vales

Seta did go back to try to find her people, but not until after her first Godsland winter had passed. In that long and cold season, following the murder of Ari, she found solace in her two babes, her sister, and amongst the other women, particularly in the friendship that grew deep and true with Halla. Seta had mostly refused the interest of the hall's men, although, in her own aloof way, she had entertained some of Torrador's attention. So when she tested her gifted freedom by announcing she wanted to try and find what remained of her family, it was not a great surprise that Torrador wore a frown and silently stewed over the news.

Eskil understood the pain caused by lost family, something he knew only too well, after the Battle of Svold. The sea conflict, an ambush of fleets, had left him missing his father and older brothers, who had been lost, if not to Christian-backed axes and blades, then to the wants of allied kings.

When spring had well and truly arrived, Eskil, Ballr and a sullen Torrador took Seta a fair distance down the fjord and across the channel, to near where she said the land opened up into several vales her extended family often passed through in late spring and summer.

The distance was a fair one, not far past the entrance to Alfvin's Golden Dale, but on the opposite shore. That put it on the same side of the channel as Lakeland, but far removed. Getting that far took enough of the day that the three men camped with her for the night before planning to return to Godsland in the morning.

And that is how she wanted it. She needed to search for what was left of her family, and she needed to do it without any Godslanders.

The night in the wilds was uncomfortable, the wind fresh and the showers of rain verging on sleet. They sheltered in a glade that grew close to the base of a small cliff, which offered some relief from the worst of the weather, but certainly no peace. Torrador offered to take the middle watch, seeing them through the heart of the night. Seta woke and rose from her furs to sit with him by the campfire.

Eskil felt for Torrador, for there seemed to be a genuine feeling in his attraction to Seta, not merely an urge to find a mate. To see the two together delivered its own comfort, despite the weather.

Torrador and Seta talked quietly, wrapped in their own furs and skins while they watched the night.

Neither spoke much at first, yet as the night stretched on, Seta attempted to ease Torrador's mood. "The wind dies."

He looked to the fire, watching it fight against the occasional spit of rain, the wind stirring it. Hot, yellow flames raced over the glowing embers and leapt up to lick at the air. "You would be more comfortable in Godsland, with your children."

She frowned, an expression so frequent on her face that it seemed its natural state, yet this once, by the flickering firelight, she looked to be genuinely unhappy. "I will return."

He looked at her, his eyes only occasionally darting away to check on the dark woodlands about them. "To stay or to merely fetch your children should you find your own people out here?" He waved a hand at the forest.

She turned away from him, gazing into the depths of the shadows.

He pursued her in her silence. "What if you find nothing, but someone finds you? You will be all alone."

She pursed her lips and shook her head.

"What if it should be Thoromr?"

She snorted. "I will kill him!"

Torrador could not stifle a smirk at her answer, but he did not doubt that she would try.

"I will!" she responded.

"I know you will. I still remember you telling him off on the boat!" He could not help but chuckle at the memory.

Her grave manner faded, melting into a smile.

He calmed himself, becoming serious, before he said. "If the two of you meet again, I know one of you will end up dead."

Seta nodded.

"But if he has an axe..." Torrador's words trailed off.

She hissed, her eyes sparkling with passion, "Give me your blade! With your iron I shall protect myself and take his head."

"I would prefer to lend you my arm, so I could be there to fight for you."

Her expression softened, her voice coming as a whisper, "I must look for my people. I must find what has happened to them."

He nodded, knowing she was not one to easily be swayed. "If you must go, then let me come with you?"

She leaned in against him, her fur wrapped body pressing along his side. "Torrador, Thoromr is not the only danger out there. My own people might kill you."

He put his arm around her, pulling her close. "You will have a blade, but I would prefer to be your iron."

They spoke long into the night, of her childhood campsites, the stream that ran down her home valley, and the great meeting of families, where the vales joined, as they celebrated spring and honoured the spirits of the land.

Together they talked, and the night drew on.

***

At dawn, the men prepared to set off back to the boat. Seta said her goodbyes, and that seemed easy enough for her until she came to Torrador. He stood there, dark and quiet, tall and strong, looming over her as if a towering mountain.

With each previous Norseman, she said she would visit Godsland soon enough, but it was when this mantra was on her tongue before Torrador that her voice broke.

He looked coldly upon her, the softness of last night forgotten. He was more aloof and distant than any withering look Seta had ever offered.

With her words stalling, an awkward silence filled the glade.

Torrador's manner stiffened even more before he opened his mouth to speak. "Such a visit, should you not be taken out here by wolves of four legs or two, or Thoromr himself, will only be to fetch your children."

Seta's bottom lip trembled. "I have to find my people."

"What of Frae and your children should you be killed?"

She bit her lip and then frowned, but had no answer.

"What of all of us at Godsland?" He put a hand to her elbow and hissed, "We have been good to you."

She swallowed and said, "I will return. We will talk then, but first I

180

must know what has happened here."

"I will see you again."

"Wait for me in Godsland."

"I will be where you need me."

She pursed her lips and nodded.

The silence that had earlier filled the glade returned, although now it held a softer edge.

Eskil cleared his throat. "Good luck Seta. All of us, not just Frae or your children, await your safe return."

Seta glanced at Eskil and Ballr and nodded. Finally, she looked back to Torrador. With nothing left to say, she quickly ducked in and kissed him on the mouth, stunning both him and the other men.

In a heartbeat, she then turned, got her pack on her shoulder and stepped out of the clearing.

The men watched her go, Torrador's surprise fading as he began to shake his head.

Before long, she was gone, lost amidst the spring growth and trees.

Eskil turned, beginning the short walk back to the boat.

Torrador stood staring at the woods where Seta had gone. Finally, Ballr clapped him on the shoulder, nodding after Eskil. "Come, we should go."

Torrador shook his head again. "Yes."

Ballr and Torrador followed the trail ahead, before long coming to the gravel beach where Eskil stood readying the boat.

Eskil looked up and said, "To the golden vale then. We shall check on Alfvin before heading home."

Ballr agreed. "Yes, with an early start, we should still make it back to Godsland before sunset." He dropped his own pack into the boat and helped Eskil push it out into the water.

The two looked back at Torrador, the big man standing there, his own pack on his shoulder, not making any effort to come near the water.

Eskil said, "Come Torrador. We have a long way to go."

Torrador remained still.

Ballr stopped what he was doing and looked to both men. He asked, "Torrador, what is on your mind?"

Torrador frowned. "It is dangerous for a woman to be on her own, even Seta."

Eskil gave a nod. "Yes, even Seta."

"I should follow her."

"We need you back at Godsland."

"I want to help her, to see her safe."

"If something happened to you, perhaps her own people mistaking you for a man of Lakeland, it would be a grave loss."

Torrador frowned.

Ballr added to Eskil's words, "Not just a loss to our hall, but to all of us."

Torrador's face was torn, grim and frustrated, yet sad and strong. Finally, he said, "I will come with you. She does not want me, or our help, so that is the way it should be."

Eskil reached out a hand.

Torrador stepped forward and took it, and he then swung his pack down into the boat as they prepared to leave.

Ballr offered, "Besides, you shall get to see Alfvin tell off Eskil, when our leader again calls the bog works 'Golden Vale'."

Eskil laughed. "Yes, and not the shorter name of Guldale, as I must remember."

Torrador smiled at that, his mood lightening.

***

Alfvin stood up from where he knelt beside Erik the Dane and the ash of their work fire, surrounded by the makeshift tools and mess of their workings. As he did, he smiled and lifted a hand to wave. Under his breath, he said, "The ironmen have visitors."

Erik stood beside him, brushing the dirt off his hands. With a nervous sigh, he whispered, "You mean again. Perhaps I should have stuck to fishing with the brothers Steinarr and Samr or collecting wood with Ballr."

Eskil unknowingly cut off the exchange, calling out as Ballr and Torrador followed him through the low hills that lay across the entrance to the vale, "How go things?"

Alfvin offered a grin, but the darkness about his eyes spoke of fatigue. "Well enough, but I did not expect to see anyone for a few more days."

Erik was quiet behind him.

All the men came together, the new arrivals dropping their packs to the ground.

Alfvin said, "The rain over the past few days has slowed us, but we already have some bog iron to take back."

Eskil nodded, pleased, but looking over the tired men at close quarters put other concerns into his mind. "You look exhausted. What has been happening?" He also noted the dead fire. "You are not working your iron today?"

Erik glanced beyond their worksite, his eyes scanning the crest of hills around them. He looked nervous.

Alfvin offered, "We have had company."

Ballr gasped, but Eskil waited for Alfvin to continue.

Behind them, Torrador could not help but ask, "Who? Lakelanders or skraelings?"

Eskil knew his mind was as much on Seta, all alone across the water, as it was on whatever threat had visited Alfvin and Erik.

"Skraelings. They came down from the vale in a group of five, but more were waiting back in the trees. They saw our smoke and came to investigate."

Eskil could see no sign of struggle or wounds on the men, only fatigue from long watches through the night. "What happened?"

Alfvin turned to Erik and said, "Can you check on them while I speak? We shall join you soon."

Erik nodded, and turned to carefully climb up one of the low hilltops, before flattening out to look across the vale, trying to remain unseen.

Alfvin began the tale, "Yesterday they arrived, five men, of the same look as Frae and Seta. We were merely working, and then turned to see them standing on the hilltop, looking down on us." He indicated to where Erik now lay. "Both Erik and I were caught off guard, completely. We had our blades on us, but our backs to them, lost in our toil. If they had wanted to kill us, they could have done it before we would have known."

"What happened?"

"We stopped and stared at each other for a good while. They looked upon us coldly, but did not move to come closer or raise their spears, so I took a chance and said hello."

"Hello, in our own tongue? What happened?"

"I did use our own tongue at first, but after a heartbeat with no reply, I repeated a greeting Frae taught me."

"And they knew it?"

"Yes."

"So they were friendly?"

"It is probably best to say 'not hostile'."

"What do you mean?"

"We exchanged a few words, and while I know a bit of Frae's language, I do not know enough to work such a meeting well, though I tried."

"What else did you speak of?"

"They asked where we were from, but their questions and gestures made me think what they were really asking was if we were from Lakeland."

Eskil considered that with a furrowed brow. "That is not good. They will not have had any good dealings with Lakeland."

Alfvin gave a knowing nod. "I told them we were not from that way, but knew of the people there. I tried to show we had no love for them. Instead, I said we were from the sea and indicated the channel out more to the north. I did not point out Godsland."

"They know of Lakeland for certain?"

"Yes, know of it and have no love for it."

"Why?"

"From what I could understand, it seems they have lost people to Lakeland, but I do not think it was to Thoromr's axe-or mostly not."

"What do you mean?"

"They spoke of some kind of sickness amongst them, an illness that has taken more than a few of them over late winter and into spring."

Torrador shifted, restless beside Eskil.

Ballr asked, "Did you speak of anything else?"

"They asked how I knew their tongue, so I told them that I married Frae."

Eskil asked, "Do they know of her?"

"It is hard to say. They did talk amongst themselves for a while after that, their manner relaxing a little. They asked afterwards where she was, so I told them back at our own camp with our son. They then seemed to relax and left, bidding us good hunting."

"They did not ask what you were doing or come to look around?"

"Erik thinks they might be scared of coming too close in case they get sick. Regardless, they did seem curious, but not overly so, at our doings."

Erik called down from the hilltop, "I can see them by the trees – only two – but campfire smoke still rises from further down the vale."

Alfvin gestured, "Come, but keep low."

They followed him up the hillside and dropped down to lie on their bellies beside Erik, as they peered through the spring shrubbery.

Eskil asked, "What else can you tell us?"

Erik answered, "We know there are more, but we have not yet approached their camp."

"How many do you think there might be?"

Alfvin spoke, "We cannot say for certain, but we saw as many as fifteen yesterday afternoon. I think it must be several families."

Erik added, "Their sudden appearance unnerved us, and they easily outnumber us, from what we have seen. Worse still, they have been around the camp after dark, taking a look at our workings."

"Did you confront them?"

Alfvin shook his head. "No, after that first meeting, there being only the two of us, we crossed to the island to sleep, with one always on watch."

"I see." Eskil was pleased they had taken such a precaution.

The five men watched the two skraelings who were digging in the soil not far out from the tree line. As they looked on, two more appeared – small children – when they chased a little creature, perhaps a squirrel, out of the woods. The youngsters laughed and squealed as they gave chase, both holding sticks as they tried to catch the speedy animal.

Alfvin broke the men's silence. "There are other children; that is what makes me think they are family groups."

Eskil gave a nod. "So you camped on the island and returned today?"

"Yes."

"To what end?"

Erik spoke up. While anxious about the turn of events, he was also growing uncomfortable with Eskil's questions, feeling they revealed a critical edge directed at Alfvin. "We took what we could to the island last night as darkness fell, and while I wanted to leave at first light, for Godsland with our news, Alfvin would not have it. He said we still needed to come back for some of the gathered iron and tools, lest the skraelings take them."

Eskil eased his tone, "That is not bad thinking. So what did you find when you came ashore in the morning, was anything stolen?"

Alfvin did not seem bothered by Eskil's previous tone; if anything, he seemed pleased Eskil was taking the matter seriously. "We buried the bog iron and the more valuable tools we could not take with us last night."

"So what did they do last night?"

"We saw footprints and saw that things had been moved. Nothing looks to have been taken."

"I wonder what would have happened if they had come and you had been asleep? Would they have left you alone or killed you?"

Alfvin shrugged. "We need this place, not solely for iron, but for the vale. We cannot last on Godsland. We have already cut down all the good timber, and if Faraldr returns with more of our own kind, the soils will never serve us."

187

Eskil agreed. "I know. What do you propose?"

"We need to return here in numbers and stake a claim."

"We lack the numbers needed to take and hold a claim if we leave bad blood between us and any who survive, should a war be fought. We need to reach some kind of agreement."

Alfvin agreed. "Frae and Seta might be able to help." He looked back across the vale to the skraelings – the children still running, the adults still digging. He sighed and added, "Well, if Seta has left us, we need Frae, at the very least."

Torrador bristled. "She has not left us; she will be back."

Ballr ignored the comment and answered Alfvin, "Perhaps we can split the vale with them? We only need the land here for iron and some space for farming."

Eskil frowned. "For now."

Torrador offered, "Perhaps we could live side by side?"

Alfvin nodded, thinking of Frae. "Or together."

***

They loaded both boats and set off back to Godsland, before midday. Alfvin and Erik were on their own boat, the craft low in the water, weighed down by tools, supplies, half the bog iron and some of the work's specially cut timbers. Beside their boat, the other also sat low as they rowed on. Eskil, Ballr and Torrador carried their own gear, more bog iron and related equipment.

Alfvin admitted he had been stockpiling some of the iron, keeping about a tenth of all he produced buried and wrapped in skins. He hid it away in case he ever lost a load or boat when heading back to Godsland. But now, with two boats and the unknown of the skraeling arrival, this seemed like the time to share the load and bring it all home.

Torrador said little while they packed the boat, his mind clearly on other things. He worked hard and quickly, but kept glancing across the water, down to where the wider channel lay, looking at the last of the visible shoreline near where they had left Seta.

Now he stirred as the boats made for the main channel and near to that shore. He raised his voice, calling out across the water to Alfvin and Erik, only a few boat lengths away. "What did the skraelings say of the sickness?"

Eskil and Ballr exchanged glances, the former turning to gauge the distance to Seta's shore.

Alfvin looked to Torrador. He had been scanning the waterway ahead, his own gaze resting on the distant Lakeland shoreline, the same as Torrador's had on Seta's landing. After thinking back to what had been said, he answered, "I cannot be certain of what they meant. The language seemed similar, but I do not know it well, as you know." Torrador had pestered Alfvin over the past season to teach him the tongue so he could try to talk to Seta, although his progress had been slow.

"I understand, but what was said? They talked of death and you think they knew of Lakeland and a killing sickness. Alfvin, is Seta safe, alone on that shore?"

Alfvin looked down the channel to where Torrador indicated with a wave of his hand. He shrugged. "I think they may know of someone who has suffered at the end of Lakeland's iron, but their real concern was of the malady. They knew of others succumbing to the sickness and had also lost one of their own to it first hand."

Torrador turned back and looked to the distant shoreline where they had landed with Seta, his brow furrowed.

They were now joining the main channel and beginning to head away from it, back towards Godsland.

He again asked Alfvin, "Do you think she is safe there?"

"I think, for now, she is safe from Thoromr's Lakeland—even if he survived his wounds. What the skraelings back in Guldale spoke of mostly was the sickness moving through their people's camps. From what they said, it sounded like many had gotten sick, with some dying. Seta may not be safe from such a plague, but having said that, she had already been in Lakeland for a long while before joining us at Godsland. Perhaps the sickness has already tried to touch her, but cannot."

Torrador gave a nod of understanding and then turned back to the landing shoreline fading in the distance.

Ballr spoke up, tackling Torrador's troubles head on. "She wanted to go alone."

"Yes, but now we know of an illness, and of people she knows nothing about."

Alfvin said, "Even if Thoromr is alive, he is not the danger. The Lakelanders will be busy working the lands close to their hall, much like us."

Torrador challenged, "We are a long way out here!"

"The only reason we are this far from Godsland is because it is our best source of bog iron. If not for that, it would be late summer before we would have time to range more, to explore and hunt."

Torrador reluctantly accepted his comment with a solitary nod.

Erik offered, "The dangers to Seta are from animals and her own kind. The skraelings of Markland seem quite peaceful, but who can say for certain."

"And the sickness?" Torrador asked.

Eskil finally spoke, noting their speed was slowing as the conversation went on, and their oar strokes seemed sapped of strength. "Alfvin is right. If the sickness was going to claim her, it would have already had the chance in both Lakeland and Godsland."

Torrador frowned, pulled his oar from the water and stopped rowing.

Eskil asked, "Torrador?"

"I will go to her."

Now it was Eskil's turn to frown, but he knew he could neither deny nor fight Torrador's response. Besides, he would not stand in the way of Torrador while he sought the same kind of happiness so few of the men and women at Godsland were able to enjoy. He pulled his own oar from the water, followed by the others. "I shall not stop you, but you know I believe we need to keep our numbers together."

"I know, but she needs me also."

"Think carefully, Torrador."

"I am sorry Eskil, but I can feel it."

"What will you do when you find her?"

"Bring her home, if she will come."

"She will come eventually. She will want her children."

Torrador nodded.

"How will you get home?"

"We will make our own way. I can build a raft easily enough to get us out on the water, and then we will paddle down to Godsland."

Eskil called out, "Alfvin, am I right in saying you want to return to Guldale soon, with Frae and more men, to claim the place?"

"Yes. We need the iron and the land. Frae might be able to talk to the skraelings now there, and see if we can live side by side or, at least, without blood. She can win their trust."

"When do you want to return?"

"Quickly, while the skraelings remain at their camp...in a few days."

Eskil turned back to Torrador. "We will check Seta's landing site for you the day after tomorrow, staying until not long before sunset. You have until then to meet us, after which we shall head to Guldale to face the skraelings."

Torrador's frown faded, replaced by a relieved smile. "Thank you."

"I want you there and ready. We will need you in Guldale."

They changed direction and got him ashore.

Eager to start his journey, Torrador grabbed his pack and said his goodbyes before heading into the woods.

***

Eskil and Ballr approached home alongside Alfvin's and Erik's boat, in the setting sun, to find Godsland well and truly alive. The shoreline held their fellows as a longship approached the shore from the direction of the sea. Gudrid stood waving to the crew, not yet aware of her husband's return from down the fjord behind her.

Ballr asked, "Faraldr?"

Eskil began to row harder. "Let's hope so, for we know him and his intent well enough."

"He seems trustworthy."

"Yes, he does. And we need what he can provide; people, seed and livestock."

Alfvin smirked and added, "And women, one each for Erik and the others!"

Erik grinned, the first time he had in days. "I hope so!" he then growled, "At least one to start with!"

Ballr laughed, doubling his efforts to get them home, digging his oar into the water and pulling it back. "It must be Faraldr. Gudrid would greet no one else so enthusiastically, except Eskil or Odin himself!"

Erik's earlier loud and hopeful agreement that it was Faraldr drew the attention of those on the beach. So as the longship emptied its crew onto the gravel, all noticed the approach of Godsland's own, which had been lost in the glare of the setting sun behind them.

THE LANDING

The ship was not alone on the beach when the two smaller boats from Guldale arrived. The quiet of Godsland soon transformed with laughter, greetings and embraces when the folk of the hall reunited and threw themselves into welcoming Faraldr and the scores of men and women he had landed.

Eskil found Gudrid striding through the chaotic throng, leading Faraldr by the hand. "What a day!" he cried out in delight as he took Gudrid in his arms, Faraldr grinning behind her.

Nearby, Halla found Ballr, just as Frae sought Alfvin's arms. About them the laughter and talk fell into a cheer, as together the people gathered to celebrate either the return of loved ones, a homecoming or a landing.

Eskil smiled at Gudrid, but pulled away to bring her beside him as he turned to greet Faraldr, "I am glad to see you!"

"And we are glad to land, all of us! Some are settlers for here or elsewhere, and others, like me, will return to Greenland after summer's peak."

"That is great news!"

"I also have someone I want you to meet." He waved over a woman who had been standing back and waiting for the summons. She moved across, her steps firm, her face holding a hard beauty about it, her ice-blue eyes framed by long, blonde hair. She also bore a likeness to the look of Faraldr.

When she stepped beside him, he announced, "This is my sister, Aldis, recently widowed when her husband was taken by the sea. She now comes to settle in lands hereabout, to represent our family interests."

Eskil smiled and offered his greetings, alongside Gudrid, the Godslander asking, "Forgive me for asking, but where?"

"Lakeland, of course...our hall and vale."

As they spoke, Eskil's mind turned over with thoughts of what Faraldr had said. He wanted very much to know the details, but there would be another time for that.

193

***

The Godsland hall was full of people, warmth, laughter and song that night.

Alfvin spoke of what had happened at Guldale, of the meeting of the skraelings, just as Eskil recounted the tale of Torrador deciding to go after Seta.

In all this, the arrival of Faraldr and his people could not have been better timed. Now, when they returned to Guldale, they could take dozens by ship, although Eskil was determined, along with Alfvin, to see what could be done to claim the vale without bloodshed.

Chapter 12

'

Torrador & Seta

Torrador spent the rest of the day trying to follow Seta's trail. When they had talked the night before, the two of them side-by-side at the campfire, she spoke about how the lands ahead, beyond the crest of the gentlest part of the slope, opened into the first of a series of broader inland vales.

She described how most of the valleys nursed narrow lakes that fed into each other by way of fast flowing streams. The waters eventually joined to become a river that flowed strongly to find the fjord even further up the channel. Another lesser network of vales headed in the opposite direction to end near Lakeland.

He could choose from several tracks and trails leading from the shore, but only one looked to be wide and fit for a person, with the shrubs and trees farther back. He stood at its beginning and looked up the green and shadowed tunnel that stretched ahead. Compared to the others, it also had the gentlest climb.

With a nod to himself, he started his jourey, remembering what she said about the gentle path. Hoping for the best, he offered a prayer,

"Odin, lead me to her, to find her whole. Seta may not be of our lands, but I think she has the heart of a Valkyrie."

And so he began, watching for any sign of the woman he chased.

***

Seta walked along the jagged ridgetop, with the fjord half-a-day to her back, and the first vale she sought ahead. She knew several spots where her extended family had often camped in spring, so she watched for any sign that they might be occupied before choosing which one to head down. The paths would be clear, in places slippery with mud because of the previous night's rain, but easy enough.

The vale itself was quiet, holding only the sounds of the birds and the wind passing through the trees. Looking down on it all, she had a feeling the land was largely empty, for she saw or smelled no telltale signs of campfire smoke. At least, she told herself, the birdsong meant no obvious threat lurked under the canopy spreading before her.

She thought of Thoromr.

She gripped the blade tightly, the iron that Torrador had given her, leaving himself unarmed. The handle felt good in her palm. With a thought of Aris and his murder, she hissed a curse and hoped Thoromr had died in agony, from a wound gone bad.

Or if not that, she might find him out here.

She imagined how surprised he would be to run into her; how pleased with himself that he could torment her afresh. She would let him approach, but she of course would run from him, feigning a fall. Once on the ground, she would pretend to be hurt and lost to cowering as he closed in on her. Then, as he reached her, so close that neither could get away, she would plant Torrador's iron into him.

She smiled at the thought as she walked, beginning to stray down from the vale's top, towards one of her people's favoured camping sites.

Her smile broadened, but it was one built of dark memories and a demanding anger. Oh yes, she would plant that iron in his belly and then watch him pull away in horror. Once he looked at the wound she put in him, she would then kick him down as his life began to bleed away. She would then sit astride his chest, pin his arms down, and cut his throat.

Seta's knuckles showed white as she tightened her grip on Torrador's blade.

***

Torrador reached the crest of the ridge late in the afternoon. From there, he looked down upon the vale opening up before him. The woods started not far down the rocky hillside, and in the distance, the shadowed green canopy revealed glimpses of water.

He knew he had found the vales, but which way would Seta have travelled?

The sun was low, soon to sink behind the snowcapped mountains farther inland. At the same time, a wind, with a chilled edge, stirred to suggest a cool night. Thankfully, the clouds that were scattered about did not look to be heavy with rain or sleet.

He contemplated what lay ahead. Seta had not mentioned much about her people's campsites, only giving the impression of sheltered places, by rock outcrops or besides streams. Torrador knew he could call out to her for she might be close enough to hear. But would she respond? She had made it plain, after all, that she did not want him here.

Besides, who else might hear his call?

No, he would call when his search was at an end, when such a risk was necessary, but not before.

He looked about again.

Here, unlike on the coast at Godsland, he could see down the vale and across expanses of land beyond, more than he could cross on foot. With that land came vast woods – no doubt more hazards – and probably many skraeling camps. Simply looking at it made his heart sink.

How was he to find Seta and get back to meet Eskil and Ballr in just two days?

He did not see any sign that anyone was near, in the foreground, but in the far distance, fully the length of the vale before him, a lone twisting column of smoke began to rise, thin and white, probably from a cooking fire.

He wondered if Seta had seen it?

The smoke was too far away for her to have reached, perhaps a full day's walk. No, Seta would not have reached it yet, even if she had seen it and headed that way. But it did tell him that he was not alone and that Seta had been right: He was the stranger here, the one in danger, not her.

The smoke also gave him an idea. He would look for a sheltered spot to camp tonight, a place with good visibility, amongst the rocks poking through the soil at the ridge's crest. He would not light a fire, but instead would spend what time he could looking around him for any sign of a nearby fire that Seta may have either lit herself or be attracted to.

While the light remained, he got to work looking for a suitable campsite. He would have to sleep at some point tonight, but he would also spend a good part of the night doing what he could to keep searching, either by walking along the crest, or by watching over the vales for signs, smells or sounds that might giveaway a nearby camp.

He would find her – maybe not tonight – but he would find her and make sure she was safe.

***

THE LANDING

Seta headed down into the vale, taking the easiest path. It soon followed a stream flowing through a series of pools, stepping down to where an age of rains and thaws revealed buried rock. The woods about her thickened the farther she went, the sounds and smells bringing back memories. The recollections sang to her of happier times, of laughter, of the promise of youthful love and of the warmth, comfort and company of family.

She stumbled over a root and fell forward.

The fall was not drastic, but set her tumbling down the path and through leaves, mud and shrubs. She careened into a thicket, finally stopping in a cluster of sapling trees. She lay bruised and sore amidst the bent and broken young trunks.

Slowly, she sat up and gathered herself, shaking her head. Looking back up the path, she could see where, lost in memories of play and laughter, she had tripped over a root and then slipped on the damp earth.

She cursed herself.

Seta was quick to rise, but quiet as she did. She was listening to what the vale had made of her loud tumble.

Nothing.

The birds had been silenced by the sudden thrashing of the wood and shrubs, but nothing else sounded or approached in answer.

Again on her feet, she looked to the saplings, noting the tallest and thickest one. The sapling stood askew, but unbroken.

Seta looked about, listening again to the valley, wondering if anything or anyone nearby had heard her fall.

Was she in danger?

How close were her people?

These vales had always held several family groups who moved along them with the seasons, ranging about to hunt.

Could she really be alone?

She listened again, this time holding her breath and searching for anything, absolutely anything.

She heard nothing, not even birdsong.

She turned back, with a frown, toward the skewed sapling and put Torrador's blade to work. She cut it free and then stripped off the branches before striking off its top, making it a stick she could use for walking. The sapling was still green, but strong and thick. After all, she had the bruises as proof after ending up sprawled against it.

Now, as she continued her journey down the trail, she worked on sharpening one end. She knew she could harden the point in fire, but she needed a safer time to try that, not today, as sun and day waned.

The birds restarted their song as she walked on. Memories of happier times returned, of a larger, extended family and of other groups, again reminding her of a life spent in this vale and the others running off it.

Until Thrainn had burst into the hall at Lakeland, flashing the whites of his eyes, mad with grief. He had charged in and lashed out with his cursed axe, cutting, hacking and slashing, even killing one of his own kind. Even his own people had not been able to comprehend the horrible, blood-drenched murder of Leif.

What followed next in the hall had been just as harrowing.

Blood, fury and violence were what Thrainn had delivered to her and her family.

The memories continued to work her, like the fast, rushing flow of a thaw-filled creek rising as melting ice dams broke, increasing the torrent, pummelling the remaining ice, while drowning the shallows.

She cursed at the memory.

Seta continued down into the valley, haunted by reminiscences that more and more drifted from childhood games in the vales to a more recent season of blood.

Lakeland, a time of terror and violence, thankfully ended with the move to Godsland. Now she left all of that behind and returned to the valleys of her childhood, even if so far she had only discovered a growing sense of loneliness, as if she had arrived after everyone had gone.

She shook her head, cursing herself as she continued the journey.

Why had she left Frae and her children behind?

And what of Halla, someone she had begun to build a close friendship with, despite how alien each had been to the other in the beginning?

And what of the others?

She sighed.

What of Torrador?

What was she doing?

She stopped for a moment and pondered why she was here.

Why?

To get answers and to find truths, the things needed to help her settle, one way or another, into a new life here in the valleys, or even back at Godsland. Perhaps even a life that might include Torrador, the man who loved her enough, despite her icy reluctance, to break Eskil's rules and give her his blade.

Visible through the leaves, the sky above spread, dotted with golden clouds that glowed as the sun sank in the west. The bright globe itself was lost to the woodlands and no doubt, soon enough, to the mountains, as the day headed towards its end.

Seta began to move again, realising with frustration, that she was wasting valuable daylight. There was nothing to debate; she was now here, so she would continue her task. Then, if there was nothing to stay for, she would return to Godsland. She might even let Torrador into her life.

He was a good man and she knew it.

Torrador did not come robed with the grim memories of Thrainn and Lakeland as Ari had. He had not been there. Although Ari and Alfvin had not been as knee-deep in blood as Thoromr and Trion, they had both been a party to the violence. That was what Seta had never been able to forget or come to terms with, unlike Frae, who had found not only peace with Alfvin, but also love and security.

She again shook her head and tried to focus on what she was doing.

Farther ahead, not too far away, should lay some of the campsites her family had often used. Clearings by rocks or groves, upslope from the stream before it reached the narrow lake's waters that marked the bottom of the vale. If she hurried she would reach the first of those before sunset.

Beyond, down by the lake were the larger campsites where families had often gathered. She would see those tomorrow.

Seta hurried on, determined to at least reach the first of the old camps.

As she moved on, the wind increased in strength, filling the wooded vale with a chorus of noises – the rustling of leaves, branches knocking against each other, the groaning of boughs and trunks – making it harder to detect any approaching people or animals.

Yet this was what leaving Godsland and searching for what was left of her extended family meant. She had left the sanctuary of the hall and traded it for the possibility of finding something similar, with her family, if they still lived.

***

Torrador found somewhere to camp, a place on the ridgetop, some large rocks standing out amidst shrubs and stunted trees. The spot offered shelter in its nooks from the rising wind, but would be mostly open to the rain and sleet if the weather turned. It was not perfect, but had good visibility on its approaches. Simply, for one night and his purposes, it would do.

THE LANDING

Before he settled in, he checked the surrounding area, ranging down both hillsides, looking for any sign of resident beasts or skraelings. As the light died with the setting sun, Torrador retreated to his camp and did what he could to make himself safe and comfortable. He would not have a fire, but he did have a fur to sleep under and dried fish to eat. While he chewed through his meal, he worked at sharpening the ends of various lengths of wood he had collected from the forest, grinding them on the rock faces that made up his meagre camp. By the time it was fully dark, he had turned the broken branches into half-a-dozen stakes. One of them held enough length and strength for him to keep it separate; that would be his spear.

While he did not begrudge giving Seta his knife, he felt exceedingly vulnerable without it.

His preparations complete, he got up and left his gear behind, aside from his new spear and the sharpest stake, which he tucked into his belt. He planned to walk lightly along the ridgetop, marching for half the night if need be, as he searched the vales below for any flickering sign of campfires.

It would be a long night.

***

Seta knew that, out in the woods by herself, she dared not light a fire. That meant she was in for a cold and long night, one of nerves and drowsing, as she tried to stay as alert as she could, while hoping for a safe time to sleep. The idea weighed on her already-flagging spirits, because she had not seen any of her people. She told herself tomorrow would be different.

During the last part of the day, she had seen some empty campsites as she made her way to a rock outcrop in which she now camped. Unlike the others, the last one seen held a fresh grave. By the sombre light of dusk, as she had looked upon the turned soil, she realised this was as close as she had been to her people since leaving Frae and their children. The realisation planted a seed of doubt in her mind.

Where were her people?

The question haunted her for much of the evening.

Some of her doubts were soothed later when she caught the faint scent of smoke from a distant campfire.

She simply had to keep going; she would find them tomorrow.

At least, that is what she hoped.

Seta chewed on some fish, the meal reminding her of Torrador, as he had packed the dried food for her before leaving Godsland.

She wondered where he was, if he had cheered up at all, and what he was eating.

But under it all she wondered; was he thinking of her?

***

Torrador had been able to smell smoke on and off through part of the night, and at one stage thought he saw the flicker of distant flames, but the light had been brief and white, possibly the reflection of the moon on water before the scattered clouds above again stole it away. With no clear sign of where another camp or Seta herself might be, he instead turned back to his own camp, hoping to get some sleep.

Getting back to his campsite was easy enough, and once there, he worked at staking the few ways in, between the stones and trees. Then he lay where he had a good view down into the vale, wrapped himself in his furs and watched the dark wood until he fell asleep.

Chapter 13

-

Back to Lakeland

Eskil stood next to Faraldr, having second thoughts, while the longship cut through the water and a light fog as they headed towards the beach. Ahead, under a midmorning sun, that spent more time hidden behind drifting clouds than not, a path climbed up the slope and into the small and narrow vale of Lakeland.

He had not been back since they had first seen the hall's smoke. Softly, so as not to be overheard by anyone but Faraldr, he said, "I should not be here."

Faraldr put a hand to his shoulder, taking his eyes from the shoreline. "Of course you should. Without you, none of your people or Lakeland's would be in Markland."

Pursing his lips as he frowned, Eskil then answered, "That may be true, and I am not afraid to come, but if he has survived, my presence will only taint your visit."

Faraldr shook his head. "Eskil, I saw the wounds. He could not have survived."

"Perhaps."

"If he has, then it is because the gods have willed it. Regardless, we already know whom Asgard favors; you were gifted with the drive to come forever west, until you reached this place. All of this was meant to be."

"I would not want my presence to sour your relations with Thoromr."

"He was destined for a slow death, falling to madness, as the wound went bad–and that is if he was not taken by one of his other injuries."

"A painful death."

"Yes. Regardless, if he has survived his wounds, you are here as my guest. Remember this is my hall and vale."

Eskil looked to the Greenlander, thinking on his words. Arching an eyebrow, he said, "I am here in case Thoromr lives, am I not?"

The trace of a smile came to Faraldr's face. "You are my guest; my people and I guarantee your safety." He glanced to his sister, Aldis, who stood nearby, peering with an intense gaze as she studied the land coming into view. He added, "You will also be a witness to any deals made."

***

They landed on the beach, the expanse empty, but the path up the slope to the vale showing plenty of wear. They left the livestock on the ship for now, along with a few men and women to hold it, but the rest of them assembled before Faraldr.

He called out to them as they gathered. "The winter has been long, and the hall housing our fellows is crude. Know that our people will have had a hard time, but we are here now, with spring, and we will build new halls and bring better times to this vale. Follow me and my doings, and also those of our Godsland host." He gestured to Eskil,

206

though they already knew who he was. "Be wary of Thoromr and Trion, if they remain, as they are not of our own people and have already stained this vale with too much blood."

The gathered group, numbering twenty, nodded that they understood.

Faraldr added, "Do not show your blades, but do have them within reach." And then he turned, and with a nod to Eskil, headed up the shore towards the path.

***

They got as far as half way into the vale before they saw someone, a Norseman, appearing from a thicket of trees, with an armful of firewood. The man had seen them and waved, as though he recognized Faraldr. He put the wood under his arm and began jogging towards them, the rising bluff of Lakeland looming at his back, and with it, hidden from view, the hall.

Faraldr said to those about him, "Well, it looks as though Young Raf has survived the winter."

Aldis walked just behind her brother and Eskil, but was not slow in offering, "Look at him and his tattered clothes and furs. He looks like he has been living with pigs!"

A chorus of murmurs showed agreement, prompting Eskil to look down at his own clothes. What he wore was of Norse cuts, but mostly made of furs and skins sewn together, if quite good compared to Raf's, but still rougher than the shirts and such of those with him.

Raf ran on, his pace steady and not so fast that it indicated anything other than an eager greeting.

Eskil looked back to the man and got a better sense of what Aldis meant. Raf's clothes, or what remained of his usual garb, hung worn, torn and stained. Some of what he wore bore patches made of animal skins or were covered by a rough-cut, hole-bearing fur he wore over his back, slits cut in at the shoulders for his arms. In addition to that, everything looked to be caked in mud and dirt.

Faraldr spoke softly as the man neared, "Remember that they have had a long winter alone, and one not planned. Ten men with Thoromr and Trion and one skraeling thrall is not an ideal hall to winter in."

Raf called out as he closed, "Faraldr, it is great to see you!"

Faraldr smiled. "And better for us to see you well!"

Raf laughed as he slowed, covering the last of the distance.

"How have you fared?"

"Come and see. We all have lasted out the ice and snow, but it was not an easy time." Eager, he turned to lead them on.

As they walked, Faraldr asked questions, the first coming easily, the rest prodded by Aldis. "Raf, tell us of how you all fared, including wounded Thoromr?"

"We are well, although Bersi sickened with a burning fever not long after the first snows. He recovered, but remained sluggish for a time. The sickness did not touch any of us, but some of our thralls came down with it, two of them dying..."

Faraldr interrupted, "Thralls, I thought there was only one?"

"There was when you left, but we have had some run-ins with the skraelings in the deeper vales. We killed over a dozen in fights and also took some into thralldom."

Faraldr gave a nod of understanding as he considered this. "And the sickness has passed?"

"Yes, a full season ago, before the heavy snows. It did not touch any of us."

Aldis prodded from behind, "And what of Thoromr?"

"Thoromr has recovered, but is a different man. He still has his temper, yet it takes more to stir it and even more for him to act upon it. He was lucky to survive, and he knows it."

"And Trion?" she persisted.

"Yes, he is also here, but spends much of his time away from the hall." He slowed his walking and turned around to meet their gaze before going on, "And from Thoromr. They have grown apart. I think Trion thought he would be king of Lakeland if Thoromr did not recover."

Faraldr grumbled, "I hope you reminded him of my own claim?"

"We did, but I do not think he believed you would return."

The path rounded a bend, past some thickets, and then the heart of the vale opened up before them. Ahead at the foot of the bluff spread the hall and the wooden frame of a new building rising up next to it. Several garden beds ran to one side of the hall, where the soil and light were best. Two skraeling women worked the dirt as another Norseman looked on.

Raf, the wintered Greenlander, said, "Trion had his own brush with death, making him both an eager hunter of skraelings, while also wishing to leave this place."

"What do you mean?"

"Some thralls escaped. They came across him while he was out in the woods hunting, and he tried to stop them. They knocked him out and left him. We found him in the snows later. He was nearly dead."

Faraldr nodded. "And Thoromr has treated you well?"

"Well enough, but he considers the hall and vale his."

"We shall see about that. Where will we find him?"

"The hall."

"We shall head there to speak to him. Can you gather our wintered people and bring them in?"

"Of course." And with that, he hurried off to fetch his fellows.

They kept walking, following the path to the hall.

Eskil shuddered as they passed by the thralls working the soil with crude tools fashioned from cut branches. The misery on the poor souls' sunken-eyed faces spoke of more than endless toil. Their skin bore bruises and pockmarks, while their limbs were thin and their shoulders slumped.

He could not help but make the comparison: Back in Godsland, Frae was not just free, but free to marry whom she liked, and her sister, Seta, was even free to leave.

***

The door was open to the hall, so Faraldr walked straight up the path, intending to go in. Eskil and Aldis followed directly behind him, and they were trailed by the rest of Faraldr' people.

With only a few paces to go, a series of small thuds and splats sounded out as if someone or something hit the floor within. A moment later, a loud curse growled, quickly matched with the sharp slap of a blow and a muffled scream.

Faraldr quickened his stride and entered the hall to find a basket rolling across the floor. Between it and a Norseman, with his hand still out, fresh from delivering a blow, lay a skraeling woman sprawled on the floor, surrounded by a scattering of broken eggs.

The Norseman looked up in irritation, but surprise quickly overcame his face. He whispered, "Faraldr?" At his feet, the skraeling woman scurried away, one hand to her cheek, the other chasing after the basket.

On the other side of the hall, a familiar voice rose, "Faraldr, you have returned...but you are late!" It was Thoromr.

The Greenlander continued on, his pace slowing. He moved beyond the entry, the broken eggs, and then past the smoldering fire pit, to make room for his people. He looked to the Lakelander, the big man sitting on a stool while he checked over two iron blades. "Thoromr, I see you have recovered from your wound?"

THE LANDING

Thoromr frowned and began to move a hand, raising it on reflex to his missing eye, covered by a leather patch. He stopped himself. "Yes, I survived." He smiled, but it was not a warm thing. "Odin wanted me to witness your return." The big Lakelander then glanced at the people following Faraldr in. The first thing he searched for was drawn iron or any sign of hostility. The second thing he noticed was the presence of so many women.

It took only a heartbeat for his manner to soften.

Until his lone eye spotted Eskil.

He sprung up as he took a blade into each hand, roaring, "What is that Godsland pig doing here!"

Faraldr squared his shoulder, but did not draw his own blade. Calmly, without looking to Eskil or to any of his own people, he said, "Eskil is my guest and under my protection. I have asked him to come here, to a hall I built with my own hands."

Thoromr considered the words, but did not like them. Yet he relented, at least for now. "Then you can look after him, for I want nothing to do with him or his people. Besides, I have already had my vengeance."

Ari had paid a high price for leaving Lakeland.

Eskil said, "I can look after myself."

Faraldr put a hand out to stop the exchange. "This is not about ravens and wolves. Let us move onto other matters. I am glad to see you healed and I would like to hear how my men, and you and Trion, fared over winter."

Thoromr beckoned him forward and sat himself back down. There were other stools about, and a step around the fire pit. "Sit and I will tell the tale."

Faraldr sat closest to Thoromr, Eskil let Aldis slip in between her brother and him, pushing him further back, so he did not become a distraction for the rest of the visit.

Once everyone had settled, Thoromr began to speak, "I was well

211

tended, and for that I must be grateful; even I can face up to such a thing."

Eskil was surprised to hear such an admission.

Perhaps Thoromr had changed, or, perhaps was not so much like his father?

Faraldr answered, "I was glad to help."

Thoromr locked his one eye on him, the glare more piercing because of its singularity. "I am sure you were. Regardless, because of my wounds, I missed much of your men's hurried preparations for their unplanned stay. Trion helped them, taking them hunting, while also gathering nuts, roots and leaves that could be stored for eating during the snows. There was also fish to be caught and dried, of course." He shook his head. "My father hated those fish, and I think, after another winter, I shall be in full agreement with him.

"Your men caught more than fish; there were birds and small animals like hares and squirrels, plus seals, and even a few wolves and a bear. The meat was cured, carcasses skinned, and then there were the skraeling camps they kept stumbling upon."

Faraldr's brow furrowed. "We have had little contact with them before. How did it happen?"

"The hunts were going deeper into the vales. Once they found one camp, another never seemed to be too far away, or that is what they told me." He leaned towards Faraldr, his eye intense. "In truth, I think your men got a taste for killing and taking thralls."

Faraldr did not respond to the suggestion. "Were they or you or the hall ever attacked? Did this all happen only away in the deep vales?"

"Nothing happened here; they would not dare!"

"How many thralls are there? We have already seen three."

"There are six at the moment, all women." He looked like he was about to leer, but glanced at Aldis and thought better of it before continuing, "There were more, but some sickened after the first snows, others escaped. Those who fled attacked Trion when they did. We killed a few who were nothing but trouble."

Faraldr said, "It is one thing to bring someone into thraldom in a world where everyone knows the rules, where one hall is surrounded by a dozen others, and those by hundreds more. But it is another thing to do it in a lone hall, where the source of thralls is what surrounds you."

"Hold your lecture. They are a placid people and are there to be taken."

"If the skraelings begin to resist and escape, as you have said they have already done, how long until they tire of your presence, murder and mistreatment? How long until they come seeking blood?"

Thoromr flushed red with anger, but thought for a moment on those words. After a long pause, one in which he dropped the two blades into the dirt at his feet, he said, "I do not think it will be a problem."

"What do you mean?"

"The sickness: Your man, Bersi, had a kind of pox, not that he was so sickly himself, but when the thralls tending him caught it, they all came down with it and were affected differently from him, as if it was a kind of poison."

"What happened?"

"Most survived, although some carry scars, but two did die. The survivors were terrified; that is when we had a few escapees."

"It is another reason for the skraelings to hate us."

"Come the thaw, we began sending groups out to hunt and get fresh meat. While we have not yet ranged far, the one time they did go into the deep vales, they came back with tales of abandoned campsites peopled only with graves and rotting bodies. That is why I am not frightened of them; Bersi's fever is killing and scattering them."

"Are you certain?"

"Yes, they are terrified. We cannot even get a thrall to touch Bersi now without them crying and pissing themselves. And out there in the vales, they no longer face us; instead, they run away."

Faraldr thought about that, mixing it with the knowledge of what Alfvin and Eskil had shared with him the previous night in Godsland. He began to nod his head, as what Thoromr said made some sense. There was indeed some kind of sickness travelling the vales of Markland, but it did not seem to be affecting the Norse and was perhaps even sourced from them.

Aldis cleared her throat and spoke into the silence, "What of the building outside?"

Thoromr looked to her and glanced back to Faraldr, prompting the Greenlander to introduce them, "Thoromr, this is my widowed sister, Aldis."

The big man looked at her, noticing the familiar features and also her noble, if stark, beauty. "We are preparing another hall. Your summer hall was never meant to house so many and certainly not over winter." With a glance to Faraldr, he added, "Also, some of the thralls are pregnant."

Aldis gave a nod and smiled her thanks for the answer before surrendering the conversation back to her brother.

Faraldr said, "To build such a hall is a good idea, a matter made more urgent with the news I bring."

"And that is?"

"I am not merely delivering words, but also new settlers. There are five couples here, but also some single men and women. I will be staying in Lakeland and Godsland with them, until the end of summer, to oversee their settling-in. By autumn, I shall leave to take some of those who have already wintered here back to Greenland."

"More people are welcome in the vale, as there is much work to do."

Faraldr narrowed his eyes. "Yes, there is, in a vale I own. But I am not blind to the fact that you are entitled some due for your efforts in improving the hall so it can be used in winter and the other works you have done."

Thoromr lost his relaxed manner, his jaw set as he waited for Faraldr to finish.

The Greenlander lifted a hand and indicated those who had entered the hall with him. "I present new settlers, all of them with tools and skills, seed and livestock. A few even have their own thralls. They will live here on land the both of us will agree to gift them, so that they can work it and build their own farms next to this one."

"They have no need to build their own halls; they can join my own."

"They are my people and I am not gifting them to you, but the vale to them. They will have their freedom, and that includes the freedom to build their own halls here in Lakeland, on land that they own."

"There is not that much good land in the vale; the soil is thin and the valley narrow."

Faraldr ignored him and pressed on, "We will divide the vale between you and me. From that division, we will gift land to these and future settlers, matching each other's losses."

In a loud voice, Thoromr announced, "You are giving me something that you plan to steal away!"

Again, Faraldr ignored him. "In return for your agreement, the settlers here, and those that come next year, will work to build you a grand hall of your own, to be finished within three summers. You will receive some livestock. You will have that, and our respect as the longest settled Norseman in all of Lakeland, a fact we will honour."

Thoromr thought on that, his face softening as he considered the offer. "How many settlers will you bring next spring?"

"I think it will be as many couples. Again, they will come with skills, livestock, seed and faith in the gods of Asgard."

"Your offer is *almost* tempting."

Faraldr glanced at his sister, who gave a slight nod, the movement almost imperceptible. He then stood, catching Thoromr off guard, but the Greenlander did not draw a weapon or step forward to threaten.

Instead, he held out a hand to his sister, Aldis, who also rose.

Into the quiet, as Eskil and the settlers, the thralls, and the wintered Norse who had now returned to the hall, listened, Faraldr said, "Aside from making you one of the wealthiest men in all of Markland, I also offer marriage to my sister."

Aldis smiled at Thoromr, letting her long, blonde hair and blue eyes woo him as her smile reminded him of what he had not seen for such a long time.

A Norsewoman.

Thoromr sat speechless for a moment, his mind weighing all he would be giving away: half a valley to which he could only lay a dubious claim, and could not defend in any case. In return, he would be a central figure in a growing settlement, one that would generate wealth and deliver him a new hall and livestock, while he retained land and won a Greenlandic beauty.

The offer was so much more than his father could ever have achieved.

He answered, "I agree." He then smiled at Aldis, his mind racing, as he added, "I shall do it not just for me, but for the good of Lakeland."

Faraldr smiled. "Then I welcome you as a brother, and remind you that you will show Aldis the same respect you will show me and demand for yourself in our new land."

***

They planned to hold the wedding that night, after an afternoon of hurried preparations for a feast. One of the newly arrived goats was slaughtered as a sacrifice to the gods, and added to many other foods being prepared, most coming from the stores of Faraldr's ship, including smoked lamb and delicacies such as the shark meat hakarl.

But a wedding feast was not the only thing that needed readying.

Both the bride and groom needed to be cleansed, as tradition demanded, though they had to make do with what Markland had to offer for the task; a dip in the lake their vale was named after.

After Aldis washed in the chilled waters, with her attendants of married women drawn from amongst the settlers, she was robed and returned to the hall to be properly dressed and have her long blonde hair combed out.

While Aldis and her attendants went to the hall, where the feast preparations were also underway, Faraldr led Thoromr and the married men to the lake, where the groom stripped and washed, as part of his own cleansing, before being given fresh clothes. During the chilly ritual, the married men advised the young man on how to be a good husband, a conversation he politely tolerated.

Faraldr watched him, occasionally prodding with questions or repeating some advice. He made it clear this was no game, but an important lesson.

Aldis would not be ignored, taken for granted or mistreated.

Meanwhile, Eskil, left to himself, spent time looking about the hall and its gardens, while attempting to speak to the toiling thralls. He found Seta and Frae's surviving cousin and asked her if there was any message she would like passed on. The woman, weary and worn by almost two years of harsh thraldom, was not only stunned and suspicious of the request, but also disbelieving of what he said about the Godsland skraelings being granted their freedom. In the end, she feigned that she did not understand. Sadly, Eskil nodded and left her.

By late afternoon, they were ready for the ceremony, in front of all the wintered Greenlanders and new settlers gathered in a clearing between the birch groves at the base of the bluff and the lake. Thoromr was almost unrecognizable in fresh clothes. Aldis was a stunning beauty.

Faraldr himself spoke the words, of a man and woman leaving behind their old selves and stations to be joined in union, not only before the community they were founding here, but for the people with which they would live.

A serving of mead from the ship was poured into a bowl, a few drops of blood added to it from the sacrificed goat. Faraldr dipped a bundle of fir twigs in it and then shook the twigs, sprinkling some of the liquid over the couple and assembled guests, thus delivering the gods' blessings before Aldis and Thoromr both sipped from the bowl.

Aldis offered Thoromr an axe as a gift, and he reciprocated by giving up his own axe, a crude thing of bog iron. She would hold it in reserve for their future son.

They then exchanged rings, as Faraldr spoke of vows to each other, the vale and their people here. Aldis agreed and repeated the vows, as did Thoromr, the young man beginning to grow weary.

After the ceremony, Thoromr led Aldis into the hall, helping her cross over his axe that lay across the threshold, guarding the door against evil.

Once inside, he lifted the axe and swung hard, slamming it into a supporting post, as tradition demanded, showing how powerful a man he was, and how strong his weapon.

Bridal ale was then brought out, and Faraldr again led Thoromr in tradition, toasting the gods, particularly Frey, the goddess of fertility and marriage. Then Thoromr shared the ale with his new wife, Aldis, leaving them married and the hall ready to feast.

Food was served and the night became an uproar of eating, merriment and drink. Lakeland had never experienced anything like it.

Eskil kept out of the way during the celebrations, and while Faraldr did what was required in the way of speeches, he found time also to talk to his own people and make sure they would watch out for Aldis until his return in a few days, after he had helped Eskil deal with matters in Guldale.

***

In the morning, before going back to his ship, Faraldr and Thoromr

218

agreed on a plot of land for the Lakelanders' new hall, and on several for the settlers. They agreed to work out the division of the remainder of the vale upon the Greenlander's return. With that, and a heartfelt goodbye to his sister, Aldis, Faraldr and his crew-and some of the wintered Norsemen-were keen to get away. The ship headed back out, first to Godsland for midmorning, and then on to Seta's Landing and Guldale.

Chapter 14

-

A Mournful Cry

Torrador came to a stop along the forest trail. Last night's ridgetop camp and the morning's descent into the vale were now well at his back, as was a good part of a day's walk farther into the unknown.

Too much of the day.

He had followed a stream that often pooled and stepped down into small waterfalls and sets of rapids meandering through the woodland. Seta had mentioned the watercourse or one like it. On that night, as Eskil and Ballr had slept, he had hoped she might change her mind about seeking out her people, but she had not.

He hoped she was safe.

Torrador tried to move quickly as he searched for her, but at the same time, he was thorough in watching for any sign of her passing or possible danger.

Looking up to the sky, he knew he had travelled as far as he could for the day, as the light was beginning to fade. Tomorrow morning, at first light, he would need to turn around and head back to the fjord if he wanted to make his late afternoon meeting with Eskil and Ballr.

But he still had not found Seta.

Earlier in the day, he had found the stand of broken saplings and saw where one had been cut and flenched. With a nod to himself, he quickly concluded it was Seta's work and with his knife. Only a metal blade would produce such a cut, and only one person in the vale had such a weapon. The discovery reassured him.

Yet, despite his determined pursuit, he never got close enough to glimpse her or even hear a hint of her presence.

As the sky bled out the day's light and gave into gloom, he also found his mood sinking.

Torrador had passed four abandoned skraeling campsites marked by cold fire pits. A few of them hosted graves. The last one he had seen during the midafternoon held three mounds that rose from the dirt, the soil still settling.

The sight, for the first time, stirred his own fears, not only for Seta, but also for her people.

For now, with the daylight dying, he had no choice but to choose the safest camp he could. He would listen and watch the night for any sign of her, but if he saw or heard nothing, come dawn, he needed to turn back and march as quickly as he could for his meeting with Eskil and Ballr.

***

Seta awoke, quietly cursing herself for falling asleep, but it had been a long day of walking down the vale and of checking empty camps for any sign of her people. In all of them, she found nothing, aside from some abandoned shelters and cold, ash-filled campfires. At one site, around noon, she also found three graves that looked recent.

The discovery had chilled her.

221

Later, after more walking, and as the sun set, she again found a place to settle in to ride out the dark. Tired and downspirited, she began to wonder, and not for the first time, whether she should have stayed in Godsland.

With Torrador.

But then she fell asleep.

Now, around her, the wind sang out as it passed through the tree branches above. The night spread cold, lit by the stars and moon. It was then she realised that she had not just woken up, but had been disturbed.

Something was wrong.

Seta tensed and focussed, thinking hard.

She had heard noises, in addition to the wind, noises, with a call mixed in.

Or had she?

Yes, she had. The more she thought about it, the more she was certain. There had been a yell of surprise or warning.

Tensing, she listened for it again.

Nothing.

The wind eased for a moment, and with it, the noise of its chorus, as it raced through the leaves and branches above. In that pause, a distant voice sounded, sung out to wail, full of grief

Seta listened, not certain if it was what she had originally heard, but that did not matter, not now.

The voice was of a man displaying the pain of great loss.

Seta did not know of the cause, but knew of the emotions behind it, of what powered such a wail and cry.

The caller had lost something very dear.

She shivered.

THE LANDING

Oh, how she knew that feeling, even if she was not the kind of person, so cold and aloof, to give it voice.

The wind rose to bluster again, drowning out the cry with its own as it whistled through the woods. The lament briefly repeated, rising to overwhelm the world, before once again being taken under.

Seta found tears in her eyes. Someone out there mourned for the very thing she was searching for; a sense of belonging, and their family.

The call rose again and then wavered, growing weak.

In the distance, a wolf lifted its own voice in ominous answer.

She began to stir, rising from her hiding place. With a pat to her side, she checked that Torrador's iron was at hand.

She would go and investigate. She had to. She knew the person who owned that voice could give her the answers she needed, even if on this very night, he was losing the same thing for which she searched.

***

Torrador had dozed off at one point, but had been awakened by the wind. What had been a rising breeze now blustered, occasionally as strong as a gale, while also breaking to unexpectedly gift the night's rare moments of peace. During those quiet times, the land spread, illuminated by the moon, a silver world of calm respite, but also poised, as if waiting for grave matters to unfold.

Torrador marvelled at the sight, but also grew tense.

In the distance, soft but unmistakeable, a voice cried out, a long and forsaken cry, one of loss and grief. The voice came from a man.

The Norseman's first thought was of gratitude to Odin that it was not Seta's, but something in the cry told him it came from a skraeling throat. These were Seta's valleys, and that meant the man out there was not just a skraeling, but perhaps her kin.

223

Torrador shrugged off the need for sleep and rose, grabbing a wooden stake to stick into his belt and picking up his spear.

***

Seta held her spear tight as she moved down the path. The night spread deep, but moonlight played through enough of the woodland, over the stream, allowing her to see. She walked into a swirling breeze, the wind carrying the mourning call down the vale to her, along with the smell of a campfire's smoke. She made good progress, trying not to take any careless risks, as she could not afford to fall and injure herself when the answers lay so close.

The cry continued on, coming loud and long.

She had camped close to where it came from, perhaps only a few hundred paces, around a bend in the valley.

Another sound arose close by, but not of the wind, though it also howled. Rising clear, to cut through the night's chorus, pierced the call of a wolf.

She hurried on.

***

Torrador followed the path running beside the stream, only detouring where the trail swung upslope as it meandered around pools, rocks or thickets. He took the time to pause when the wind quietened, listening to check for the call, also making certain nothing stalked him as he passed through the woods. On his first stop, he could still hear the call. On his second, a good while later, he heard a different call that chilled his blood – a wolf's howl.

With a frown, he gripped his spear tight and continued.

THE LANDING

Seta went on, closing on the mourning voice. The call persisted, breaking only occasionally, as it sang out and into the night. She followed a bend in the stream, coming around to spot the glow of a campfire ahead. The flames were not yet visible, but they illuminated the trees, shrubs and rocks crowding about the rugged landscape that nursed the clearing.

The snap and growl of a wolf cut through the gloom. The beast sounded nearby, and unlike the tales she had heard of the old wolf in Godsland, she knew this one was not likely to be alone. The mourning cry itself suggested death, and the pack would have caught the scent of it in the wind–if they were not the cause.

Seta worried; previously wolves had rarely come so far into the vales. She knew continuing on might be the last thing she would ever do, but she needed answers.

Where were her people?

Seta tightened her grip on Torrador's blade, the handle reassuring in her hand. She grasped her spear tightly in her other hand, knowing if it came to fighting or defending herself, the spear was better, since it would keep both wolf and man at a distance.

Determined, she closed on the distant campfire.

***

Torrador knew his actions were foolhardy and quite likely doomed, but he was committed to it, and so he continued. He constantly listened to the forest for clues of what might lay ahead–or behind–while his eyes searched the moonlit path for anything useful.

Whenever the wind stilled and the silence settled, even if only for a

225

heartbeat, he would stop and listen. Such breaks confirmed the direction of the mourning voice and, that he was nearing it, just like the wolf.

He continued onward.

***

Seta rounded the bend in the vale and could finally see the fire's flames ahead. Relief flooded her, doubling when she saw a small encampment of her people's shelters, though they looked tired, with one leaning precariously.

At the centre of the camp, the fire blazed unexpectedly bright. A man stood beside it, with his back to Seta, holding a burning brand in one hand and a spear in the other, tense and ready, as he peered into the woods.

He watched for the wolves.

A twig snapped near Seta, breaking uphill of the path and well to side. She turned in time to hear a rising snarl, and the rush of movement, as a beast, seemingly built of fangs and shadow, launched itself through the air at her.

She stumbled back a step in surprise, one of her feet slipping out from under her in mud, dropping her to a knee. The clumsy move startled her almost as much as the sudden attack. But it also put her temporarily out of reach of the wolf, as the beast flew through the night, aiming to land on the path where she would have been if she had taken another step forward.

Seta cursed, but worked to right her balance.

Seta brought the spear up and swung it around. The angles were all wrong, so she was not in a position to stab the animal with the makeshift weapon. Instead, she brought it about, fast and hard, trying to club the beast and stun it. As she poured her strength into the swing, she let out her own growl.

THE LANDING

She needed some luck, or she would never see her twins again or get her answers.

The blow hit the wolf across the back of the skull with a loud crack, coming hard enough to throw the beast off balance as it landed. The wolf rammed face first into the dirt, one of its shoulders also hitting the ground. Carried by its momentum, the beast tumbled over itself to roll down the slope towards the stream.

Seta sprang to her feet and raced for the campfire. She heard the wolf crash into the water behind her.

Other snaps and snarls arose from the woods around her.

She was not far from the camp now, so she sprinted straight down the winding path, past trees, shrubs and rocks, her spear out on one side, blade on the other.

She would soon reach the safety of the fire and her own people.

Step after step, she closed the distance, the flames not just a beacon of light and warmth, but a weapon against the dangers hidden by the night.

Just before she reached the clearing, her eyes fixed on the back of the man, who continued to face off against something in the woods on the other side. He seemed exhausted, his shoulders slumped, his back exposed by torn furs and marked by bloody rakes from a previous fight. Grey streaked his dark hair, marking him as an older man, as weary as his fading, mournful cries that now only came as a whisper.

The treeline in front of him erupted; a fierce growl accompanying the flash of claws and teeth as a wolf launched itself at the man.

Seta hissed in anger as fate tried to steal him, and the answers he might have, away from her.

The wolf leapt for his throat, claws ready to tear him up at the same time it sought to knock him down. As the wolf reached him, his spear was knocked aside, but he managed to bring the burning brand up between the wolf's maw and his throat. It was not enough. He took the hit of the beast's weight and began to fall backwards.

As Seta charged into the clearing, she could see some of what had happened to throw the man into grief: Two bodies, one a young man, and the other a little girl, both with gruesome wounds, were scattered about the fire. The girl looked like she had been sleeping and still lay half wrapped in furs. A dead wolf lay near a corner of the slumping shelter made of skins and branches.

The man went down under the wolf's weight, but the old skraeling managed to keep the beast's teeth at bay with the length of the brand.

The wolf easily avoided the sputtering flames at one end of the brand. The hungry beast knew the man was drained of strength and was beaten, as it raked his chest with its claws and reached forward, trying to lock its jaws onto his throat.

Seta threw herself at man and wolf, casting the spear's length impulsively across the wolf's face. She hit it hard over the nose, distracting it, the beast ducking its head back.

The move spared the man another snarling attempt by the wolf to rip out his throat. But only briefly.

Seta tightened her grip on Torrador's blade and jumped straight over the man's head to get behind the stunned wolf. She spun about, grabbed a handful of the wild animal's hair and skin at the back of its neck and jerked it hard, while leaning in to use her weight to pin it down.

The wolf recovered from its surprise and tried to turn, snapping at her, with spittle flying, but she was already swinging in with the blade, stabbing at the wolf's own throat.

The man's eyes bulged in surprise at her unexpected arrival, encouraging him to redouble his efforts to keep the wood of the smouldering brand between him and the wolf. He pushed back hard, forcing the ferocious animal's head up and exposing only more of its throat.

Torrador's blade hit home.

She felt the knife sink deep into the beast's neck, sticky blood welling up over her fingers.

228

In one last burst of chaos, the beast struggled to get away.

She slashed hard and fast, dragging the blade through the meat of the wolf's throat. The beast's neck opened, the parted flesh releasing a flood of blood.

Elated, Seta let out a triumphant yell as the rich store pumped out over her fingers and washed across the old man on the ground.

She pushed herself off and away from the beast, the animal enraged and turning to focus on her. The monster let out a deep and gruesome rumble that gurgled while it bubbled through its own escaping lifeblood and ruined throat.

Seta kicked out to push herself further back, past the fire, until she sat near the other edge of the clearing.

***

Torrador could see the path begin turning with a bend in the valley ahead. Light shone, that of a blazing campfire, the flames themselves still hidden by the lay of the land, but the glow of it was apparent as it lit the surrounding trunks of the forest's trees.

Between him and the light, a good distance in front, a dark silhouette flashed across – a wolf. The beast was about sixty paces away and launching itself from the hillside, to strike at another silhouette that only became clear as it spun to meet the snarling threat. The figure stumbled, but recovered, and then lashed out with a stick or spear to knock the beast off balance, sending the wolf tumbling past and down the hillside. The animal tried to regain its balance, but failed, ending up in the waters of the stream.

Torrador looked back to the figure, a woman, now dimly lit as she recovered and ran for the campfire.

It was Seta!

Torrador sprang into action, launching himself into a sprint as he

229

chased after her, resisting the urge to call out lest he attract any other wolves lurking in the woods.

He whispered as he ran, "Aid me Allfather!"

The wind picked up to bluster in a sudden swirling gust.

He charged on, following the path as it wove between shrub, trunk and rock, running along and just upslope from the stream. He soon came to the spot where the wolf had dived at Seta, the beast now scrabbling unsteadily as it tried to get out of the water, still shaking its stunned and bloody head.

The animal heard him and looked up snarling.

Torrador stood ready, with his spear in hand.

Like Thor striking with a hammer, he rammed the sharp point into the ragged beast's maw, shoving it down the wolf's throat.

The animal gagged and whined, before finally thrashing about.

Torrador pushed forward, putting all his weight onto the grinding shaft, until he pinned the wolf down. The struggling monster let out a desperate yelp that tapered off, falling into a rattling sigh. A moment later, aside from one twitching foreleg, the beast lay still.

Torrador stepped on the wolf's head to hold it down as he pulled the spear free. The rough shaft did not come easily, but since it was the only weapon he had, aside from the stake, he persisted until he could drag it out.

He heard a rush of movement from far off in the depths of the woods, the pad of hurried paws and brush of bodies as they parted branches, leaves and shrubs. Torrador got moving again. He knew other members of the pack would be out there. Refocussing on what had brought him here, he set off at a run and renewed his charge for the campfire and Seta.

His boots pounded the trail as he tried to put on as much speed as he could. Ahead, the flaring yellow flames of the campfire were now visible, promising light, warmth and safety.

The sudden growl of a wolf cut through the night, coming from ahead, and jagging his attention.

Torrador watched as Seta ran into the clearing just as another figure, a skraeling man, went down under the weight of a wolf that launched itself from the far side of the clearing.

The Godslander redoubled his efforts, pumping his arms and tightening his grip on his spear.

As Torrador ran to help, he watched as Seta unbelievably tossed her makeshift spear at the beast's face and then jumped past it as the stripped sapling hit the creature's snout. The wolf already had the skraeling pinned, raking his chest, while trying to tear out his throat. Her actions distracted it, but did not dislodge the animal from what looked to be an easy kill.

Seta grabbed the beast by its coat, at the back of its neck, and jerked its head back as it tried to turn on her. But she was ready, and she lashed out with the blade.

Torrador kept running, closing on the clearing, but had a way to go yet. As he did, he heard the fast movement of parting bushes and stirring leaves as other hungry wolves rushed in behind him to end the hunt.

He was their prey, not Seta. The thought chilled him.

The rising beat of yet another wolf's chase also drummed on the earth along the trail further back.

With his own heart racing and Seta needing help just ahead, he threw everything into increasing his pace.

He had to get there!

If he did not, he knew he would never see her again.

Ahead of him, the wolf she confronted turned its neck, attempting to latch onto her. She restricted its increasingly frenzied movements by putting her weight on its back, while the old man pushed its chin up with the brand to expose the beast's own throat.

The knife struck home.

Running for his life, Torrador could not help but grin as he whispered, "I'm coming!"

***

Blood fountained and caught the firelight, spraying red and rich.

Seta sat near the other side of the clearing in exhausted elation, panting, one of her hands covered in blood as she clutched Torrador's blade.

Unsteady, the wolf started to get off the man.

The wound was good and deep, the beast doomed.

An instant later, the uneasy quiet broke as another wolf appeared in the trees, right behind Seta. The frustrated beast lunged forward with slavering jaws, trying to get the odds back to where the pack had worked them over the course of the evening.

With teeth flashing, it darted in and tried to latch onto the back of her neck. Seta reacted to the sound and ducked forward.

Seta felt the wolf's wet snout hit her nape, just as its rancid breath blew her hair. But the creature missed.

The beast may have missed her neck, but its sharp teeth did catch on the edge of her furs. With a hard jerk, the wolf worked to stop her escape.

Desperate, Seta turned around, slashing with the knife, while working to shrug off the fur.

She had to get away.

She *needed* her answers!

The blade found meat, but it was only a glancing blow.

The beast's teeth were still caught up in the fur that now slipped up and over the top of her head as Seta tried to pull back. With limited vision, she slashed out blindly again, trying to stab at the wolf's shoulder or face, trying anything that might make it release her.

She only had moments.

She needed to get lucky, or she would die.

Seta struggled, still slashing and stabbing, but to no avail. From the world outside, now smothered by her furs, from a place she could mutely hear and no longer see, she heard the approach of other wolves as they surged forward.

She cursed herself.

She should never have left Godsland!

What about her poor children?

What about Frae and Halla?

Or Torrador?

And it was then, when she knew she was out of time, the wolf beginning to shake her hard from side to side, rough and fast, that she heard his voice.

His tone was urgent and came to her, smothered by her furs, but the first words were clear, "Get down!"

She began to shed tears.

***

Torrador moved as fast as he could, but knew he was running out of time. He had watched Seta, with admiration, deliver a mortal wound to a wolf all by herself, and then he had seen her escape, throwing herself across the clearing to safety.

He prayed to Odin that he would get the chance to hold such an amazing woman again.

But, for now, he had more immediate concerns: The wolves were right on his heels. The closest of two was only moments away from trying to bring him down; he could hear its ragged breathing behind him.

Yet, he was only a few dozen paces from the edge of the clearing. He merely needed a dose of good luck.

The desperate Norseman watched for anything that might aid him, but in an unfamiliar nightscape, his vision increasingly blinded by the blazing fire ahead, nothing looked of use.

The closest wolf snapped at his heels.

Torrador somehow managed to shake it off and keep running, though the effort made him misstep and lose balance. He veered off the path, putting his arms out to steady himself, but he clipped the trunk of a big tree. He pushed himself away from it with his spare hand and kept going, charging through the undergrowth.

The wolves still followed, only encouraged by his troubles.

Ahead, he saw Seta facing him, with her back to the woods at the far edge of the clearing. She suddenly bent forward as a wolf took her from behind, the beast trying to lock its jaws around the back of her neck. The beast seemed to miss, but still managed to get a grip on her hair and furs.

The sight of it, after what she had just done, made Torrador's blood boil. He screamed out, "No!"

Recovering from his glancing collision with the tree, but still not back on the trail, he raced through the undergrowth, only to be confronted by a series of rocks that stepped up in height in front of him, rising from amongst the gloom.

With the wolves right behind him, he had no choice but to leap up the first one and keep going. Before he knew it, he had stepped up three of them and was flying through the air, crossing the last of the undergrowth and then passing into the clearing.

THE LANDING

In front of him, Seta had spun about to face the wolf and swung wildly with the knife, but her furs were being pulled up and over her face so that she could not see. She was fighting blind.

The wolf began to tug the fur side to side, roughly shaking Seta back and forth, with fast and frantic jerks. The beast was trying to knock her senseless or break her neck.

Behind the animal, two more wolves came into view. One was big, the other much younger. They darted in to join the attack.

Torrador, arms out and spear wide for balance, was going to pass right over the campfire and land on the wolf and Seta.

With grim determination, he brought his spear around and called out, "Get down, I am behind you!"

She heard him, and despite having so little control over her position, tried to lower her body.

***

A moment later, regardless of Seta's desperate efforts, the wolf brought her fur-wrapped head crashing down into the dirt. The sudden move stunned her, but at the same time, the thud and thump of something heavy landed right in front of her, backed by the crunch of bones.

It was Torrador; she knew it!

She could hear the other wolves whine and cry out in surprise as they pulled back, but the attacking wolf had not let go of the fur, even if it no longer moved.

Both hopeful and desperate, she quickly drew herself back and slipped out of her fur.

Torrador stood before her, his back to her, with one boot on the wolf's crushed neck.

The beast lay in front of her, prone, with blood running from its jaw. It was not moving.

Torrador's other leg was out to one side, steadying him, along with a makeshift spear, which he had pinned through the beast's ribs.

Unbalanced from his landing, he staggered back towards her.

She got up and put a hand to his shoulder, supporting him as she led him back towards the fire. "I have you."

The wolf was dead, the makeshift spear shattered and still sticking out of its carcass.

The other two animals, recovering from their shock at Torrador's sudden arrival, slowed their retreat and skulked at the clearing's edge.

The old man, now on his feet behind them, called out in the skraeling tongue, "More come!"

They turned to see the two wolves that had been chasing Torrador cautiously enter the other side of the clearing.

The animals took in the bloody scene; two of their pack-brothers were already dead, while in front of them staggered the beast with the opened throat. As all foes across the clearing sized up each other, that wretched animal finally collapsed into a pool of its own blood.

Seta stepped over and retrieved her spear from where it lay. With it again in hand, she passed the bloodied blade back to Torrador. Simply, she said, "It is good to see you."

He grinned as he took the blade from her, and then drew the stake he still had tucked into his belt, the rough piece of wood giving him a longer reach. "I came when you needed me, as I promised."

She smiled, licking her lips as she stared down the two wolves that had just arrived. "Yes, you did."

The wolves began to growl, one snarling and snapping, spittle flying from its slavering jaws.

Seta took a step forward, stabbing with her spear.

THE LANDING

The skraeling man, with the burning brand still in his hand, stared with wide eyes, his gaze switching between the wolves and Torrador. He spoke quickly in his own tongue, too fast for Torrador to hope to grasp, despite his lessons with Alfvin.

Seta grimaced as she glanced at him, and then shot a sharp answer back. She then took her anger out by stabbing her spear tip at a wolf and yelling at it.

The two wolves facing her fell back a step, one then turning and disappearing into the night. The other snapped at her again, but then turned and ran.

The old man cursed the animals, and then used the opportunity to drop to his knees and rummage in the nearest shelter.

Seta turned to the remaining wolves on the other side of the clearing, striding over to them, past Torrador, and again stabbing with her spear as she advanced. With an angry fire in her eyes she hissed, "They have already lost three of their number. They will go."

Torrador came up beside her with his own weapons. "I finished off the one you knocked into the stream. They are now a much smaller pack than what they were at sunset."

Another wolf turned and ran.

The last beast stood its ground for a moment, snarling, but then also backed away.

After a few moments, the night fell silent.

Seta looked around the clearing, checking it over, before throwing some more wood on the fire to build it up. "They are not usually in the valleys this deep. My people keep their numbers back." But as she said it, she realised that the only reason the wolves had come so far, even if it was only a small pack, was because her people were no longer about the vales to stop them.

Her gaze drifted across to the shelter where the old man dug through a pile of furs.

A figure moved within, lost in shadow.

237

She cursed. Children were in there!

Torrador looked over his shoulder and saw them also.

The old skraeling nodded to her, but threw a glance of concern Torrador's way. He turned back to Seta and hissed in their tongue.

Seta snapped back, "He is mine. We are together!"

Torrador tensed, understanding enough of what they discussed, even if he could not be clear on every word's meaning.

The skraeling grunted something verging on disapproval, but turned back to the children.

The little ones began to emerge from where they had been hiding amongst the furs. Their movements were hesitant at first, but the longer the silence reigned after the pack's departure, the more confident they became.

There was a girl and a boy, both only a few years old. They reached for the old man and threw their arms about him. Eventually, when their affections subsided, he looked up to Seta and asked, "Who are you?"

Torrador let Seta answer. He barely knew enough of their tongue to be able to follow the question and was certain any attempt he made at an answer would only sow confusion.

She wasted no time. "I am Seta and this is Torrador."

The old man frowned, while his eyes showed both confusion and discomfort. "He is of the Sea People." He indicated a direction with a dismissive wave of his hand.

Neither Torrador nor Seta had to guess at where he meant – Lakeland.

Seta explained that Torrador came from a different group, even if of similar kin.

The man looked unconvinced, but he acknowledged that Seta thought him worthy-and that Torrador had undisputedly saved him and his kin.

He and Seta spoke for a good part of the night, while Torrador helped them bury the bodies of the skraeling dead.

The old man, during that toil, spoke of the many deaths in the valleys caused by the Norse of Lakeland, some in misunderstandings or outright fights, but worse had followed those first incidents. He told of how some of their people were taken back to the hall, and made to work in thraldom, with the women taken as mates. That had been near the end of fall, not long after the first snows had come.

Seta and Torrador could both imagine the scene all too easily.

Later, some of them escaped, but one of them was sick. His fellow escapees helped him back into the vales, but his return seeded a terrible trail of pestilence, one that claimed several members of each camp and scarred many after they were racked by fevers.

The violence and sickness, the latter of which had spent the last of winter moving deeper into the vales, valley to valley, and camp to camp, caused Seta's people scatter. In the wake of it all, the way lay open for wolf packs and other predators to stalk the land.

Seta listened to the tale, of a bloody autumn, followed by a terrible winter, and of heartbroken survivors dealing with a spring where they were hunted and overrun.

The man, Doroba, looked exhausted, but he became re-fuelled by a smouldering bitterness. Tonight the wolves had taken his son, after mauling his sick granddaughter, the fever having already claimed his son's wife earlier in the evening. Her body still lay in one of the shelters.

With so much death, and no hope of help coming from a people scattered and weak, he had begun to mourn those lost, while he got the little ones to hide and he stood to keep the wolves at bay. He had not expected his mourning song to summon any aid; it was merely a means to farewell his family's spirits and set the scene for his own demise.

Seta listened to his story, offering her understanding as he went on.

Beside her, watching over the edge of the clearing, while working to skin the dead wolves, Torrador understood enough to feel the truth of what his people's arrival had meant for Seta's kin.

By the time Doroba finished his tale, his surviving grandchildren asleep at his feet, Seta knew there was nothing left for her here. Her people were now in thraldom, scattered or dead. The life she had known was no longer here, only in her memories.

Even if she could find a group to join with, things had changed and would never be the same again.

She found the truth of it hard to believe.

But it had been two years since she had been in the vales...

It was then she realised she had no better choice than to return to her children and Godsland.

She looked to Torrador beside her, to where he worked at skinning the wolves. He was a good man, and capable.

He had come back for her.

Tentatively, she reached out and patted his knee.

THE LANDING

COLIN TABER

Part V

The Golden Vale

COLIN TABER

COLIN TABER

Chapter 15

-

To Guldale

Eskil stood at the ship's bow, beside Faraldr, as they made their way up the waters of the fjord under the midafternoon sun. A steady breeze meant their progress came by sail. The ease of passage gave most on board, especially the new settlers, a chance to look upon the surrounding shoreline's climbing slopes, scattered woods and the distant, snow-dusted inland heights.

Despite the fine weather both Faraldr and Eskil were preoccupied by their thoughts, if not of what lay ahead at Guldale, then of what lay behind.

Lakeland.

The lakeside hall seemed stable, but troubled and tense, and built on a short and bloody history that could all too easily erupt like tinder touched by a spark. It was true to say Thoromr was calmer now and perhaps even more considerate, and that came courtesy of a newfound sense of caution that had settled in as if to replace his lost eye.

The brute knew he had been lucky to survive the injuries he had suffered following the murder of Ari. He also knew he had been even luckier to have Faraldr and his people in Lakeland to care for him. Yet those exposed to the hall over winter had also been touched by its corrupting blight.

Now, at the end of spring, with a full summer ahead, the new settlers presented a chance to change Lakeland. An opportunity to build a place that would last; a hall that might be the seed of a thriving new settlement instead of a sickly sprout doomed to being stamped into the dirt by its own, or those surrounding it.

The future held so many possibilities.

Faraldr spoke, breaking the contemplative silence, as the ship cut its way up the fjord's smooth waters. "Lakeland was a sorry place when we first arrived last year, and yesterday it seemed that it was becoming such again."

"The men of the hall are too quick to reach for their blades and axes. It is a land of brute strength, blood and fear."

"It was not as bad as last year."

"Perhaps, but not so different either."

"Things will change. Besides, of the ten men I left there, five now have their wives to help temper their actions. The other five have a promise that I shall bring them single women next year, if they are not returning to Greenland with me. "

Eskil nodded. "Your sister is your best chance of making Lakeland a more civil place, but you are a brave man to leave her with Thoromr."

"Not as brave as she is."

Eskil looked further down the channel, hoping their early arrival for Torrador's pickup would not see the lovelorn Norseman caught out. Faraldr's ship meant they could get around much quicker, so they would get to the shore where they had dropped off both Seta and Torrador much sooner than planned, and still get to Guldale before sunset.

His thoughts turned back to Lakeland, the topic at hand. "I do not see why you do not settle all your people with us, or in Guldale, and forget about Lakeland?"

Faraldr offered a nod. "I know what you mean. Lakeland will be an ongoing effort, as well as draining. Thoromr will never be someone I can trust, but working with him does two things; one being to keep alive my claim on the hall and vale; the other is to give our people, as a whole, more chances in this new land."

"But the men you left there last winter became almost as wild as Thoromr and Trion. How can you know that every person you put into that hall will not also become a murderous beast? What if your sister fails, overwhelmed by internal dissent, Thoromr's temper, a long winter or other trial?"

A grin cracked the Greenlander's face, one built of secrets. He lowered his voice and said, "Eskil, I am going to share a bit of information with you, news that will become common knowledge, soon enough."

"What is it?"

"Those I left behind last year were volunteers, many of them young and full of a hunger for adventure, fighting and lust."

Eskil snorted. "Like Thoromr?"

"Indeed, but nonetheless, they are from my own family's farms, and owe an allegiance to me that will be reinforced now that half of them have their wives and the other half have women promised to them, either here or in Greenland."

"Alright, but I guessed they had some kind of link to you. Is that your secret, because I fear it is not enough."

Faraldr's smile broadened. "The secret is not about those I left there last year, but those who have willingly come here this spring."

"What is it?"

"Aldis is my sister, but not my only relative in Lakeland. Those we left behind today are not only loyal to me because of bonds of service through my own hall, but because they are family. All of them. The men and women will work as a block, to do what I want and secure my claim on Lakeland, because the claim is also theirs, through blood."

Eskil's eyes went wide as he laughed. "How many of them, surely not all?"

"All of them. Each and every one of them is either a brother, sister, cousin, or niece or nephew, or married to one. Nothing will happen in Lakeland without me learning of it, and soon enough, nothing will happen that my family does not will."

Eskil pursed his lips. "And what of the settlers in Godsland? Are they all relatives, too?"

Faraldr laughed. "Eskil, how big a family do you think I have?"

The Godslander shrugged.

"No, I am sure you shall have some of my family arrive sooner or later, but not now. Godsland and you are not what worry me. You are a clever man, wise beyond your years, looking to both immediate needs and the future. Thoromr, on the other hand, if left alone to live with his anger, will either be murdered, or die in a fight. With him, Lakeland may also die, for he is likely to turn the local skraelings completely against our kind."

Eskil agreed.

"We are here, and this land will be ours, but that does not mean we need to wash it in blood."

Eskil listened and liked the sense he could hear in Faraldr's words. "There may yet be a time of blood before we can truly hold this place."

"Yes, there may be. If it comes to that, I will be at the front of the charge, doing what has to be done for our people. But if that has to happen, I would rather we chose the time-and that is not now. We need greater numbers. Right now our hold here is too fragile."

Eskil could only agree.

***

The shoreline where Torrador was to wait came into view up ahead, although the original arrangement was for Eskil and Ballr to return closer to sunset. Looking ahead, Eskil could not see the Norseman or Seta. He frowned. He did not really expect to see Seta, but hoped Torrador would have at least had a chance to look for her, perhaps found and talked to her, and then returned to wait in safety. He wondered, not for the first time, if he should have tried harder to convince Torrador to return to Godsland and let Seta find her answers alone.

Ballr arrived beside him, as did Alfvin and Frae. The Icelander asked, "This is it, is it not?"

Eskil nodded. "They are not there, not yet."

Frae looked up and down the shore, peering where the trees thickened. They were still a fair distance out from the gravel beach. "I do not see anyone."

Alfvin frowned, knowing his wife constantly worried about Seta's insistence she return, by herself, to the vales. "We did say to meet us by sunset. We are early."

Faraldr shrugged and turned to Eskil. "You said that Guldale is close?"

Eskil gave a nod and, with a tilt of his head, indicated the distant shoreline on the other side of the channel. "It is over there, just back around that last point. You merely follow the other waterway to the north."

Ballr asked, "Can we wait?"

A good part of the afternoon remained.

Eskil shook his head. "No, we should take advantage of the daylight and land in Guldale now. But we can send one of the small boats ashore here, as we have brought two. The boat can wait until sunset and then meet us in Guldale."

Ballr volunteered to take a boat and wait, for he was close to both

Torrador and Seta–and Halla would never forgive him if he did not try to help her dear friend. Steinarr offered to row ashore with him, as Alfvin, Frae and Eskil needed to continue to Guldale.

They parted, the ship waiting until Ballr and Steinarr reached the woods. After they checked the area for safety and saw that Torrador and Seta were not there, they waved and called out, bidding the ship get on its way.

***

Torrador set as fast a pace as he could, Seta following hard, with both of them weighed down by wolf pelts, gear and carrying one of the children each. They managed, but were tiring, as they climbed up the slope and out of the vale. Behind them, burdened by his wounds, Doroba struggled along.

The old skraeling was doing well to keep up; he was exhausted, bruised, and had lost some blood from his various bites, scratches and gashes, but he did not complain. He knew he could not last by himself in the valley and therefore could not protect the two little ones. The realisation had been a hard one for him to accept.

Last night he fought Seta's suggestion to go with them, but she told him the truth of his fate if he stayed.

Death.

The end would come for him because either he would not recover from his wounds, the pack would return or he would face some other calamity. At best, he might last until the next snows, but at some point, the winter would bury him.

Once Seta got him to accept that, she only had to ask what would happen to the children.

Finally, at dawn, he agreed to go with them, also reluctantly letting them carry the little ones. From then on, he simply locked eyes on the carried children and followed, regardless of how tired and sickly he felt, or how often he tripped or stumbled.

Above, the sun began to sink, heading for the horizon at their backs. The crest of the hill rose ahead, and then it would be downhill all the way, on a gentler path. That trail ended at their destination by the water.

Slick with sweat from their efforts, their muscles burning, they continued their journey. All three knew they had to leave the vale, if not by boat this sunset, then some other way. The wolf pack they had confronted might not return for them, but eventually another would, or perhaps a bear, or some other threat.

***

Ballr and Steinarr watched the ship leave, their boat pulled up beside them on the gravel beach. The ship was a beautiful sight, turning on the wide and calm waters of the channel. It headed to round the point that would take it into the waters of the Guldale shoreline. Such a ship would not take long to cross the distance.

The two of them surveyed the area again, looking for any recent signs of passage or any hint that Torrador had returned. They found nothing aside from the traces Ballr, Eskil, Torrador and Seta left in the days previous. Even the nearby and sheltered campsite held no sign of recent use.

With an eye to the waning afternoon, Ballr and Steinarr sat and waited, watching the approaches to the shoreline.

***

The ship came into the gentle waters off Guldale, after rounding a small promontory and making its way along the shore. The breeze slowed and the sun seemed, if possible, to brighten, despite the growing cloud cover.

To the ship's left spread the shore of Guldale, with the low hills behind. On the other side of the ship, small waves lapped against the island that had been Alfvin and Erik's refuge. Ahead, the waters continued, the widening channel eventually turning back towards the sea and passing by Godsland's distant, far-northwestern coast.

The hills behind the shore, green and covered in shrubs, hid much of what lay beyond, yet the wide spread of the vale and the two much higher ranges of hills, one studded with rocky bluffs, were visible. For now, the bottom of the valley lay hidden by the low hills backing onto the beach. But those on the ship could see parts of what lay beyond as the land rose to climb, with wooded slopes, towards those siding bluffs and heights.

Proudly, Eskil announced, "Welcome to the Golden Vale, or Guldale, as we know it!"

Faraldr smiled and was not the only one to do so. He clapped Eskil on the back as others about him began to nod and voice their agreement that the vale was indeed worthy of such a grand name.

Faraldr said, "It looks better than the valleys of Greenland, though I am certain the winters will still be white, long and hard."

Eskil said, "The valley floor is wide, and the land around the lakeshore and along the river shows promise."

Alfvin grinned. "Good land with iron and plenty of timber. This is where we need to settle!" He stopped and cast a sheepish look at Eskil, before whispering, "Only do not tell Gudrid!"

Eskil laughed to hear such a thing. "Do not worry. Godsland is serving our purpose for now, as the gods wanted, but I think it is clear, even to my Gudda, that we will outgrow the island."

Behind them, the excited conversations of the new settlers came punctuated by the bleat, oink and call of their livestock, as they joined in agreement.

Faraldr asked Alfvin, "Well, let us not waste any time. Where do you want us to land?"

He pointed. "Make for the beach up ahead, by the river."

***

They came ashore quickly, but left most of their belongings and livestock on the ship. For now, most of the Norse carried nothing but their weapons, while a small group stayed aboard, ready to set sail if need be.

Eskil and Alfvin led Faraldr into the low hills, towards where they had been working the bogs for iron. The path appeared recently trod, tracks and trails marking its length, but as they moved along, they set great clouds of insects to rise, making Alfvin feel that no one had been through the camp, at least recently.

Faraldr, and those with him, spoke about all they saw; the variety of plants and small animal tracks, so many new to them, and a few familiar in one way or another.

When they reached the bog workings, Eskil could see things looked much the same as when Alfvin and Erik had left them a few days before.

Alfvin searched for Erik, waving for him to move to the head of the line. "Take a look from the hilltop. We will work to keep everyone quiet, until we know if they are still camped in the valley."

Erik nodded and began to climb the hill opposite, crouching as he got near the top, until he finally slid amongst the shrubs at the very crest.

Aided by Faraldr, Alfvin and Eskil, those waiting below grew quiet, despite more than a few looking as though they wanted to follow.

The question was on countless lips, "Were the skraelings there?"

No answer came from Erik, not at first.

Frae moved down the line and joined Alfvin.

He shook his head and frowned, whispering, "I told you to stay on the beach, near the ship!"

She simply smiled at him and shrugged, the gesture melting his anger. He knew her well enough to know she would do whatever she wanted if she deemed it wise. "You will need me here if they are near."

She made a good point.

Erik cursed, drawing the attention of everyone.

Back on the hilltop, he began to wriggle backwards so as not to be seen. That alone said the skraelings were there, but the curse added an ominous weight to the moment.

Eskil noted the sun was already sinking towards the distant hills. Soon enough they would be out of light, so they needed to make a decision on where to spend the night: here, the beach, the ship or on the island.

Erik extracted himself from the shrubs and crawled down the hill enough so he could stand.

Alfvin was already stepping forward to meet him. "Well?"

"I saw a skraeling running, crossing the vale, heading from our hills here to the woods, where camps are beyond the trees."

Alfvin asked, "Camps? How do you know, what did you see?"

"Smoke rising from fires."

"How many?"

"Perhaps as many as a dozen."

Eskil shook his head. "That skraeling was watching for us, and now hurries to report our landing."

***

254

Faraldr and Eskil sent groups to comb the low hills and make sure that they were alone. Meanwhile, Erik took a different path, heading for a spot that would give him a view down the river and across the valley to survey the extent of any skraeling camp.

Through all this activity, the day began to wane. From the beach, where many of the Norse gathered, they watched and waited as the sun sank towards the horizon at the far end of the vale. With each passing moment, they knew they were losing the time they needed to properly prepare their own camp.

Concerns and worries grew as the shadows lengthened and the land about them began to look wilder and more alien.

**

When the sun began to set, some of the scouts returned. They announced that the low hills were clear of skraelings and that they had checked over some of the taller rises about the bogs. The hills were so good that they had left some of their numbers behind to continue watching the beach, vale and approaches.

Faraldr, Eskil and Alfvin spoke to Erik when he also returned, jogging from down the riverbank, where it cut through the hills.

The Norseman looked anxious, glancing to the nearby hilltops and down to the river as he spoke. "I cannot give a good count, but if there was fifteen or twenty a few days ago, that number now must be closer to a hundred. My tally includes all of them; men, women and children."

Erik worried about the skraelings, ever since they had first confronted Alfvin and him in Guldale. The Norseman seemed quite disheartened now that they had returned, only to find more.

Frae listened and offered, "They have gathered for spring."

Alfvin gave her a nod, understanding some of what she meant through their discussions of her people and their traditions. "You may

255

be right, but what does that mean for us?"

Frae gave a weak smile. "It would normally mean they might be open to strangers, even those who come in numbers like ours."

Eskil could see she was troubled. "But there is something else?"

She nodded. "They think we have brought a sickness to the land, an illness that is working its way through their camps. If they truly believe this, they will not welcome any of us."

Eskil asked, "Frae, even if they are not your people, Alfvin says they spoke a similar tongue, and looked much the same."

She nodded. "There are many groups, not all of them the same or related, with some welcoming and others happy to kill. There are also different people up and down the coast. Some work the sea, with boats and spears, where they fish and seal, using the ice and living in the snows. If these people are camped in the forest, near a lakeshore, then they are more likely to be of my own kind. Our people are few now, with our neighbours forcing us away as they take the best fishing grounds. They have made us a people of wood and vale."

"What would you suggest we do?"

Frae looked to Alfvin and the others. She knew they needed the land. "We should set up our camp, but watch them. They shall come soon enough, perhaps tonight. We can talk to them then."

"Will they attack us or just come to talk?"

"With the bloom of spring, they may be emboldened, helped by their greater numbers."

"So we should plan for an attack? Is it that simple?"

"If they attack, we know our iron will weigh heavily, cut hard and quick and perhaps let us win, despite their advantage in numbers. They will not expect it or know the danger they are in until they face it."

Alfvin looked to her with a stern face. "We have nothing to fear, but you worry that we will slaughter them, if it comes to fighting?"

She nodded, her eyes reflecting her worries. "They will come, perhaps to talk, but also perhaps to fight. Such a meeting need not end in the slaughter of anyone."

***

Ballr and Steinarr paced the beach and again walked the nearest trails. The light was fading.

Where was Torrador?

The sun had dipped below the heights of the fjordside, and they waited in shadows that grew only deeper.

Where was Seta?

Steinarr had always been close to Torrador and was reluctant to be the first to say it was time to leave. However, as the light faded, the woods along the shoreline became not just mysterious, but ominous. And none of that accounted for the channel's dark water, the unknown depth that showed off swirls and bubbles, where unseen animals hunted beneath the surface.

Such stirring movements only reminded the men of Manni, long since dead, his leg taken by a monster at sea.

Were they safe to try crossing the water under the stars?

Ballr spoke after they had walked the shores and looked up the paths for the umpteenth time, "I suppose we should go?"

Steinarr frowned, the expression weighed down by sadness. "If we leave, we are saying he is as good as dead."

Ballr sighed, looking around and up the empty paths again. "No, we are saying he missed our meeting." The Icelander pointed to where the sky showed over the fjord, the scattered clouds aglow in amber. "It is sunset; we need to get to Guldale, while we still have light."

The noise of a passing flock of birds came from above, calling out as they beat their wings. Many of them seemed to slow and circle, as others settled in the branches above, rather than moving on.

Something must have been good for feeding.

Steinarr turned from the sky and looked back to the trail they both felt Torrador had taken. The path meandered, but widely climbed the gentlest part of the slope.

"Steinarr, as much as I would like to, we simply cannot stay."

The big man bunched his fists and began to grumble as he stepped down from the start of the path and made strides back towards their beached boat.

Ballr sighed, looking up the path again himself. He whispered, "Torrador, come friend, come back to us now-or is this the end?" With a shake of his head, he turned and followed Steinarr, who was already throwing his gear into the boat.

***

Torrador stumbled, his legs heavy as though made of rock. Seta struggled along behind him, not in any better shape. Neither of them felt the burdens of their gear, the wolfskins or the children they carried. They were merely numb, and almost senseless, as they pushed themselves on.

Unbelievably, Doroba still followed, although he regularly fell.

The sun was setting in the vale behind them, the sky lit in amber and shades of pink. Thankfully, they had crested the ridge and left it behind, now well on their way down the slope towards the water. Yet, on their descent, they unmistakeably walked a path of deepening shadows.

Torrador did not say anything, but he thought they were too late. For the fjord in front of them, the sunset had already occurred.

Regardless, they continued the trek.

***

The din of the birds in the trees above filled the fjord.

Ballr cursed them.

Steinarr growled, angry at the world, "We would not be able to hear, even if Torrador and Seta were near!"

Ballr picked up a rock off the beach and threw it into the branches. The attack elicited a flurry of movement, but did not make any real difference as the birds continued to call to each other.

Ballr cursed again and shook his fist.

Steinarr sighed. "Come, let us get going. Otherwise we will be crossing the fjord in the dark."

The Icelander went to the end of the boat, waited for Steinarr to get in, and then began to push the last of it off the beach. With a final shove, he stepped in, grabbed an oar and sat down.

He turned around and stared back into the darkening woods, any sign of trails or camps erased by the deepening gloom. He called out, "Torrador!"

Steinarr added his own voice, "Seta! Torrador! We must go!"

The boat drifted out, both of the Norseman quiet as they listened for a reply. Above them, the chorus of the birds continued on, in a mix of chirps, screeches and screams.

Nothing else sounded.

Resigned, Ballr said, "Let us go."

***

The sunset began to wane, the lurid colours above glimpsed through the canopy, bleeding away into dusk. Torrador and Seta continued on, both focussed on staying up and moving, their legs following the downhill trail as they carried their burdens. Fatigue numbed their bodies, their limbs heavy and sore, but they dared not stop. If they did, they knew neither of them would be able to start again.

Behind them, stumbling on, Doroba followed.

They both knew they were not far from the gravel beach at the end of the path. About them birds raised a racket in the shadowed canopy.

Torrador gasped, "We are nearly there."

"Will they wait?" Seta asked.

"Perhaps, if they have brought supplies to set up camp."

Doroba stumbled behind them, tripping over a rock or root, or perhaps his own sluggish feet. He fell forward with a crash, but did not get up.

They both went to him, putting down their wolfskins and children.

Seta bent over him, putting a hand to his cheek. "Doroba, are you alright?"

Torrador added, "We are nearly there."

The two young children squatted down beside their grandfather.

Doroba moaned. "Leave me, I cannot go on."

Seta met Torrador's gaze. "There is nothing else to do but for you to run on and see if they are there. I will stay. If you find them, you can tell them to wait and come back for us."

Torrador glanced at the shadowed woods about them, remembering the previous night's fangs and claws. "I do not want to leave you; that is not why I came back."

She smiled, the gesture mostly lost in the gloom. "Torrador, go and find them. I will be here. You only need be gone a short while."

"I will not leave you."

"We need to catch the boat."

Faint, yet managing to be heard over the birds' chorus, Ballr's voice sounded out in the distance, "Torrador!"

"Go!" she hissed.

He nodded. "I shall be quick; call if you need me."

Another distant voice called out, also faint, "Seta! Torrador! We must go!"

Torrador dropped his gear, handing her the blade, and then sprang off down the trail.

He went as fast as he dared in the dying light, trying to keep his footing as he flew over tree roots, gravel, rocks, and dealt with the bends in the path. Once he was on his way, he took in a deep breath and called out, "Ballr!"

The birds' din continued, growing louder as he neared the shore. He hoped that if he could hear them, they could hear him.

By Odin, how he hoped they could hear him!

He called out again.

***

Ballr and Steinarr listened for long moments, both reluctantly beginning to pull on their oars. The noise of the birds dominated the sky but were joined by a rising breeze.

One slow stroke through the dark water became two, then three and then four. Ballr looked back to the shadowed shore, but saw nothing. Quietly, he asked Steinarr, "Do you think he is alright?"

Steinarr grunted before clearing his throat. "Who can know?"

The wind gusted briefly, the noise of the shore's rustling trees drowning out even the birds.

***

Torrador hurried on, hoping that finding his way back in the dim tunnel he passed through would not be too hard. He occasionally yelled out Ballr's name, but he was so exhausted and out of breath that he doubted he was above the birds and wind.

Behind him Seta also called out, her voice loud and commanding, "Ballr!"

And the path then came to an end.

Torrador was on the beach, but it was empty.

He fell to his knees in the gravel and took in a few deep breaths, looking about as he did so. The boat was gone, that was certain, so his eyes searched the channel's waters ahead.

He could see something – a silhouette!

Torrador got back to his feet, whispering, "Please Allfather, we need to get home!"

The birds above had begun to grow quiet now, with the dying of the light, joined by a stilling of the blustering wind. As Torrador bent down and picked up a rock, he heard Seta cry, "Ballr, we are here!"

Torrador drew back his arm and let the stone fly, trying to get Ballr's attention. Once it was off and on its way through the night, he took a deep breath and bellowed:

"Ballr, come back!"

A new quiet settled, one even the birds and wind were not prepared to disturb.

Torrador held his breath.

THE LANDING

The rock splashed as it broke the water's surface.

Desperate, he yelled out one last time, "Ballr, come back to us!"

The sound of hurried oar strokes came to him, splashing and slapping the water as the blades were enthusiastically redirected and pulled.

Ballr's voice came loud and clear a heartbeat later, "Torrador, Seta, we are coming!"

"Thank Odin!" he whispered, faliing back to his knees.

He could hear Seta's exhausted laughter in the distance. Never had he heard anything so sweet.

Chapter 16

-

The Beach

Eskil watched over the beach camp as the colours of sunset faded above.

A few tents rose from the rough pasture growing between the gravel of the beach and the first of the low hills, not far to the side of the reed-edged river. Yet the protective ring created by the small driftwood fires, not the pitched tents, better defined the camp. Tonight, most would sleep in the open, ready to react to any sign of a skraeling approach. Likewise, to avoid any risk, any heavy or unnecessary belongings and livestock remained on the ship.

Amidst these defensive arrangements, the only things threatening to dampen the Norse's tense spirits were the rising buzz of insects and the heavy clouds.

Regardless, they would manage.

The number of Norse in Guldale was not as large as Eskil or Alfvin had wished – around thirty in total. Both of the men would have preferred to handle the skraelings here, before Faraldr had dropped off his settlers in Lakeland, when they would have tallied closer to fifty, but it was not to be.

Faraldr's settlers were his to do with as he wished.

With that in mind, as the last of sunset's hues drained from the sky, both Eskil and Alfvin were eager to see the return of Ballr and Steinarr, hopefully with Torrador.

They needed the extra numbers; even three more could make a difference.

Eskil worried as he looked over the camp, a position holding only half of the people they had brought to Guldale. One third of the remainder were on the ship, just off shore, the other two thirds on the separate hilltop, watching for any skraeling attempt to approach their camp.

Standing there, lost in thought, he did not notice Faraldr approach, until the Greenlander asked, "Ballr should be heading back by now?"

"Yes. They will not delay."

Faraldr nodded, but movement amidst the low hills grabbed his attention.

Eskil turned to see.

One of their watches rushed from the hills, the whole group on the move. The lead man pointed to the river and called out as the gloom of dusk deepened.

Alfvin scanned the hills and reported, "The other watch is also coming in."

They turned to see the men from that hill, the watch closest to the river and the camp, also racing back.

Faraldr called out, "Get your arms!"

The camp burst into activity.

Alfvin growled out, "Feed the fire closest to the water! Let them see our great ship!"

Eskil yelled out to the closest of the watches as it neared camp, "How many?"

The lead man kept running, stumbling on unfamiliar ground, but his answer came clear, "Two score at least. They are coming along the riverbank, straight for us!"

Faraldr cursed.

Alfvin shook his head. "Frae, where are you?"

The two groups of watches were nearly back with their fellows, but as of yet, there was no sign of the skraelings' approach.

Eskil said, "We need to be smart about this, to not simply get in a fight. We need to use all our advantages."

Faraldr nodded. "The fires will blind our vision–and theirs."

"We can still use it."

The Greenlander nodded. "We should send a small group to hide out in the dark as night falls."

"Do it...get some of your most trusted. Instruct them to wait until they hear your command. If it comes to fighting, they can take them from the rear."

He grinned. "Hear my command? I shall be with them!"

Eskil patted him on the shoulder. "Go along the beach and into the river's reeds. There you can shield your vision from our fire's glare and hide in the shallows, at the skraelings backs."

He nodded. "Yes, the reeds."

Frae arrived.

Alfvin said to her, "My wife, we do not desire any blood, but if we must fight, it will be theirs that flows. You can help us try and avoid that by translating."

Her face was grave, but she agreed. "Yes, Alfvin."

Faraldr grabbed four of his men and sped off into the gloom.

Alfvin reached out and gave Frae's shoulder an affectionate squeeze. "You will do well; I shall guide you."

She smiled at him. "I shall try."

Eskil said, "You can only try, but you will need to speak up, loudly and clearly, so the others can understand what is being said."

She nodded.

"This is important. You will not only be translating for Alfvin and me, but for Faraldr and those on our ship."

***

It was some time before the skraelings finally came into view. Dusk was long gone, and nightfall had settled in the sky.

The strangers came along the riverbank, at a steady pace, massed together, many of them carrying axes and spears. They easily doubled the numbers of the Norse.

Eskil took in the scene with concern. Although he knew the skraeling axes and spearheads would most likely be of stone, flint or bone, used against Norse iron, he could not ignore the fact of the size of their force. The Norse on the beach stood armed with their knives, axes and spears. They also had half a dozen bows aimed at the new arrivals from the deck of the ship.

The skraelings continued their advance, nearing the edge of the firelight cast by the smouldering campfires. The Norse gathered to meet their visitors inside that ring, but with their backs to the water and the biggest and brightest of their fires.

The skraelings came to a stop, leaving a space between the groups.

Eskil stood next to Alfvin and Frae. "You have spoken to at least one of them before; see if he is among them. If so, have Frae ask him what they want; try and keep things open and peaceful."

Alfvin nodded.

"If we have to fight, too many are going to die on both sides. I do not want to win a battle here, only to lose the increase in strength that Faraldr's settlers gives us."

Alfvin said, "I understand."

Frae began to tremble beside him.

Her husband did not ignore it or utter reassuring words, but instead, put a firm hand around her wrist and said, "We shall never see our son again if this does not go well. We need to be brave."

She nodded, licked her lips and stilled her trembling.

**

Ballr's boat headed towards Guldale unnoticed, lost in the gloom, and over a hundred paces from shore. The cramped boat held Ballr, Steinarr, Torrador and Seta, and was crowded because of the two children and Doroba.

As they approached, they realised something was happening on the beach. The Norse, lined up, had put their backs to a blazing fire while facing another group at the edge of the light. The dark silhouettes they faced were clearly skraelings, evidenced by their bulky furs. Many of them also carried arms, and their numbers more than doubled that of the Norse.

Using a voice strong and firm, Seta told the children to be quiet and asked the Norse to do the same. She then told Ballr to continue rowing on, behind the longship, and head around it towards where the river's flow met the fjord's waters.

While the Icelander did not argue, Steinarr whispered, "Why?"

She hissed at him, "I did not survive the wolf pack to watch my people, old and new, slaughter each other!"

He was taken aback by her intensity.

With a flick of her head, indicating where they were headed, she said, "We will land where there is cover amidst the reeds."

Torrador asked, "What will we do?"

The boat coasted now, lost in shadow, heading for the nearest stand of greenery.

She put a hand to his. "Whatever we must."

***

From the throng at the edge of the glow, a lone skraeling stepped forward into the firelight. Behind him stood a solid mass of silhouettes, spiked with spears, and standing with menace. That lone figure, an older man, levelled his spear and swung its tip to pass over the gathered Norse standing fifteen paces away. In his own tongue, he growled, "You should not be here!"

Frae whispered the words so Eskil and the others beside him could understand.

Eskil said, "Louder, so all can hear."

Frae repeated the skraeling leader's line.

As she did, Alfvin whispered, "It is the same man as before."

Eskil nodded and with a loud voice told Frae, "Tell him we come to live in peace, to settle and fish."

She did.

His answer came in a harsh tone, loud and rough-edged.

Frae translated, repeating his message clearly, "He says we cannot stay, that this is their land."

The skraeling barked something, showing his anger at her.

"He says we are bad, that we kill, and that our presence is sickly." Her voice broke with the last words, her nerves shaken by the man's growing animosity.

Eskil looked at the skraelings arrayed in a line several deep. They numbered at least forty, perhaps as many as fifty.

Eskil said, "Tell him they have met and heard of a different people, that we live in health and in peace."

She called the words out, but her shadowed audience tensed, as if only needing some kind of spark to launch an attack.

The man growled back, something Frae barely needed to translate. "You lie!"

Eskil felt the anger building. He spoke loudly, wanting Faraldr, positioned in the reeds, as well as the people on the ship behind them, to hear every word. They hopefully had their bows at the ready. "We did not make them sick. Frae, tell them you live well with us, that you have a son, and that your sister was well enough to have twins."

She did.

The skraeling did not answer immediately.

The Norse heard hissed exchanges, but they were soft and unclear.

Eskil grabbed the chance and said, "Frae, tell them the truth; you choose to live with us."

She nodded and did.

The old man listened, as did those behind him, some of them pestering with advice. He hushed them, frustrated. Finally, after a long moment of consideration, he barked, "You are nothing but their pet. We have heard how they take women and use them. We have heard that not all sicken!"

Frae's translation was wrecked by her breaking voice as she relayed the accusation.

She was giving into her fear.

Alfvin put a hand to her shoulder, trying to reassure her.

The old man saw it and accused, "You are his, you are beaten! Your body may be well, but your spirit is defeated!"

Alfvin understood enough to withdraw his hand in shock, as if burnt, but only for a moment. His anger stirred a heartbeat later.

Frae kept translating even though she was now succumbing to tears.

Eskil shook his head, a hand sliding to his knife.

The atmosphere moved beyond tense, ready to spark and snap with fury.

The old man dared her, "Show me a sign that you or your sister have any worth and that you are not just their slaves!"

Frae did not know how to answer the man, who fed by his anger, then encouraged by those who stood behind him, did not want to listen. How could she say or offer anything that would be acceptable or get through to him?

She knew the truth of it; she could not.

A silence fell across the beach as everyone waited for her to answer his charge, but she had nothing to offer, nothing he would understand. Even if he could comprehend her answer, she knew he did not want to hear of her love for Alfvin, or his kindness, or the beautiful son they had made together.

Or of how he had sheltered her from the worst of the violence in Lakeland.

No, he did not want to hear it.

She stood there, with everyone watching, and then opened her mouth to speak.

But no sound came.

She had no answer.

Nothing he would believe.

Not now, while he was so worked up and angry.

***

The man lifted his spear and yelled a fresh threat.

The skraelings behind him also raised their spears and added their voices to back him with a roar.

Shaking his spear, he again called out, challenging the Norse.

Those behind him echoed him and took a step forward.

***

Seta stood in the shallows, amongst the reeds, with Torrador at her side. Doroba, Ballr and Steinarr remained in the boat with the children. Beside them were Faraldr and his men, who intercepted them as they drifted into the reed-cloaked shoreline.

Faraldr had been surprised to see skraelings on a Norse boat but, in the gloom, was quick enough to discover Ballr and Steinarr, and ordered his men to stay their blades.

Seta listened to the failing negotiation on the beach, the skraeling side poisoned by anger and grief. She felt for her sister, a gentle spirit, as Frae struggled to dispute the skraeling leader and then failed to answer and defend herself, opening the way for a challenge.

The challenge came and thundered through the night.

But Seta would not have it.

She hissed to Steinarr and Ballr, "Quick, give me the pelts...all of them." With a look to Torrador, she then put her arm about him and drew him close. "Give me your blade."

He handed it to her without hesitation, ignoring the startled looks from the Norse about him.

She tucked it into her belt.

A moment later, the bloody wolfskins were handed across.

Torrador took them and passed them on to her.

She grabbed them under one arm and hefted the weighty things up on her shoulder, holding them there. With a last look, she turned and faced Torrador, a smile on her lips. "You will be my husband for this." And then she turned and strode off, trying to maintain both her quiet and her balance as she climbed up the beach.

***

Frae was terrified.

Blood and slaughter seemed only a heartbeat away. The thought pushed her rudely into the realisation she would never see her son again, and that heartbreaking moment melted her paralysis.

She took a step forward and opened her mouth to speak.

At the same moment, the beach flared white, illuminated by a bolt of lightning overhead. The unexpected light gave pause to the skraelings, while stirring the Norse.

Alfvin hissed, "The gods are with us!"

And then thunder cracked to roll over the standoff.

Frae raised her voice and said, "I am a woman, a mother, and have fought my own battles against what the world has thrown against me. If you dismiss my survival of those trials, then you are no better than the men you claim to hate!"

The head skraeling lowered his spear, caught off guard, first by the lightning and now, by her speech. After a moment he called out, "What battles have you survived, what trials have you lived through?" his tone was dismissive.

Frae licked her lips and answered, "I was once a prisoner in Lakeland, where the one your anger is against lives. He beat me and threatened my life. I escaped to Godsland where I have found only kindness and peace."

He frowned. "It is not enough. Show me some daring, some bravery! Why should I believe any of this?"

Lightning flared again, starkly bathing the landscape in its glow, and thunder rolled over the land, buzzing the air with power.

Some of the skraelings called out in surprise.

The Norse hoped it was a sign that the gods were with them.

All of them, as the blazing light faded, were lost to darkness, their vision overwhelmed by the blinding display.

Until a heartbeat later.

A softer flash of lightning lit up the sky above and the beach below. As it did, coming backed by a low and rumbling roll of thunder, both parties found that the space between the two groups was no longer empty.

Seta stood there.

In a voice loud and laced with contempt, she said, "If you think my sister has not been through enough in the way of daring, I offer up my own from just one night."

She cast down the pelts at his feet.

The lead skraeling jumped back, startled enough by her appearance, even before he took in the sight of four bloodstained wolfskins.

She went on. "Last night, while you were sitting around a campfire, I was killing wolves. I was doing it to save a stranger and his grandchildren!" She drew Torrador's knife, pointing its glinting blade at the leader's belly. "Now, I dare you to say I have no will or courage!"

Silence took the beach.

Doroba hurried up beside her, urging Torrador before him, the Norseman carrying the children, one in each arm.

Some of the skraelings called out in alarm at how close the

Norseman was to them, but Torrador followed Doroba's guidance. He dropped to his knee beside Seta and put the children down so they could stand.

Doroba called out so all could hear, "They came to me last night, my family dead from a season of ill-fortune, sickness and, lastly, under attack from a pack of hungry wolves. Seta charged in first and slew one with that blade, not long after her man, Torrador, flew in like a hunting bird to join the killing. They beat back the pack, slaughtering countless beasts and saving my grandchildren. Seta is a warrior!" His words came in a gentler way than Seta's, but also flowed with passion.

The lead skraeling remained speechless.

Frae translated what he said for the Norseman.

A fresh silence settled, also held by the sky.

Slowly, a whispering of murmurs and queries sounded through the skraeling ranks.

Their doubts were clear.

Finally, the lead skraeling said, "You have shown great courage, that is true. But some of our people do not want to lose this land."

Seta, despite her bravado, was exhausted, and the emotions that had driven her a moment ago were now fading. All she wanted to do was get some sleep, ideally with Torrador beside her.

She knew what Alfvin wanted; the low hills and the beach, and some land to farm. She had heard him talk all winter long in Godsland hall about Guldale. She said, "Have you or any of the warriors behind you killed four wolves?"

The leader looked to those behind him, but already knew the answer verified by shaking heads. "No, it is a great feat."

"What of three?"

Again, the answer was no.

"Two?"

One skraeling had, and more offered that they had killed a wolf or injured one.

Seta, emboldened by the stature the wolfskins gave her, even if in truth she had not killed all of them on her own, offered, "I will give you the skins if you give me and my sister the land of the beach and these low hills, to share with our husbands."

Torrador whispered, "And the land along the river, back up to the lake."

She went on, "And the land along the river, up to the lake. You can keep your right to come and go, as long as you come in peace."

"You ask for much."

Lightning flashed again, followed by a crack of thunder.

With no need to lace her words with bravado, she said, "My husband and children need land for our own hall and space to hang more pelts, as does my sister and her family. If any would deny me my place, I will skin them like these wolves."

His eyes widened at the threat, but he gave a nod and stepped back amongst his people. His kinsmen immediately swamped him with counsel.

Seta waited, putting a hand out to Torrador's shoulder, as he was still on his knees beside her. She whispered, "Did I forget anything, my husband?"

She could see his cheeks move as he smiled. Quietly, he whispered, "No, my wife."

"Good."

The skraeling man stepped forward again and raised his voice. "We will take the skins and you can have your land, as long as our people can still cross it safely and, in peace."

Relief overcame Seta.

Frae, behind her, translated his words, and drew a cheer from the Norse.

Once the noise died down, the skraeling stepped forward and added, "But we will take it all back if the halls you raise bring sickness."

***

That summer, the settlement of Guldale was founded, with Alfvin and Frae the first to raise a hall, although Faraldr's people were also quick to build. By the time the snows returned, three halls sat clustered across two low hills near the river's mouth. Around these spread the first farmyards, fields and Alfvin's iron grounds and workings, along with a jetty running off the beach.

Seta and Torrador were married in Godsland, their family consisting of the orphaned grandchildren and the twins Seta had delivered to Ari. Soon enough she was pregnant again with a child of Torrador's.

They spent the next winter with Alfvin and Frae, the Guldale settlers and, also Doroba, although Seta missed the other Norse greatly, Halla in particular.

While Seta and Torrador eventually built their own hall in Guldale, Seta would forever spend the summers hosting Halla or visiting her in Godsland.

And all about them, the Norse settlements grew.

COLIN TABER

Epilogue

Smoke on the Horizon

COLIN TABER

Epilogue

*

Smoke on the Horizon

Godsland, Markland, twenty years later.

Ulfarr awoke to the sound of a distant horn. He threw back his bedding without delay and sat up in the sleeping alcove, the hall about him dimly lit by the smoldering fire pit and the dull light before dawn.

Beside him, his wife, Bryn, stirred "What is happening?"

"I do not know. I will go and look."

She looked across the wide expanse of the new hall, the grandest in not just Godsland, but all of Markland, and only finished at the previous summer's end. She offered, "I shall go and check on Eskil and Gudrid."

He nodded, "Do it. My father will want to know, if he has not already woken."

Ulfarr quickly rose and dressed, pulling on his boots last. He had grown into a strapping man – blonde and broad – so big that some called him the Godsland Giant. He patted Bryn's leg as she began to dress herself, but he did not wait as he hurried off to find what was happening.

By the time he left their sleeping alcove and began crossing the hall, he could see his childhood friend, Brandr, had also risen, summoned by the distant call.

Brandr had his father's brown hair and lean frame, but he was also taller, and more muscular than Ballr the Icelander. Quick to meet Ulfarr, he asked, "Any idea why the horn sounds?"

"No, but let us take a look."

The two men visited Godsland often, but spent a good deal more time on errands for both of their famous fathers, or exploring, or in Guldale or the settled vales beyond. Regardless, whenever either found themselves in Godsland, they stayed at the new hall – the original hall still held within its foundation – that rose atop the hill. Around the magnificent hall, a structure of cut stone and carved wood, spread a growing village, wharf and breakwater.

As they approached the doors, Ulfarr observed, "I can smell smoke."

Brandr hurried. "Me too...something is wrong."

In the distance, another two horns called out to stir the coming dawn.

"Where are the horns sounding from...Guldale?"

Ulfarr pushed the doors open, "No, Guldale is likely too far away."

The opened doors revealed the view from the terrace outside the hilltop hall, the vista spreading across the channel and down the coast, including a handful of islands, and the cove and lands of Lakeland beyond.

The mournful call of other horns arose.

A column of thick smoke climbed darkly over the far shore's

ridgetop that hid the Lakeland vale. As they watched, two others rose to join it, climbing high into the sky as they took on the colours of sunrise. The smoke glowed at the base of the plumes, lit by flaring oranges and yellows.

Half-a-dozen more plumes of smoke billowed up in the distance, just as the sun rose, coming not only from the Lakeland vale, but also from the inland and southerly vales settled over the past twenty years.

The two men were stunned. Finally, Ulfarr whispered, "Lakeland burns!"

A voice spoke deep and sure behind them, "Sound our horns and rally our people!" It was Eskil, gazing upon the doom of Lakeland. "We go to help!"

***

Sign up for Colin Taber's emailed new release alerts at:

www.UnitedStatesofVinland.com

COLIN TABER

Continue your Markland adventure!

Loki's Rage

Book 2 of The United States of Vinland will be available in the second half of 2013. **Sign up for a new release email alert from the author at:**

www.UnitedStatesOfVinland.com

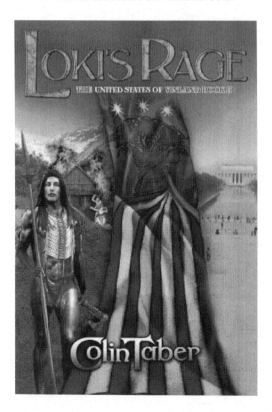

COLIN TABER

The Landing:

-

A Note From The Author

COLIN TABER

288

The Landing:

A Note From the Author

What if?

That's a great question, a favourite of mine, and one here applied to the topic of the Vikings and their journeys west across the Atlantic.

The thought first came to me years ago while on holiday in the United States – and I've been thinking about it ever since.

What if?

This series will work its way through that question presenting an entire alternate history. Along the way I will research, add some twists, elaborate on some not so well known facts about the relevant areas, such as Greenland being subject to a warming period back then, thus extending growing seasons (if only marginally), while also taking advantage of the gaps in what we do and don't know, like the extinctions of previous peoples who lived in Markland. It's also true to say that I may use some artistic licence.

Eventually, as we travel with each book through the generations, we will reach other areas of North America and finally our destination of a very different version of the world we know today.

In the end, what I am hoping to create with this series is an exciting narrative that many of you will join me on, as we explore what might have been.

Welcome to Norse America.

Colin Taber – March 7th 2013

The Landing:

-

Characters

COLIN TABER

The Landing:

Characters

The Godsland Hall:

Ballr: An Icelandic friend and supporter of Eskil, married to Halla. He has many skills, from those of a warrior, to builder and carpenter.

Brandr: The son of Ballr and Halla.

Drifa: Another victim of the shipwreck, married to Manni.

Erik: A Danish farmer, also widowed by the shipwreck. He has come west to seek unclaimed land after finding he was unable to secure a farm in Iceland.

Eskil: Orphaned as a child by the Battle of Svold, this bloody event fostered Eskil's distrust of the rising kings in Scandinavia and his loathing for the White Christ's missionaries who were one by one converting the region's monarchs to their alien faith. Eskil is leader of the expedition and driven by a dream that would see him claim land so the old ways of his people may live on. He is married to Gudrid and father to Ulfarr. Originally from Norway, he has spent time in Denmark and Iceland before finally launching his expedition west across the ocean.

Gudrid (Gudda): Wife to Eskil, mother to Ulfarr, and also strong in her faith. Gudrid is a wilful youngest daughter of an established, but poor Icelandic farming family.

Halla: Wife of Ballr and friend of Gudrid, from a large and well established Icelandic family.

Manni: One of the ill fated to not survive the landing, married to Drifa.

Samr: Younger brother to Steinarr, a warrior and trader.

Steinarr: A Norse warrior and older brother to Samr.

Torrador: Widowed by the shipwreck, but loyal to the cause and accepting of his fate. Torrador is a broad and tall man, a warrior from the Norwegian west coast.

Ulfarr: The first son of Markland born to Eskil and Gudrid.

The Lakeland Hall:

Alfvin: A Norse man of fair mind and broad skills. Alfvin, with his cousin Ari and their thralls, shifted allegiance from the Lakeland Hall to Godsland.

Ari: A widowed woodsman originally of Lakeland, but who also moved to Godsland with his thrall Seta and his cousin Alfvin.

Frae: Thrall of Alfvin and survivor of the first meeting of the local indigenous population and the Lakeland Norse. Sister to Seta.

Leif: The charismatic leader of the expedition's second ship and the only natural rival to Eskil's leadership. Leif died within hours of the Lakeland landing.

Seta: Thrall of Ari and sister to Frae.

Thoromr: Son of Thrainn, a strong young man born in Iceland, only held in check by his father's overbearing ways. Cousin to Trion.

Thrainn: Widowed by the shipwreck and assumer of the leadership of the Lakeland men. Oldest of all the survivors, father of Thoromr, and uncle to Trion. This giant Swede had settled in Iceland prior to seeking land in the west.

Trion: Weary of the new lands he finds himself in. Iceland born nephew to Thrainn and cousin to Thoromr.

Others:

Aldis: The widowed Greenlandic sister of Faraldr and destined for marriage.

Faraldr: The Greenlander who originally built the Lakeland Hall, as well as claimant on the Lakeland vale. Brother to Aldis. He is head of a large family with many links back to Iceland.

The Landing:

-

Locations & Terms

The Landing:

Locations & Terms

Helluland: The lands to the north of Markland and west of Greenland (Baffin Island).

Markland: The rugged and partially wooded coast to the south west of Greenland (Labrador).

Skraelings: The name given to some of the indigenous peoples of the westerly lands. In Norse mythology the term is both attributed to dwarves and wretches. Historically, the term was applied by the Greenland Norse to the Inuit populations of that region.

Thralls: The Norse term for slaves.

Vinland: The island to the south of Greenland and Markland (Newfoundland).

COLIN TABER

Enjoyed this read & want
to see more of my work?

The Ossard Trilogy

The Fall of Ossard is a dark fantasy that tells a coming of age story, as a wealthy city-state of merchant princes spins out of control. This is a slower and considered read in a dying world, not an action adventure, and may not be for all readers of The United States of Vinland series. Please, feel free to give it a try, but be warned it is a layered and brooding story.

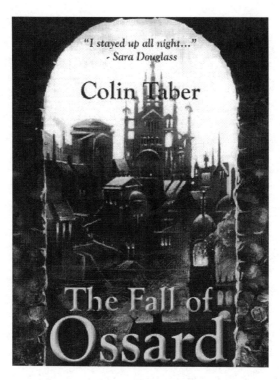

Book 2, Ossard's Hope, is also available.
Book 3, Lae Ossard, will be released in the last half of 2013.

COLIN TABER

About the Author

Colin Taber was born in Australia in 1970 and announced his intention to be a writer at the innocent age of 6. His father, an accountant, provided some cautious advice, suggesting that life might be easier if his son pursued a more predictable vocation.

Colin didn't listen.

Over the past twenty years Colin's had over a hundred magazine articles published, notably in Australian Realms Magazine. In 2009 his first novel, The Fall of Ossard, was released to open his coming of age dark fantasy series, The Ossard Trilogy. The second installment, Ossard's Hope, followed in 2011 and was supported by a national book signing tour. Currently Colin is working on the final book in that trilogy, Lae Ossard, and his new series The United States of Vinland.

Colin has done many things over the years, from working in bookshops to event management, small press publishing, landscape design and even tree farming. All he really wants to do, though, is to get back to his oak grove and be left to write.

Thankfully, with an enthusiastic and growing readership, that day is coming. He currently haunts the west coast city of Perth.

www.UnitedStatesofVinland.com

Made in the USA
Charleston, SC
02 September 2016